The Ivory Knife

A Kayne Sorenson Mystery

Thomas Paul Severino

Thomas Paul Severino

The Ivory Knife

A Kayne Sorenson Mystery

Thomas Paul Severino

Copyright 2022

Pollywog Pond Communications, Ft. Lauderdale

https://www.tomseverino.com

tomseverino100@gmail.com

The names, places, and incidents in this work of fiction are either a product of the author's imagination or used fictitiously. Any resemblance to actual persons, living or dead (except for satirical purposes), is entirely coincidental.

Cover: AdobeStock 391642747

ISBN: 978-1-7369769-8-2

The Ivory Knife

Also by Thomas Paul Severino

The Kayne Sorenson Mysteries: The Quartet of Blood

Seed Blood

Tribal Blood

Stage Blood

Ancient Blood

The Kayne Sorenson Mysteries: The Quartet of Evil

The Evil Genius

The Shadow of Evil

The Pearl of Great Evil

The Evil League

The Kayne Sorenson Mysteries: The New Adventures

The Crystal Orb

The Flower of Gold

The Ivory Knife

The Amazing Adventures of Rebecca Quinto

The Frozen Diva

The Lost Museum

The Last Maya

Thomas Paul Severino

The Ivory Knife

For all who struggle

for truth, equality, and justice.

Fight on that we all may be free.

and for Stephen

Thomas Paul Severino

The Ivory Knife

Seek strength, not to be greater than your brother, but to fight your greatest enemy -- yourself. -- an Inuit Proverb

Thomas Paul Severino

Dramatis Personae

The San Franciscans

- Kayne J. Sorenson, Ph.D., President, Sorenson and Sechi Consulting Detectives, Inc.
- Nicola M. Sechi, Vice President, Sorenson and Sechi Consulting Detectives, Inc.
- The Honorable Kristof Saxe-Coburg Gotha-Koháry Sorenson (The Kris); Student at the University of San Francisco
- Andi S. Rodriguez, Executive Business Partner, Sorenson and Sechi Consulting Detectives, Inc.
- Jessamyn R. Trasker; Housekeeper
- Matthew A. Crowley, RN
- Eric N. Sorenson, Commander 1st Degree, The Order of the Dannebrog (Denmark)
- Oscar Stål, Ph.D., Occupational Therapist
- Raul Dos Santos
- Austin R. McDaniel, Head Soccer Coach, University of San Francisco;
- Jesse L. Okeyo, Soccer Team Captain, University of San Francisco
- Declan Starr, Photographer
- Chouko, an Akita
- Alice, an Australian Border Collie
- Christine, a Domestic Shorthair

The Russians

- General Secretary Marie Mikhailovna Lissemskaia
- Colonel Demitri Ivanovich Malenkov
- Colonel Vasily Pavlovich Bounine
- Captain Sergei Andreivich Sarov
- Hegumen Stefan (Stefan Lebedev), the Holy Abbot of the Andronikov Monastery of the Theotokos
- Lieutenant Colonel Katsitsanóron Isapoinhkyaki, aka Katya Sidorovna, the Russian Foreign Intelligence Service

Thomas Paul Severino
- Captain Ivan Illyich Korolenko, 11th Spetsnaz Brigade

The Americans

- Rebecca Quinto, President and CEO, The Fritcher Museum of Fine Arts
- Mark R. Gadarn, Journalist, CBN, Inc.
- Micah Valez, Executive Assistant, The Fritcher Museum of Fine Arts
- Hudson Ch'en, CEO, The Preston Foundation
- Mary Chance, Special Agent, FBI
- Amy Simmons, Tour Guide, Seattle Department of Cultural Affairs
- Jissika Pitka Delutukl, Arctic Researcher, Prudohoe Bay, Alaska
- Darren Uralic, Manager, SkyCity Restaurant, Seattle
- Mrs. Honoria McCave, Innkeeper, Cecil Bacon Manor, Seattle
- Benjamin Waska, Landscapist, Program Technician, Levitech Systems, Inc.
- Pauline Inokapti, MD
- Regina Netsilik, CEO, Levitech Systems, Inc.
- Captain Ciarán David Farrell, U.S. Coast Guard Intelligence
- Rysam Keal, Field Agent, CIA

The Canadians

- Aleksei Volkov, (Aloysha), co-owner, Pysanka Bar
- Tim Chernoff, (Timofe), co-owner, Pysanka Bar
- Grigorij Kovalenko (Grisha). Bartender, Pysanka Bar
- Michael McDowd, Captain, HMCS Rusalka
- Eva Nakoyak, Cook/First Mate, HMCS Rusalka
- Cameron Yakecen Jakobs, Ship's Steward/Cabin Boy, HMCS Rusalka
- Cleatus Lee, Server, Ranger Bar
- Léo Gauthier, Bartender, Ranger Bar

The Ukrainians

- Vasyl Belous, Director, BurshtynPower
- Pavlo Dydenko, Director of Technical Operations, BurshtynPower

The Moldovans

- Vadim Shatralev, an entrepreneur
- Livinia Shatralev, an entrepreneur

The Bulgarians

- His Highness Lyuboslav Saxe-Coburg Gotha (Cousin Pesho, "The Flea"), Bulgarian Ambassador to NATO-OTAN
- Mikhal Yordan, Assistant to the Bulgarian Ambassador to NATO-OTAN

A.I. Entities

- Mycroft, data analysis program (Sorenson and Sechi)
- Eris, data analysis program (Mark Gadarn)

Thomas Paul Severino

Prologue: Beyond the Circle
70°12'59"N 151°0'21"W (Give or take...)

Snow is your friend. — Inuit Proverb

So much white. Need to sleep for a while. Not sure what ... arms ... legs...? Numb ... that light? I saw it ... it was there ... Gone? Don't want to fall again.

"Hello. You there? I brought it. Where?"

The storm-ravaged man could not hear his voice. He wasn't sure if the roaring wind was too loud or if anything was coming from his throat. Was it just his head voice?

So cold.

"I followed the instructions ... you out there? Hey. Hello?"

The blizzard raged like a maelstrom of wind, ice, and snow. The fugitive's footing was unsure, but he had lost most of the feeling in his feet and legs a while back. Rocks and ledges suddenly caused him to fall on the hardpack. Each time he tried to get up, it took longer.

The all-terrain had flipped over a rocky outcrop masked by the snow blow. The traveler imagined that his vehicle had been batted by the paw of a gigantic Arctic beast, insane and ferocious. He unbuckled and rolled out of the capsized truck and tried to figure out if anything was broken.

Never even saw it coming ... couldn't stay there. That light ... up on the crest ... a way off ... an outpost?

"Help!"

He had scrambled away in time. The explosion and fire turned everything into a negative of the landscape — lighting up the night sky and turning the swirling snow into a black rain.

They were close ... will see the fire ... and they will come for me. Have to go.

He expected his arctic gear would keep him from freezing. The man was dry, and all surfaces were covered and insulated. His goggles were cracked, however-- eyes watering.

He trudged in the direction of the light, hoping it was not just a star on the horizon. His staggering twisted in the blasting maelstrom like a forced dance of death. He was unsure of the direction now. Just forward ... forward ....

Stormy skies – no starlight. No horizon, the darkness, and the white of a frozen Hell. That's crazy. Must be people. Help. Help is on the way ... help is up ahead ... PLEASE HELP!

A blast of wind knocked him to his face. Again, he took a while to get to his knees. He checked his satchel.

Yes.... still there. Keep it safe, Stefan. Gotta deliver.

The fallen man stood but dropped to one knee as a torrent of snow flipped up like a little whirlwind that powered into and around him, screeching like a wounded beast. He grabbed his head and pulled his face down.

There was no feeling now.

Tired ... pale sleep ... there ... there in the dark ... I can make that ... yes, but first sleep a bit. Then tomorrow ....

***

"What's up with you gizmos? Such a racket. Just a wolf or a fox or something that lost its way. Minus forty, and the wind chill kicks it out a lot lower. Damn deadly gusts. No, kids. Settle. You are not going out there. Go to sleep ... Good dogs."

Jissika Pitka Delutukl looked out an ice-encrusted window glass of Amaruq Outpost 3, a small extension site of the Gray Wolf Research Center fourteen miles north of Nuiquist, North Slope Borough, Alaska. The town was one of the most northern habitations in the world -- the far north – above the Arctic Circle.

The Ivory Knife

The storm was a killer, ramming down the Nechelik Channel from the Beaufort Sea. Inside the thick walls of the facility, the dogs were usually very calm, even with a storm of this intensity. Not tonight ....

Something was out there ....

Pulling on her Arctic gear, she spoke to her team.

"Yeah, you can tell I am going out in the frozen bitch, can't you? You see my boots and parka. Fine. Nope. Nope. You settle. Anji, No. Stay with your pups. Good girl. Just Yura and Tulok tonight. Doing a two-sled. Way too bad out there for a bigger team."

In the garage with her most robust and best tracker dogs, the bundled-up woman checked the heat and lights – all good so far. This was no night for the truck. It would not go very far in this wind and blowing snow.

She hooked up the dogs and opened up the small door. The white beast barged in-- a furious barrage of freezing wind. The dogs lowered their heads and pulled as Jissika pushed.

She raised the night vision goggles and scanned. Nothing.

Yura was barking, and as they went forward, Tulok also raised the alarm. But, there was nothing out there ... nothing. In this storm, the world of the outpost was a deadly blank.

A quarter of a mile from the station, the wind flipped the sled, the researcher, and the dogs. They huddled briefly, but the woman quickly righted her transport and considered returning to Amaruq station.

Wait. Fire? There's no oil station in that direction. Wonder what it is? In fact, there's nothing to the back of that crest.

She started to pull up the night visions to get a better look. That was when Tulok broke free of his reins.

"Tulok! Tulok! Come!" She yelled into the heart of the storm.

"Go, Yura. Mush, girl."

The dog's tracks were quickly snow-covered, but she heard him or thought she did. Jissika stopped the sled and raised the goggles.

Dog ass – for sure. Stuck in the rocks. Cornered a fox? Shit!

"Tulok!"

He wasn't trapped. The dog was face-first in a hollow between boulders. Tulok turned around and did his best "Timmy's in the well, Mom."

It was then that she saw the snow boot.

Chapter One: Goodbye
221 Baker Street, San Francisco, California

Nick Sechi's Journal

"Seal off the gallery until we get there. Andi is booking the next flight to Ft. Lauderdale. "

"I will arrange to have you picked up, Dr. Sorenson."

"Micah, there is no need. Airport Avis reservations ... we will need a car anyway."

"I can forward Mr. Sechi Ms. Quinto's car service contact information."

"No, thank you. Mark?"

"On assignment, Sir. I'm afraid it's impossible to ...."

"I will contact him."

"Let's go, Boss. Kris packed our stuff. The Uber arrives in eight minutes."

Kayne gave me a nod and made signals to Andi Rodriguez, our professional assistant, concerning our appointments. Our nephew, Kristof, stepped into the office.

"The bags are downstairs, Unks. Gotta get to class. Love to Aunt Rebecca."

We got man-smooched.

I called out to the open phone, "Micah, Rebecca?"

"At this moment, stable."

***

"Please have Andi get the following message to Mark, my love.'The wifi is temporarily unavailable at the condo. Requires your passcode.' At once if you please."

"Boss?"

"It's code, Nick. It is a message that he needs to return home."

The Uber pulled out of Pacific Heights and headed to the 101 freeway to San Francisco International.

I asked, "Any idea where he is? You realize his gonzo journalism activities often put him at the heart of severe international danger, right?"

Kayne tapped his phone and showed me an email.

"Yeah, it's from Mark. So? He sent it to congratulate us on the Japan case. And? Wait, what's that? That is not a typo. Too weird. Looks like he leaned on the keys."

"*Swarrtotmaal* is Burmese for goodbye. He is somewhere in Myanmar."

"Holy shit! Rebecca must have been ...."

"Upset? Yes, that is an accurate conclusion. Look at the message."

I read aloud, "She writes, 'Please keep an eye on the WiFi for me. It has been acting up.' Means she's super pissed."

"Quite so. Our gal wants Mark out of all that. And we both know that Mark Gadarn will never be satisfied being the kept trophy boy of the President and Executive Director of the Fritcher Museum of Art."

"Yeah, trotting Studly Man out in his formal wear whenever she has a gala. Not gonna happen."

Kayne looked away for a moment and said, "This is not logical. Myanmar? I think he is elsewhere, and his cover doesn't allow him to reveal his location. Nick, I am concerned for both of them in many ways."

"Micah say how it happened?"

"Only that the exhibit piece came crashing down, and she was under it. More information will be forthcoming once we arrive. You're breathing seems headed for panic mode, my love."

"I'm cool, Boss. Hopefully, will sleep most of the way."

The Ivory Knife

My combination of acrophobia and aerophobia had been somewhat under control – no Xanax this time. I was learning to control the intense anxiety with meditation and breathing exercises. It would be a long trip, but I had been up against tougher outfits than this. Being married to the foremost psycho-criminologist and modern consulting detective was filled with thrills and danger. Sorenson and Sechi, Consulting Detectives, Inc., had been piling up some major wins against the "Big Bads."

Crossing the globe in a plane a few times a year -- I considered it the price of admission. I was hooked on this guy from the git-go – he was my instructor in a graduate course when we lived in Ft. Lauderdale. I was a ballsy cop for Wilton Manors, and he taught graduate courses for Florida Global University. The passion for each other and for crime-solving continues to be smoking hot.

BFD – another plane ride. But, this had all the markings of one unusual case.

***

Andi spoke to the device, a round, black muffin-like dingus that softly glowed when connected.

"Mycroft?"

"Good morning, Ms. Rodriguez. I hope everyone is well. I see that Dr. Sorenson and Mr. Sechi will arrive at Ft. Lauderdale Hollywood International Airport at four-thirty Eastern Standard Time."

The artificial intelligence program spoke to her via her earpiece as the device blinked.

"Yes ... please follow these instructions, Mycroft."

The "cyber detective" listened carefully and said, "There is a fifty percent probability that Mr. Gadarn will receive this message from Eris, my similar operative in his office. There is a high-percentage chance that he has been captured or is, in fact, dead."

"O.K., so there is this thing we humans practice, Mycroft. It's called discretion. What I am saying is keep your mouth shut on that one."

"Received. I will not communicate that information."

Thomas Paul Severino

Right, you don't even have a mouth. This is totally strange.

Chapter Two: Denali
The Fritcher Museum of Art, Ft. Lauderdale, Florida

Nick Sechi's Journal

"Sedated, Dr. Sorenson. The repairs were made to Ms. Quinto's spine only a few hours ago. I can tell you it all looks good. The spinal cord was not injured, but some bone and surrounding tissue have suffered intense compression. We have alleviated the pressure on the nerves and mitigated most of the damage. The head injury was minor, but we are watching it. I expect she could see you in the morning."

"Thank you, doctor. We will be back."

Rebecca looked pretty messed up through the window of the ICU. She was in some kind of suspended contraption to lay on her face. Tubes in and out .... machines beeping, and a symphony of graphics in white and blue on small screens. She slept.

It's good to have friends who remember you. My buds at Broward General let us get close with no questions. One of the nurses recalled me from a rather nasty murder spree case. He actually patched me up from a stabbing. The camaraderie felt comfortable. As Kayne always says, "There's family, and there's family, my love,"

***

"Only the police, Dr. Sorenson. Well, the paramedics, too. And museum security. Um ... That's it."

Micah Vélaz, Rebecca's professional assistant, cringed slightly. He knew the situation. Kayne hated a disturbed crime scene, or in this case, a potential crime scene. My detective was frustrated, although his expression was totally deadpanned.

"Boss, I have the report from Lauderdale PD. They are calling it an accident -- faulty installation. That is so not the case. Five will get you ten that they read this totally wrong."

Thomas Paul Severino

He looked up at the exhibit of the giant blown glass chandeliers, part of the exhibit "Borealis: Art and Culture in the Frozen Realms."

"These are done by the Iñupiat artist, Irene Hopson Okpeaha, five of her 'Northern Lights' series. The white one with touches of black is 'Nanuq,' Polar Bear. The grey and white cluster is 'Qimmiq,' Sled Dogs. 'Qimuqsuq' is Drifting Snow – it really scatters the light. The brown and green one is 'Tuktu,' The Caribou."

The glass creations were imaginative fantasies of blown glass curves, spirals, and twisting shapes that exploded in four sunbursts of light and color. I would guess that each was about six to seven feet in diameter, hanging from the gallery ceiling in a grouping with one conspicuous gap in the middle.

Kayne stepped carefully around the blue and white glass pieces covering and surrounding an orange telescopic scissor lift platform. He bent to inspect the remains of the glass bomb.

Pointing to the collapsed high-access equipment, he asked, "This?"

"No, Doctor. The installation on the piece entitled 'Danali' was completed and inspected by our curating engineer. The lift had been rolled under it inadvertently. And that was fortunate because Rebecca was half under the lift machine when the artwork dropped on her. I believe it actually saved ...."

He was a bit overcome, but we got the idea. As Micah regained his composure, Kayne led the assistant."

"The upper part of her body was shielded when she ducked under, but she hit her head hard when she fell? She took most of the impact with her back?"

"Yes, Doctor."

"I understand."

He mounted the platform and used the controls to reach the gallery ceiling. After inspecting the attachment, he took iPhone pictures and rolled the lift to examine two of the other chandeliers. He descended. Again he studied the debris from the shattered Denali piece. This time, noting our friend's blood on a few of the shards.

The Ivory Knife

"Thank you, Micah. I would like access to Rebecca's office if you would be so kind. Please have the head of security keep this area off-limits for the time being. I would like to speak to him on the sixth floor. Thank you."

***

Ken Underworthy, the Director of Museum Security, stepped off the elevator. Kayne spoke to him privately, and he left the executive suite.

"Most of the staff has left for the day, Micah?"

"Yes, Doctor Sorenson, the Museum stays open until nine on Friday, but most staff leave at five."

Kayne looked around Rebecca's office, carefully opening desk drawers. The CEO was one of those exceptionally neat executives. Everything was electronically filed – no paper.

Micah said, "Ms. Quinto is allergic to hard copy. It is either on her computer or on my desk."

"Anything suspicious? Her emails?"

"Nothing, Sir. We have been swamped planning the opening of 'Borealis.' The gala is two weeks from tonight. Now with the accident with 'Denali,' we will be delayed. It was the signature piece for the exhibit."

I picked up the media copy and observed, "Yes. The artwork for the show is all the Denali chandelier. It is the exhibit's icon. That blows."

"Micah, please find me the artist's contact information. I have her as Ms. Irene Hopson Okpeaha. Thank you."

He went back into his office.

Kayne pressed a button on the desk, and the glass walls of Rebecca's office darkened. He turned to me.

"Well, where is it?"

I pointed to a framed print of Wassily Kandinsky's "Upward" on the wall above a walnut console.

"There are the scratches of long fingernails on the wall just to the left of the frame, Boss."

"Excellent, my love."

Kayne stepped to the print and opened it on its hinges. He punched six numbers on the keypad and opened the wall safe.

"Mark's birthday. Our girl is so very predictable."

For you, maybe.

The bond between Kayne and his best gal pal went back to their younger days. The two of them, fresh out of undergrad, went wild and daring in Europe. In the course of getting into completing their degrees in the EU, they managed to court a shit load of trouble. Amazingly intelligent, magnetically sexy, and willing to take life by the balls, they complimented each other to the max.

I heard her familiar voice in my head.

"I am much more gregarious, Nick, darling. People adore me. And I make it work—couture, class out the ass, and a drop-dead body.

"Now, Kayne has to work on personal interactions. He can be quite aloof, and that puts people off. Definitely needs a warmth intensive. That and the fact that he is such a fuckin' breathtaking man-beast."

I smiled as I recalled the convo.

"You know exactly what I am talking about, Beefcake. Like attracts like. It's a hotshot bro club."

Sexually, Kayne and Rebecca had the same hot libidos and were attracted to identical male body types and cocky attitudes – athletic, self-assured, and stunningly gorgeous. The variation, of course, was a matter of the erotic mysteries of the gay/straight passion dance. A hot hunk in the sensual sites of these two had a few options, to put it simply. Rebecca and Kayne could hardly help their innate friskiness. He was Australian of lively hooligan stock, and she was a fiery Latinx.

Hunky men should heed the warning.

Now, my Bossman rifled through a small pile of papers and pocketed one. He closed the hiding place.

The Ivory Knife

A knock announced Micah's return along with Security Director Underwood. The sturdy black man placed a device on Rebecca's conference table. Kayne added a piece of the ruined 'Denali' and opened his phone.

"So here it is, gentlemen. Mr. Underwood, please proceed?"

"Right where you said it would be, Dr. Sorenson, the AC duct close to the destroyed glass piece."

"The cleaning company came the morning of the 'accident.' Please provide security tape showing me any activity they may have had inside or outside the museum."

"You got it, Sir."

"What is this, Boss?"

"That, my love, is the potential murder weapon. It is a sonic device that produces a frequency tuned to a glass of a specific chemical makeup. Only Denali is blue — glacier blue, at that. That glass additive that created the color caused the vibrations to zero in on this piece and cause it to explode."

Micah said, "So, not the fault in the installation?"

"No. Check the video. Slow motion if you please … There, see? The glass shatters *before* it descends. The chandelier's attachment was not among the shards on the gallery floor. It was still intact on the ceiling. I recommend a physical chemist take a look at the pieces. They will confirm the structural disintegration caused by high-frequency sound."

"Boss, are we looking at an attempted murder?"

"I cannot say. I need more information, Nick. At the very least, someone is attempting to sabotage "Borealis."

Thomas Paul Severino

Chapter Three: The Phantom's Note
Wilton Manors, Florida

Nick Sechi's Journal

"Sleepy?"

"Hungry."

"Le Patio. We can walk."

"An excellent suggestion. We can unpack later."

I pulled him in for a hot smooch up.

"You are amazing, Boss."

"Quite famous for it, my love."

He returned my ardor. I swatted his ass, and we left the room.

Ed Lugo Resort is a collection of completely renovated 1950's Florida bungalows located in the heart of the gay paradise that is Wilton Drive. The adult-only, male-exclusive, and clothing-optional resort is steps away from all the shops, gay bars, and restaurants in Wilton Manors.

Oh yeah, who's up for some hot trouble, boys?

We walked five blocks to the tiniest, cutest restaurant in South Florida. Le Patio was a delight of European comfort food tucked between a day spa and a small parking lot. The eponymous courtyard was romantic and charming; the food and the wine simply spectacular.

It was a bit past the usual dinner hour, so we had some privacy, tucked back in the shadows among the tropical plants and artistic touches. Kayne had Shepherd's pie, and I tucked into an amazing Lasagna. Almost as good as Mama Sechi's.

"So, the note. Boss."

Kayne retrieved the stolen paper and passed it to me.

Thomas Paul Severino

My iPhone flashlight feature revealed one of those cut-out newsprint ransom notes.

"You have to be bustin' my ass. Seriously? So 1930's."

I remarked, " Whoa. 'Two million cash or a disaster beyond proportions will follow.' She was being hustled. Murder?"

"No, mayhem, my love. There was no camera on the sonic device for the berserker to determine the position of anyone in the gallery. The intent was to destroy the piece. Perhaps with the intent to shatter the other installations once the realization was made that threat was real – relatively innocuous, to be honest."

"Why?"

"No money was paid; one art piece was destroyed. It would not take much to shut down the entire enterprise and protect the museum's investment. Finding the sonic element was quite easy. Furthermore, the note specifies no way of contact for the ransom. No, the intentions of these criminals are not yet apparent."

"Kayne, the phrasing? Broadway queen or what?"

"I am afraid I do not follow, Nick."

"It's the note from 'The Phantom of the Opera.' 'A disaster beyond proportions?' Verbatim. Then the chandelier crashes down into the audience. Andrew Lloyd Weber did it first."

"Ah, Gaston Leroux's novel. Quite right, my love. I never saw the musical."

"Boss, excuse me for saying it, but I am frequently amazed that the essentials of popular culture are often beyond your experience. You know just about everything about everything. Seriously? Broadway musicals? I may need to revoke your gay card."

The hostess brought us two after-dinner drinks. Kayne's was a glass of whiskey, and mine was a Mich Ultra. Responding to my surprised expression, she turned and pointed to two dudes in the shadows at the other end of the patio.

They came over.

The Ivory Knife

"I know we got the beer right, Nick. I think I remember Hibiki, Doctor Sorenson."

We both stood to welcome our generous guests.

Micah started to introduce his partner as Kayne offered his hand.

"Mr. Hudson Ch'en, it is indeed so brilliant to see you again."

I smiled and shook the hand of my ex.

Thomas Paul Severino

Chapter Four: Glamour
221 Baker Street, San Francisco, California

Nick Sechi's Journal

"I can see your ass."

"And a smoking hot jock ass it is, gurl."

"Not that I haven't seen it many times around this place, but Kris, really?"

Andi Rodriguez scrolled through the file. The photographer had captured the naked jock in some breathtaking poses. The adage, "the camera loved him," was never more true. His body was an exceptional work of art.

"Hold it, is that Chouko? Holy crap!"

"Yeah, Declan had some great ideas, and Cho almost stole the shots -- two sexy beasts. I like the bathtub and shower sequence. Wet is very hot. Also, check out the Muir Woods shots – very cool."

The Administrative partner for Sorenson and Sechi scrolled through the portfolio. Kris flopped into a chair in his training togs, propping his running shoes on the edge of her desk. He stretched his athletic frame and brought his arms back down.

"Feet."

He shifted but kept them there

"Pretty good job at hiding your, um .... the ahhh."

"Yeah, Declan said if I use any of these in my acting job files, shots of my man business are off-limits. Unless the job is in the wonderful world of adult entertainment."

"Boyfriend, do not even ... I mean, seriously. You-know-who and his ... well, and the other you-know-who are gonna flip when they see .... holy crap!"

She stopped all keyboard and mouse action and looked at the rascal doing his best full of himself meme. She could not decide who Kristof resembled more, his Uncle Kick, aka the Hot Mess, or his father, the Prince of Darkness. These Sorensons were some troop of monkeys.

"Really? Really Kris? And you want to be an associate in the firm. Brother!"

Kris seemed to lose a bit of the initial bravado he had when he made the big reveal. The boy figured Andi was sort of a test case. If she was cool with all of this, then chances were that Kayne and I would not completely freak. His dad would be down with it. He was never known for any kind of prudishness.

And then there was the other thing ....

"Feet." Andi swiped him off.

"O.K., so, your Nona Sechi? Not to mention that Trasker is going to have a stroke. Yeah, that'll kill her. There won't be enough masses and rosaries for them to erase this mess. Your royal relatives in Transylvania ... done."

Kris had walked to the window and looked down the hill towards the Haight. There were a few people on the Baker Street Steps – an urban street park in our neighborhood.

"Folks just gotta realize," he said like he was trying to believe it himself. "This man is going places. I work hard to stay in shape, so why shouldn't I ... well damn, what are we, a family of Puritans? I needed some real high-end photos, Andi. Declan Starr is the best. My Aunt Rebecca recommended him – well, not him exactly, but ...."

He faltered and twisted the edge of his athletic tee. Andi kicked back from her computer and turned to look at the boy/man in the window.

"Kris."

He turned a bit too quickly to face her.

"What?"

"What are you *not* telling me?"

"Naw, nothing, gurl. That's all. That's it, really."

The Ivory Knife

"Bullshit."

His weak expression seemed a remnant of his signature cockiness. The mask was slipping.

Andi said nothing more. Pointing to the keyboard, she made room for him at the computer.

At first, all there was to be seen in his expression was a serious look – big-eyed and regretful. Kris reached over and tapped some keys and slid and clicked the mouse pointer.

The video played.

Thomas Paul Severino

Chapter Five: A Three-Pipe Problem
221 Baker Street, San Francisco California

Nick Sechi's Journal

"I said I don't know where he is. How many times do I have to say it?"

"Calm down, Red. Police?"

"FBI, Eric. Special Agent Mary Chance. She has nothing to go on. They interviewed the club staff. They checked CCT recordings at the Airport, Port of the Everglades, and toll booths on the major highways. She has some of her people working on MIA and the port of Miami. Nothing so far."

I paced the library.

"He was there, and then he wasn't. Fuck!"

"Nick, Uncle Kayne would not have been abducted without a fight. No one saw a free for all – Hunter's parking lot?"

"No, Kris. Mary even reviewed highway camera recordings along I-95 out of Ft. Lauderdale for anything that looked sketchy. It is a full-blown manhunt. But, I need you all to know that we are keeping this as quiet as possible, given certain reputations and so on. Lock it down, folks – very important. No emails, texts, or reports of any kind. Check with me on everything."

Chouko and Alice tried to interrupt my fretting with some soft nuzzling. They knew I was nutso with worry. I went down on one knee to take some dog love. The soft clicking from our housekeeper's apron pocket meant that Mrs. Trasker was saying the rosary.

"This inaction is driving me crazy. Andi, get Mycroft on this. What the fuck good is artificial intelligence if he isn't in the mix?"

Slowly, I looked up at the former super spy. He and I needed no spoken communication. My brother-in-law knew what I wanted.

Eric nodded. He turned to Oscar, his partner. The man placed a hand on the former secret agent's shoulder and said, "You have no choice."

Eric left the room.

"Kris, I know you have school and all, but ...."

"Uncle Nick, I can be in Ft. Lauderdale by tomorrow. Your man on the scene."

"No, bud. Mary has a full force working on this. I need you to research our latest cases and develop some theories. If this is a revenge move, who's got our man? There may be something in the files we overlooked."

I could tell that our young man of action was totally disappointed. Regulated to be the firm's research bitch again. Fuck it. It's for the best.

"Above all, stick to your school work and the soccer. It is what Kayne would want. Your pop too, Kiddo."

"Mr. Sechi, the Sorenson brothers, your father-in-law, the Captain?"

"To be honest, Andi, I wanted a bit more than 'vanished into thin air' before I got in touch with Kick and Mitch. Too late now. I will call them tomorrow first thing. Ace? Nah ahh. Kayne would want that to happen delicately and much later should ... anyway, he's about to become a father again and ...."

"Mr. Sechi, I am very sure you haven't eaten anything today. If you will please excuse me, you look terrible. I will fix you something."

Trasker left the room.

Kris dropped down, put his arms around me, and buried his face in my neck.

"We'll find him, Uncle Nick. He's O.K. That's a fact, and ... we'll find him."

***

I thought I was alone in the library. Trasker had set out some sandwiches and laid a fire. It was raining — a cold and desolate spring downpour. The tall windows were blurry with the storm spew. I drank

The Ivory Knife

Kayne's preferred brew, Hibiki on the rocks. Sitting on the floor, my back against the sofa's edge, I stared into the fire.

Alice and Chouko watched me as they lay before the fire. Their droopy eyes signaled they would not be able to keep the vigil. I figured everyone had either left or gone to bed. The house seemed cavernous.

Breathing deeply, I longed to feel him in this place. His presence seemed just out of reach, like he would be returning from an errand any minute now. Nevertheless, I was unable to go up to our bedroom. Kayne's smell, his things, and aura would be even stronger there, and I'm not sure I could keep it together. And I had to. I had to stay tough as the point person on his disappearance.

I was surprised when the tears came. I mean, WTF? Talking snot crying. Soundless at first. Then I covered my mouth as the sobbing got louder.

So, here's where Kayne would hold me and tell me it would be all right. He'd settle next to me and pull me into a hug – yeah, like that, solid and reassuring.

I should have kept you close, Bossman. This shit is all my fault. We protect each other. I am so sorry, Kayne.

In my delirium, I pulled him closer, still crying like a five-year-old. My arms locked onto him as if I were drowning, and he was a life preserver.

"You did the best you could have done, Nick. You are not to blame for this."

Oscar held on to me in the flickering firelight. He said softly, "You must try and sleep."

Thomas Paul Severino

Chapter Six: An Iron-Clad Offer
The University of San Francisco, San Francisco, California

Nick Sechi's Journal

"Uncle Nick. I am really sorry about this. You need this right now like you need a hole in the head."

"Whatever. So used to this, let me tell you. Also, I will go nutso banging around 221, waiting to hear some news. Anyway ... let's do this."

I looked at Eric, grinding out a cigarette in our only ashtray.

"No offense, Commander, but I don't want you going into the university vice president's office and getting all wild-assed on the reverends."

Eric smiled and put a hand on my shoulder. "Pretty smart, Red. Calm, cool, and family. That's how we'll roll with this. Then we'll find the professor."

The morning sun on the patio promised another beautiful early fall day.

I said, "Deal."

The Commander straightened his son's tie.

Kris avoided eye contact.

Keeping his hands on Kris' neck, Eric said, "Following this meeting, son, we will need to deconstruct this episode. For now, you are repentant and filled with remorse. Your Uncle and I will do the talking. Nick knows Catholics. Rumor has it he was one once."

***

"It will not be much longer, gentlemen. Father Cipolla and Coach McDaniel will see you soon."

I had been mulling over the last 48 hours in my waiting room chair. To be honest, I had said very little on this subject since finding out, except to insist on being a part of the meeting. Kris expected my anger would be monumental, but emotionally, I was only concerned with the whereabouts of my husband.

Kristof was wiggling like a strip of bacon on a grill. (So much for calm and cool.) He stood up a few times and walked around the reception area. This was big trouble, and he knew it.

Eric was likewise super uncomfortable. I suspect it was more about having to wear a collared shirt and a pair of slacks than attending a disciplinary meeting about his son. I could tell he wanted a cigarette and was in a mood where he would tell anyone who said, "no smoking, please," to go fuck themselves.

The vice president's office door opened, and his assistant motioned us in. We shook hands, all but Kris. He just nodded – up from a slightly hangdog position. Father Cipolla asked us to join the soccer Coach and him at his conference table. The assistant asked us if we wanted something to drink.

Whiskey, neat.

I joined the others in saying, "Nothing, thank you."

"Can I smoke in here?"

"No, Mr. Sorenson."

You would have thought Eric had asked if he could kick a puppy.

Around us, saints and apostles, together with portraits of distinguished administrators, looked down from dark paneled walls. An enormous fireplace dominated the space behind Father Cipolla's large wood-carved desk. The surroundings were like a scene from a movie about Boys' Town in the 40s.

The vice president began with a summary of the traditions of the very Catholic University. He droned on about what was expected of its students' moral behavior. He cited the student handbook and the disciplinary code.

Pointing to the young culprit, the VP continued, "While this is not about homosexuality, the sexual behavior of Kristof Sorenson on a viral tape will bring dishonor to the University to an intolerable degree. To this end, the

The Ivory Knife

University's academic board has decided to suspend his athletic scholarship.

"Fuck the money. Are you going to throw my son off the team?"

"Yes, Sir. We cannot .... well, to put it bluntly, board members are urging me to encourage the family to find another school for the boy."

"I am sorry to interrupt, but I have a few questions."

"It is I who am sorry, Sir. Who are you, and what is your relationship with this boy?"

"I'm Nick Sechi. I am Kris' employer and former guardian. I am married to his Uncle, Dr. Kayne Sorenson. My father-in-law, Thomas M. Sorenson of Alice Springs, Australia, is one of the University's major donors, as are we."

I sensed a different level of interest had made its appearance.

"Mr. Eric Sorenson is my brother-in-law. You will no doubt remember our consulting firm in the affair of the DaVinci painting a few months back. I understand the Vatican was very appreciative of our work."

So, O.K., all of our street creds were on the table. Name-dropping the Pope – nothing like it. I took a deep breath and continued.

"All due respect, Father, my nephew is not a boy. He is a man and a very fine man. Frankly, considering how institutional scandals go, the sexual misbehavior of a 20-year-old engaged in a consenting act has little potential to bring down this auspicious institution or even besmirch its reputation."

Draw your own inferences, Father.

"Therefore, I believe our focus should be on what is best for this young man, given his serious mistake of judgment."

Eric pointed to Austin McDaniel.

"Is he a good athlete?"

"Kris is one of the finest players I have ever coached, Mr. Sorenson."

"Damn, right, mate."

He looked at the vice president.

"His grades?"

The administrator shuffled some papers, looked up, and said, "Exceptional."

Eric said, "I also understand he is quite a good actor in the University's theater company."

Hold on, folks, here goes.

I added, "Since coming to the University, my nephew has been honored for his community service for two consecutive years. He regularly serves mass at St. Ignatius and is the Cardinal's favorite master of ceremonies. Kristof founded the University's Kid's Soccer Camp, which trains physically and emotionally challenged children in athletics and coordinates university academic and life coaching resources. I understand both your Dean of Social Work and your Vice President for Medical Science Education think he hung the moon."

"Gentlemen, it is not only this tape with an outsider. There are rumors regarding an illicit relationship with one of our faculty members."

"You fire him?"

"No, Mr. Sorenson. *She* is still employed by the University."

Eric tried hard not to look like he was hearing about this for the first time. He said, "Interesting."

"I thought for a moment that you would preach to us about illicit sexual behavior, Father, but considering the current controversies about ...."

I did not finish. I let it hang right there. My point was made without any elaboration.

"Gentlemen, please. The many sins of the church notwithstanding, this tape will offend our alumni and drive our donors to desert us. It is everywhere. In this age of social media hysteria, we cannot afford to put the University in a bad light."

"Would you be so kind as to pull up the offending video on your computer, Father?"

The Ivory Knife

The vice president lifted a keyboard set into the underside of the conference table and cued up the PC. The monitor on the wall flickered to life.

Error. There is no such web address.

He tried again. Same message.

I handed him my phone. The screen showed the same message. The Coach had the same experience. He held up his iPhone.

"Gone."

The priest stepped out of the office for a moment and returned.

"I don't understand. Our tech department finds nothing anywhere."

"It seems we have a lack of *habeas corpus,* Father. Wouldn't you say?"

"But how can this be?"

Coach McDaniel said, "I believe we can tame this bronco down on the field, Mr. Sorenson. Father, he'll be too tired for any mischief for quite a while. Be in your gear and on the pitch at three, Sorenson."

Salute, Coach. You sure can try.

I said nothing.

As we stood to leave, I pushed the envelope across the desk.

"My husband and I would like to endow an athletic scholarship for an LGBTQ+ student. The details are outlined in the letter of agreement attached to the check. I would like a request for a donation to cover the expenses of the Soccer Camp to be forwarded to our firm at the appropriate time So that my husband and I may consider a donation before the end of the fiscal."

Eric added a second gift.

"This comes with a request for masses to be said in your church in memory of *Kralsko Visochestvo,* Princess Margarita Koháry. She was my son's grandmother."

Thomas Paul Severino

Chapter Seven: A Clue
Trouble Coffee, 4033 Judah St, San Francisco, CA

Nick Sechi's Journal

"Dad. I will take care of this."

"You've done enough, lad, no fault of your own. It's in your genes. Sometime remind me to tell you about my undergraduate days at the University of Notre Dame. Sex has a way of making people crazy as a pack of wet dingos. As your uncle, Kayne, would say, time to think with the big head... Ah, here we are. Thanks for meeting us, Starr."

Declan Starr was a photog of hot renown. He was handsome and fit, and he knew it. Smug and superior, Starr was instantly unlikeable. As he sat, he said, "I'm sorry. And just who are you? My secretary said Kris wanted ... so, I am rather confused."

"Yeah, so I'm the lad's father. Nah, nah, nah. Sit, Mr. Starr. No worries. We just have some questions."

Kris looked like he wanted the earth to swallow him up.

"This is my brother-in-law, Nick Sechi, a partner in Sorenson and Sechi Inc. They are consulting detectives – quite famous, actually. Kris has class, so we'll check in later, son."

Kris left without a word or a look at anyone. Talk about "his tail between his legs;" the kid was mortified.

Eric began.

"Ya see, the thing here is ... *I said* sit down, mate."

Wavering but not sitting, Starr said, "He's of age. You have nothing on me. I'm leaving."

Eric stood and placed a hand on the man's chest. The Commander pushed him carefully back into his chair. He lit a cigarette and continued. Eric's voice changed to a tone one would expect from a demon in an M.

Night Shyamalan supernatural thriller – the devil gives voice to the terror -- chilling.

"I am not used to being interrupted, so sit there, ya bitch, and listen to what I have to say. If he has told you anything about his father, you know what I am capable of. So I will tell you precisely what you are going to do as soon as we leave you.'

I could tell that Starr was becoming unglued. Eric was a star psycho in my blog and books. That reputation caused the photographer to sweat.

"My son volunteers at a mission in the Tenderloin. I believe Starr Photography will become a significant lifetime sponsor of that charity. You will do a photo series, *gratis* of course, for this website."

He passed the now quivering man the editor's contact information.

"You are mistaken, Mr...."

"Also, you will discuss a short documentary with this company on the work the University of San Francisco does in the community. The Soccer camp and the kids they serve will be the centerpiece. Again, you will assume all expenses."

"Well, this is just...."

I broke in, "If you were told not to interrupt, it is best not to, Mr. Starr. Commander Sorenson has gone to a lot of trouble to ensure that the incriminating tape has vanished. I'm talking everywhere, dude. That shit never was. In this age of all things viral, I would think twice about what you record with your intimates. My firm has taken on quite a few ahh ... blackmailers. You have made it very easy to watch you."

Eric lifted his cup and looked at me. I retrieved it and headed into the shop for a refill. I remained inside and watched. Eric was speaking with his face very close to Starr's. The man was visibly trembling.

Then the dude slumped forward.

Holy shit, he killed the son of a bitch.

I dashed out.

The Ivory Knife

"Thanks, but on second thought, I may have had enough caffeine, mate."

I put two fingers on the man's neck.

Fainted.

***

"I have that effect on people when I want something. Shall we steal his britches?"

"No, too juvenile. And yeah, dude. You can make someone's scrotum shrivel just with just the sound of your voice."

Eric shrugged.

We were joined by a familiar young man with a smiling face and a shock of brilliant white hair. He bent to kiss the Commander and nodded to me.

Pointing to the unconscious photographer, Oscar Stål said, "Ahh, the nefarious Mr. Starr. Have you killed him?"

"Nah, just about to cut off his balls, is all. Best to do that when he's unconscious. Kris will be home late, and we will wrap this up."

Oscar dug in his pocket and handed me a key.

"Andi sent this along. It came just a bit ago marked 'Mr. Nicola Sechi confidential.' It was not sent by mail, Nick. Someone dropped in the firm's mailbox."

I turned the very odd-shaped metal. There was a number etched onto the rounded part.

"A post office box. Let's move, dudes."

We left Starr. Eric went back for the man's pants.

Thomas Paul Severino

Chapter Eight: Mycroft
221 Baker Street, San Francisco, California

Nick Sechi's Journal

"It was Mycroft. Took him about ten minutes to hack every copy in the cyberverse. The tape, in effect, ate itself."

"Like it never happened, Andi. They thought they had been seeing things," I said.

"Please see what our artificial genius can make of this. There are about five hundred post offices in the Bay Area. That doesn't include the private mailbox and package companies."

Andi took pictures of the key and uploaded them to our investigator program.

"How'd it go at the university?"

I spread my hands wide.

"No tape, no problem. The solution was a bit expensive, but whatever."

"Lesson learned?"

"What do you think?"

"Nick, I have my doubts. When do you guys get to stop rescuing him? Kris needs to learn the difference between having a pair of balls and growing a pair of balls. This crap about everyone having a sex tape these days is fucked up, if you'll pardon my language, Nick. Kris is on the cutting edge of doing something amazing with his life. Making the wrong choices will default him to douchebag status. Believe me, I know."

"Andi, you know, I think it's about time the kiddo had a Father. A real Father and not a couple of subs. I have a feeling the Commander is getting into the role. You know what I mean?"

She nodded her head.

Thomas Paul Severino

I continued, "I don't know if it's the eyes or the voice or the muscled-up daddy body, but when Eric turns on the heat, knees crumble. Whatever he said to Starr – the dude passed out. Right there in Trouble Coffee, face down on the table. I am positive Kris will get a taste of that realness soon if he hasn't already."

Andi said, "I know what you mean. Commander Sorenson is stone-cold scary when he wants to be. Gives me the chills when he ... wait, Nick. Here's Mycroft."

"Good afternoon, Mr. Sechi. I am happy to assist you. The key is from Mailboxes Incorporated, 2386 Lombard Street. Box number 534 is a package-sized chamber in the fifth row. It was recently rented by A. Lorax yesterday. The address given is fictitious."

"Thank you. Mycroft, I want you to watch Declan Starr, the photographer. Should you find that he posts more salacious material on the internet, we need to know about it. I'm talking about content like the tape you made disappear. Be on the lookout for any pornographic situation where the participant seems unaware of the recording, and Starr could violate privacy rules."

"It will be done, Sir."

"Please remember, this surveillance should be within the law also."

"Understood."

"Mycroft, anything on Dr. Sorenson?"

"Mr. Sechi, I am currently tracing twenty-three persons of interest who were active in Ft. Lauderdale on the night of Dr. Sorenson's disappearance. However, my information is somewhat redundant as Agent Chance and her team are exploring these individuals. The probability that Dr. Sorenson is alive is ...."

"Stop. Thank you, Mycroft."

That was a statistic I would rather not know.

I turned to Andi.

"I'm out."

The Ivory Knife

"Anything I can do, Nick?"

I shrugged and pointed to her computer.

"Find him."

Thomas Paul Severino

Chapter Nine: Cleaning up

The University of San Francisco and 456 Burnett Street, San Francisco, California

Notes by The Kris

"So what have we learned from this experience, Sorenson?'

"Oh, shit, Coach. I mean, Jeeze. This gonna be another KPIP lecture? I am up to here with all that."

The squad was doing drills and scrimmaging. McDaniel pulled me off the field to bend my ear.

"KPIP?"

"Yeah, Keep Pecker In Pants. Look. I like sexin' up. Always have. All good. No one gets hurt."

"Say that last part again."

"Coach, no one gets hurt."

"We're going to need to come back to that, Sorenson. I think you're total bullshit on that one."

He took a step closer.

"Two things. You are a talented jock, kid. You think it's about the team needing you in this, huh? Don't kid yourself, hotshot. Look at me right here. Sorenson, you need the team. If anything is gonna pull your head out of your ass, it is the twenty guys who call you a teammate. Do not do anything to get you thrown out of this University. And, kid, think carefully before you play in the sack.'

"What's the other?"

"Always, always, always, check the room for cameras, you dope."

"That it, 'cause I gotta get going?

Thomas Paul Severino

"No, that's not it. Fifty wind sprints. Now. Suppose we add this to your daily workout. You so need to calm the fuck down."

***

"Ouch. Hooo hoo. Blond Baby Boy's in trouble again. Gotta clean the locker room for a whole month yet. Team laundry and everything. Hey, gay boy, wanna get all pervy over my sweaty gear? Mac here will post a vid of you on TikTok. Know you like that."

It's hard to love these guys 'cause some of them are real dicks, ya know? I was tired and still a bit on edge and these guys gotta start, right? I turned away and looked for a broom.

Evan Lassiter is a senior, plays backfield, and has a real problem with The Kris. Thinks I'm too cocky, up and coming, and a total showboater. I'd say he's got twenty pounds on me. Handles it well. Defenders do a lot of weight training for size. But The Kris has the moves.

His buddy, Joel MacAllister, is a total hanger-on suck-up. Probably the dumbest dude on the team. Lassiter pulls his strings. Together, they can really ride my ass, but I got this, you know? Teamwork is essential and all that, but the bottom line is getting the soccer ball in the net. Understand? Respect comes when you score, and The Kris scores. Oh yes, he does.

"Heard your bare ass and faggot dick made the internet, Baby Boy. What, you do somebody a favor to make it go away? More of the nasty nasty?"

He did a pouch grab as he undressed. They threw their dirty practice uniforms and gear at my feet. Other guys watched, chuckled, and waited to see how far these two would go with their shit. Team Captain Jesse Okeyo seemed uninterested, being late off the practice field. He stripped and towel-wrapped. Intended destination – the showers.

So now, the big jerkwad is getting loud.

"Ya know, Mac, my dad told me they used to stuff queer boys in lockers when he was in school. Shouldn't be checking out the asses and business of real men like they do, in the showers and all, ya know?"

Here it comes. The bully motioned to the locker room door.

The Ivory Knife

"Billy, keep an eye out for Coach. Mac, roll the laundry cart over near Sorenson's locker.

"Whadda say, Sorenson? You wanna kiss my ass, huh? Do ya, fag? Answer me."

Lassiter's big mistake was that he then touched The Kris. Just a grab on the shoulder but in violation of rule number one: The Kris is never deliberately touched unless he allows it.

Okeyo dropped down on a bench and folded his arms. Spectator. Lassiter went right, and Mac rolled left.

My roundhouse kick across the solar plexus knocked the beefy fullback into an open equipment locker. Asshole Evan looked like somebody threw a rag doll, and he was it. Balls and nets tumbled out on the big jerk. Next, Mac Allister was in on the charge. I caught him with a back-thrown elbow to the throat, and he staggered. Turning, I grabbed him by the front of his t-shirt and delivered three bitch slaps that sent him head over ass into the restroom, slipping and tumbling against the urinals.

Sam Casey, our goaltender, reached over and took an iPhone from one of Lassiter's boys. The guy was filming my rampage. He spun and tossed it. It went up, over, and dropped into the mop pail of soapy water.

"I think we've had enough of that for a while, dumbass."

A third doofus started for me, a second-string defender. I pulled off my tee and did a rage flex like some MMA movie dude, teeth gnashing and eyes bulging. (I'm an actor, after all, Uncle Nick. I rock all this muscle to intimidate. GRRRR!!!)

"Bring it, Wilson. You hot to join your buds licking the floor? Huh? Huh?"

I stomped like a Mauri doing the Haka.

The guy backed off. In fact, he left the locker room. Two other kiss-asses also did, unable to meet my eyes as they went.

Dead silence.

The claps were a single, then a pair, a ripple, then a cascade, and next, what was almost an ovation as Jesse Okeyo was joined by the other team members. He walked forward and shook my hand.

"Straight out of High School, Kris. Those jerks reminded me of nights and days in the tenth grade. Well done, mate. You can do my laundry any day, my man."

Got a bro hug, then a few more. I walked over and attempted to untangle a semi-conscious Lassiter. Jesse was trying to right MacAllister.

"Sorenson, what the hell is going on?"

"Nothing, Coach. Just thought 'cleaning out the locker room' meant taking out the big trash first."

***

"What's up?"

"Your Uncle Nick invited us for dinner."

"I pass."

"No. Not an option."

"But, Dad."

"Son, shame will destroy you if you let it. You messed up, but it has been resolved. There is to be no hiding. Nick is in a tough place, and we should care. You're going."

Oscar looked up from repairing the kitchen backsplash. Turns out he's a pro at remodeling stuff. The house on Divisidero was looking better than ever these days.

"Kris, hold this tile for me, please. A little pressure. Good."

He stepped back and measured. I couldn't run or hide. My dad stood in the open doorway smoking. Oscar allowed no smoking in the house.

"Starr?"

"Not a thing. Not anymore, anyway. My journalist bloke told me the drongo contacted him about the photo piece."

The Ivory Knife

I wasn't sure if I liked the sound of that.

"No lecture?"

"Now that you mention it, I have something to say."

He pointed, and I sat.

This is gonna be bad, my fans and loves.

I started to sweat.

"Sometimes institutions have their head up their collective asses, Kristof. But to focus on the failings of the University's response to your bullshit, and it *was* bullshit, would be another mistake, one that your family will not allow. You need to fix this in yourself."

My dad stepped closer to me making sure I looked him in the eyes as he spoke. When I was in school in Sofia, I used to anticipate his coming to visit. Having a heart-to-heart when I was a kid was something I looked forward to. When it was time to reprimand my ass, it was usually Prince Kirill, my grandmother's husband, who brought the house down with a military discipline quality. This was pretty unnerving – taking the wind out of my sails.

"See, here's the thing. We bought you off. If that teaches you that you can get away with shit, your uncles and I are failing you miserably. That being said, the causes we are throwing money at are worthy in themselves. If our philanthropy caused the University to rethink some priorities, perhaps that is a happy ending, no pun intended."

He stopped and seemed to make sure he was making his point.

"I realize that I am a fine one to be giving advice on sexin' up and public displays of lustful behavior, but you need to remember not to put yourself or anyone else in a compromising position because you are letting your lust do the thinking for you.

"Finally, there was a lot of cash represented by those envelopes. Your uncles came through for you in a big way. Knowing what Nick and Kayne stand for, you will tell me how you intend to make this up to them. And you have to the end of the week to tell me."

Throughout this lesson, he never lost eye contact and would not allow me to look away. My father's last point was made using his Commander Sorenson voice delivered as he stepped even closer to me. I noticed that Oscar, standing behind him, was very interested in what his partner had to say to his wayward son.

"Do I make myself clear?"

"Yes, Sir."

He walked to the sink to wash his hands and nodded.

"Good. Help Oscar."

We went back to the backsplash. I assisted the tiler by pressing where instructed. I could tell Oscar wanted to weigh in but waited for the right moment. He released me from my Mastic tile adhesive bondage with a thank you.

"You are very quiet on this one, Dr. Stål," I tempted. What the hell? Everybody gets a shot.

As I stepped back, he slathered up another row of freshly cut subway tiles. Without looking at me, he said, "I am a quiet man, Kris. But, perhaps some advice."

I wiped my hands.

Oscar took the rag and rubbed the new tiles, pleased at our work.

"It is, perhaps, quite simple. Kris, there is an old saying in Finland that my grandmother used to say. *'Et vittu missä syöt.'*"

Off to the side, my dad chuckled.

"Do you know it?"

"Any chance you been talking to my Nonna Sechi, dude?"

Oscar shrugged. I headed for my room to get cleaned up but turned and said one last thing.

"Yeah. 'Don't shit where you eat.' It is Viola's line. Only she serves it with Pasta alla Norma, and you gimme backsplash adhesive. I'll get changed."

The Ivory Knife

Oscar said, "A wise woman."

Thomas Paul Severino

Chapter Ten: Joe
221 Baker Street, San Francisco, California

Nick Sechi's Journal

"It's GI Joe. My cousin, Nolo, and I each had one when we were kids in the Bronx. We played soldier a lot. But this one is way different."

Oscar poured another round of a 2019 Syrah from one of Kayne's favorites, St. Supéry Estate Vineyard in Napa. The spring evening brought on a bit of a chill, but the night was clear.

The wine and the fire pit ("Alexa, turn on the fire pit." "OK.") warmed us up. Eric, Andi, Oscar, and Kris had come to dinner – one of Trasker's best, and we were kicking back on the patio. Raul, Andi's main man, and Matt Crowley, Kris' 'usta be' or 'sometimes be,' I can't keep track, showed up for an after-dinner drink.

We got excuses in stereo.

Raul to Andi: "Work, bae. Went over. You get my text?"

Matt to Kris: "Work, bae. Went over. You get my text?"

Kris and Andi retrieved their respective plates from the kitchen where Trasker was keeping them warm.

The main attraction was the contents of PO Box 534, a shirtless military doll in camos and boots. We rewound.

Andi placed a plate of Chicken Maricaibo in front of Raul. To me, she said, "It's different? How so, Nick?"

"Someone's done a number on it with a Sharpie, Andi. Look at the designs in the drab-colored patches of his uniform pants."

Eric said, "It's Cyrillic lettering. Kris?"

Considering recent events, the family's youngest member had been uncustomarily quiet. He stopped talking to Matt at Eric's query and turned

GI Joe in his hands. Kris had become fluent in his family's native tongue in his boyhood in Bulgaria.

"Not Bulgarian, Russian. Hold on ... yes."

He turned the toy.

"Marvelous ... ahhh ... marvelous professor. I guess the dude's playing you, Uncle Nick. See, this as a mime for Uncle Kayne – soldier of fortune and all that. But, this word is 'marvelous' in Russian. Kayne the Marvelous Professor? Odd."

Andi said, "We are getting a lot of crap about Dr. Sorenson's disappearance. This could be a considerable nothing."

I took the overly muscled soldier from Kris and repeated his translation. I think it was Raul who said, "Reverse it. Professor Marvelous. Nick ...."

His dark eyes sparkled as the synapses clicked in his brain. Raul and Andi said it simultaneously.

"Professor Marvel!"

"Fuck me. I know where he is."

***

"If they are coming for us ... and that is something Kayne has believed for a while, Eric. We have interfered with some real criminal masterminds. They will come for Kris or any one of us."

The Commander looked into the dark night and across the Bay. He was doing well in recovery under Oscar's tutelage. The irregularity of his eye had just about cleared up. He still cut an imposing figure physically – those sexy Sorenson genes. But domestic life was beginning to soften his edges a bit.

"Nick, Oscar would kick my ass if he knew. I still have some contacts in that spy cesspool that made me a monster, so yeah. V for vendetta, boyo. The 'big bads.' as you call them, want heads. This smells of the Russian bear. They got Kayne, I've no fuckin' doubt."

"Asguard."

He exhaled blue-grey smoke in the coming fog.

The Ivory Knife

"The billet is playing it cagey, lad. Russia for Asguard is a real challenge, so they're not really saying. I will stay on it, though."

"Andi set up my trip. My flight leaves tonight. Stay safe, you fuckin' crazy ass."

He grinned.

"Always wrap the big guy when I ...."

"You know what I'm talking about, Commander Nutso. I have too much to worry about without you pulling shit."

He looked at me. Was it a grin or a maniacal leer? Who knows.

I felt strong hands come around me from behind.

"Just wanted to say sorry for the most recent shit I caused."

"Kris ...."

"Naw, Uncle Nick. You thought I was gonna do a tag-along. Right? Last thing you need is me on this. Sticking to school and my sports and the volunteer stuff. Matt, ahhh, he was ... well, that's not important right now. Anyway, please keep me in the loop and let me know if I can help with details and shit."

This was unexpected. Kris seemed to be a bit humbled by the whole Declan Starr affair. Another episode of loved and lost? Nah. My nephew was far too bright to overthink a sex-up from a troll who was into muscled jocks. He knew he did not lose a love of a lifetime.

Could this be Eric's paternal success where Kayne and I had failed? The Commander had the resources of one very sensible Oscar Stål. Too good to be true if you ask me. My brother-in-law was still quite a bit batshit crazy. Just sayin'.

"Kiddo, I was going to ask for your help but need you to remain in San Francisco. I can say this outside, Bud. I don't trust Mycroft. Something. Maybe I just got a bad case of paranoia, but he has been relatively little help with the abduction right from the start. We also need more on who rented that PO Box. See what you can do. I need to pack."

"Count on me, Uncle Nick. I'm a changed man."

Eric walked off. I took Kris by the shoulder.

"Not sure I want you to change – all that much anyway, kiddo. It just so happens there is a young man over there who will take you any way he can get you, Kris. Why? I am not sure I know."

He looked at me with wondering eyes.

"Be kind whatever you decide, kiddo."

Chapter Eleven: The WhistlePig

456 Burnett Street, San Francisco, California

"You're soaked."

Eric put down the bottle of WhistlePig 10. Pulled a packet of cigarettes from his jeans pocket and tossed them on the dresser. He pulled the white cotton undershirt that clung to his upper body like a second skin over his head.

Oscar shuffled his portfolio and made notes from his place on the bed. He said, "You're dripping, Eric."

He pointed with a pencil but did not look up.

"Bathtub, Commander."

With one hand, Eric balled up the t-shirt. The other snagged the whiskey for another pull. He sauntered to the bathroom and made slapping noises tossing his wet clothes into the tub. He returned naked, holding a bath towel to wipe his torso. He shook his head like one of the family dogs.

"Not funny. So very not funny."

Oscar snatched the corner of the bedsheet and wiped his papers. He glared up at the naked man.

"You are impossible."

The returning comment was low-pitched and almost a rumble.

"You left out how smoking hot I look. And you can't handle all this trouble? Is that what I'm hearing?"

Sorenson, the Fallen Angel, stretched his arms — a surrender, a reveal, or a tease?

Oscar ignored the inference.

"As I say often, I see where Kristof gets his cockiness. Sit down. Where were you?"

Thomas Paul Severino

The younger man took the towel and dried the broad back of his love. He lightly traced the scars, some prominent, some faint, on his man's body. Oscar knelt behind his partner and rubbed the water from Eric's hair.

"I was in the garden, smoking, and haven' off a that rippa of a bottle of ten-year small batch. Nick and Kayne gave it to us. It's raining, boyo."

He reached for the bottle and took another whiskey pull.

"Yes," Oscar said. "It was a gift for our housewarming. You were doing your deep thinking. I wonder what about."

He leaned over Eric's shoulder and kissed him. The Commander brought his hand up to Oscar's head and shared the flavors of caramel, burnt orange, and smoke with the invading mouth.

They were silent for a bit. Oscar went back to his papers. He said, "I have been rethinking the kitchen. Much too small. Perhaps removing this wall ... would open it up a great amount. It is, after all, the heart of the house. We want people to gather there with us."

He pointed to a place on a blueprint page. Eric turned and took the papers. Standing, he plopped them on the club chair.

Not to be brushed aside, Oscar pressed.

"By the way, what did you think of my proposal? There is a chance that flipping houses could be quite lucrative for us. Stål and Sorenson – no, we do not want to use your name. Perhaps not mine, either. So anyway, 'Something Something Homes.' I will be the brains, and you can be the muscle – you know, lift heavy things and demolish the walls, et cetera."

Eric ignored the direction of the conversation.

"And here I thought you'd be up here having a flog -- getting up your energy to give your man some sizzling body heat. We're putting this shit away."

"Sit back down. Truth be told, I *was* having a bit of a fantasy."

Eric knew. He said, "Drake Culver... ya dirty blugger."

The name just hung out there.

The Ivory Knife

"You are so full of shit, Oscar. Ya do that to get me mad as a cut snake. Your pervy contractor is even older than me. And ...."

The ex-paramilitary ran a hand down his chiseled torso.

"Uh-huh. I will be the first to admit that daddy issues are my own private fetish. But this is something you know well, Commander. You also know you are my total fantasy man, which may be a disadvantage – it makes you too sure of yourself. More Sorenson overconfidence. Interesting."

Oscar knelt and dried Eric's feet and lower legs.

Eric snagged the man's white-blond hair in a clenched fist. Pulled his face into a deadly eye contact position.

"You love playing a dangerous game, don't you, boyo? You would love to be my little 'slapa' tramp. You know just the right buttons to push to savage up the game -- fucking master at antagonizing my libido."

The smile and the steely blue-eyed gaze were those of a first-class tempter. They both loved the game of wild passion.

Eric leaned down and pulled the man by the throat on top of him. Oscar somehow managed to lose his boxer shorts.

"You should shower before ... the bed and all ... Huh?"

"After, bitch. Just do as you are told."

***

"He feels guilty. And I am cold."

"Some bloody Viking."

Eric pulled the man closer to him as they sat on the open window ledge. The rain had stopped. The Commander flicked an ash into the alley below.

"Oscar, was I over the top this afternoon with Kris? I was thinking, who really gives a bloody piss that Kristof pounded some blugger in front of the whole bleeding universe? That lad ruts like a Sorenson and knows how to get on social media. Should do one of those fans-only thingos. Moffies will pay to see ... anyway, I just wonder."

"Eric, that sounds like pimping your own flesh and blood. And wait a minute, I thought your kitchen lecture was just what the boy needs. Sounds like you are switching horses in mid-stride. Where is this coming from?"

"Haven't you heard, boy? I'm schizophrenic. What the fuck ever, and what in bloody hell is he mooning about? Swear his balls are shriveling."

Oscar came out of the grip of the smoking naked man on the windowsill and reached for the duvet. Wrapping it around himself, he sat at the feet of the man he had loved since those first moments at the Finnish asylum. His back was against the tall Australian's leg.

"I will make you a case, Commander. Nick feels that what has happened to Kayne is somehow his fault. In like manner, Kris thinks that what has happened to Kayne is somehow his fault. What do these two sets of feelings have in common?"

"Catholic guilt."

"Precisely. Flavorful by any and all means. The Bulgarian nuns' flavor... the Jesuits flavor, the Italian American sisters of Bronx, good fathers of the Archdiocese of New York."

"*The* Bronx, Doctor."

Oscar waved a "whatever." And shared the Whistle Pig

"Interesting, *Rakkaani*. Please listen to what I say. Do not attempt to make the boy over in your former image. Raise him up and encourage his responsibility. You each have a noble heart."

He winked and added, "All evidence to the contrary notwithstanding. *Rakkaani.*

This was the second time Oscar used the Finnish word of endearment.

He caressed his beloved, tracing a hand over the bigger man's leg as he continued, "And in each of these cases, please consider how these men have responded. Nick, on the one hand, is feeling lost. His identity is so merged with Kayne's. We say this portends an authentic mourning experience."

Eric tossed the smoke and slid down to his cocooned lover.

The Ivory Knife

Oscar went on, "Kris is feeling shamed. He is often at odds with both Nick and Kayne. Kris is the new gay man — another generation with so much to assimilate and apparently not learning his lessons fast enough, according to your brother, nor appreciative enough to behave, according to your brother-in-law. He feels that Kayne has been taken from him because he is bad. Most interesting."

"Sometimes, I think I was better at waging dirty wars. This fatherhood and family shit has always been a wank-off for me."

Oscar fell silent, letting these new feelings wash through. Then, he said, "This is new territory, *Rakkaani*. You did not raise him. Your mother did, and later, Nick and Kayne. You will learn."

Eric said softly, "And just who is raising whom?"

The big man stretched out alongside Oscar but opposite, head to feet. He folded his arms beneath his head. His body was a slightly scarred work of art honed by years of combat in the most deadly spy games.

"Matt?"

"Ha. A charming lovesick lad with a masochistic side. He keeps coming back for more. They need to decide who they want to be to each other. But that may be in a while. Such is youthful love, Commander. Adolescent angst — it lasts many years."

Eric held the bottle of WhistlePig 10 up to the bedroom's ambient light. It twinkled amber and green. The rain gusts started again, soft, salty, and chilled. A police car raced up the hill beyond the house. Out in the Bay, a foghorn moaned in the gloomy darkness

"Why are you so smart? So smart and delicious? Huh? Oh yeah, Kris asked if Matt could stay. I said that was O.K."

"I have a question, Commander?"

"Yes?"

"Why are we lying here on the floor? In Finland, we have beds with blankets for *vittu*."

Eric sat up and removed the comforter. A light rain blew into the room and spritzed their two naked bodies.

Thomas Paul Severino

"That is because now *I* am given over to fantasy. You remember ... the asylum, the warm rain, the scorching rut against the courtyard wall? You wanted it, that is for sure – going bloody bunta, ya hot devil."

He crawled towards his shivering man like a panther, muscles tight and flexing in the teasing shadows. Oscar was transfixed.

Hypnotically soft, Eric's husky voice returned as he continued, "Yeahhh ...how you looked. Wet. And how you yelled into the night air."

The old bedroom window sash descended slowly, blocking the rain as the room heated up.

Chapter Twelve: The Savant
The Cecil Bacon Manor, 959 Broadway, Seattle, Washington
Nick Sechi's Journal

"It doesn't make any sense, Nick. I will level with you. Someone messed up with the security cameras at the Lombard Street mailbox place. I sent an agent there but came up with Nada. I am thinking, not a coincidence. What did you find inside?"

I picked up my iPhone and continued my FaceTime conversation with Special Agent Mary Chance. I gave Joe a camera shot.

"That is what was in the box. Yeah, fucked if I know. Anyway, keep me posted, and I will do the same."

We ended the call, and I gazed into the room of the bed and breakfast Andi had booked for me. Another night, I hadn't slept. I landed at SeaTac Airport around half-past midnight. The Uber through the city to the Capitol Hill District was utterly painless. It was raining—typical Seattle weather and the driver was uncommunicative.

As I got out of my clothes, my thoughts were rambling. Was I in the right place? My mind returned to the kindly charlatan and the little girl in the gypsy wagon.

The kindly man with the white mustache gazes into his crystal ball and "reads what's inside of her." Professor Marvel tells Dorothy that she thinks the folks at home don't understand her, and, with some help from the gathering storm, she is on her way to a place beyond the sun and moon.

I sat on the bed and held my head.

O.K, Sechi. Seattle. The Emerald City. Thank you, Kayne-GI Joe-Professor Marvel. What the fuck now?

I paid little attention to the features of my destination, given the rain and all. At the ornate wooden house, the night key was under the mat. On the hall table was a welcome note with directions to my room. So, the inspection of my surroundings began from a queen-sized bed in the inn's second-floor Venetian Room.

Thomas Paul Severino

The dawn light through the suite windows caused the Victorian appointments to glisten and shine like a jeweled box. Storm clouds had fled, trailing out over Puget Sound and moving past Lake Washington and into the mountains to the city's east. The front left behind what appeared to be a gorgeous morning in the temperate rainforest – all drippy, breezy, green, and under a brilliant blue sky.

After checking in with Mary, I pulled on some sports togs and my runners -- my exploring kit, and headed downstairs to get some coffee.

O.K. Professor Marvel, "Read my past, present, and future in your crystal ball.

"Good morning. I'm Mrs. Honoria McCave. Welcome to the Cecil Bacon Manor."

The rather attractive woman was fortyish and beamed like the morning sun in the leaves of the house's garden. On the dining room floor, behind Mrs. McCave, was a sculpture of a chubby pig. There was a story here.

"Please let us know if there is anything you need, Mr. Sechi. What brings you to Seattle, if I may ask? Business?"

She paused. The inn's hostess fixed ole Nicky Boy in a stare that seemed to penetrate his psyche, friendly but a bit passing strange. Mrs. McCave continued, "No, no, don't tell me. Love, I believe. Such a handsome young man. You are up very early."

"Thought I'd go out for a run, to be honest. Yeah, here to hunt up a close acquaintance. And, um ... see the sites, I guess. First time here."

"Ohhh, you will find our city quite delightful. If I may give you a bit of our history."

She did a hand sweep meant to include the entire bed and breakfast.

"The Cecil Bacon Manor is located in one of Seattle's few historic preservation sites, the Harvard-Belmont Landmark District. We like to say the inn is nestled elegantly in the neighborhood."

She poured me orange juice. I propped on a window seat and listened.

"The Manor's design is classic Queen Anne, and the house is over one hundred and seventy years old. Much has been left in its original elegance

The Ivory Knife

except for our modern conveniences, the plumbing, and the electric wiring. The chandeliers and sconces in many rooms are original, converted from gas."

As I looked up at the glass crystal and shining brass, I thought, *Hopefully, all firmly fastened.*

"Here in the main house, we have guest rooms on three floors. Here on the ground level are our common rooms. The Venetian, your room, as you know, is on the third."

The pleasant woman gestured through a large bay window. The dew or the leftover rain on the trees, bushes, and lawns looked like melting jewels. The morning light revealed a neighborhood of visual wonders. The glistening sidewalks and streets sparkled with a type of well-polished glamor.

"We are incredibly proud of our grounds. Our landscapist – ahh, here he is now. Benjamin Waska, our first guest to arise, is ...."

The young man in kitchen livery did not make eye contact. He stayed to the room's perimeter, placing breakfast ware on the sideboard. Cooking smells wafted through the swinging door.

"The Sechi. You are the Sechi. Sechi. I know the Sechi."

He carefully adjusted the breakfast fare on the sideboard, overattentive to each detail. My man here was in his twenties, I'd say. Kinda ordinary looking. He was rocking the messy trimmed hair of an almost auburn tint.

"*Mr.* Sechi is from San Francisco, Benjamin. I was telling him about the gardens and the lawns. What a good job you have done for us."

Turning to me, she added, "Our Benjamin has an extraordinary gift for flowers and plants. He can make such beauty."

There was something indiscernible in her eyes as she spoke. The staffer gave me a quick glance and hurried back to the kitchen.

I spoke carefully, saying, "Autism in many folks often brings with it savant syndrome."

"Quite right. But Benjamin's extraordinary gifts are in the world of technology. He also works at the downtown Levitech offices. Computer things are well beyond my limited intelligence. The Manor's website and WiFi operations -- all the boy's doing for which I am grateful."

The kitchen door opened, and the curious dude came forward again with his head down. He placed a water bottle on the dining room table near me but was careful not to come too close. He spun and retreated, stopping only to turn a bowl of flowers a quarter of an inch to its right.

"Hey, thanks, bud."

"Sechi."

Bam! Another door swing ... woosh ... he was out.

People come and go so quickly here.

"He appears to like my name."

Mrs. McCave smiled.

"Your exercise. Yes? Left out the front door is Volunteer Park. To the right, just follow Broadway. That will take you through the Capitol Hill Business District. There you will find our museums, more parks, indie shops, dining, and unique attractions. If you go right on Olive Way, you can follow it all the way to Pike Place Market and Downtown Seattle. It's a distance, but a fit gentleman like you will have no problem. You really must get to know the market."

She took a brochure from the sideboard and handed it to me. Maps and attractions of the Emerald City – *a good start, Nick Boy.*

"Breakfast is served until nine, but we always hold victuals in the kitchen for our guests. We want our friends to feel at home and settle into the *Gemütlichkeit* at the Bacon Manor Bed and Breakfast.

Kayne would know precisely what that meant. As if reading my mind, Honoria McCave did a website quote, "*Gemütlichkeit* is German for warmth, friendliness, and good cheer. It can also mean coziness, peace of mind, and a sense of belonging and security from social acceptance. Let us know if you need anything to make your stay more enjoyable."

"Wow. I am totally jazzed that our business associate booked me here."

The Ivory Knife

The somewhat chatty woman raised another theatrical hand, twirled, and left me with, "A very wise woman."

Thomas Paul Severino

Chapter Thirteen: Ashes to Ashes
Arkhangelsk, Russia

"The body was incinerated entirely, Comrade Colonel. Identification will be a long and arduous process."

The army officer said nothing but examined the ruins of the corpse in what was left of the penthouse. He held a handkerchief to his nose and mouth. The body was unrecognizable as human. Clothes, skin, and viscera had been burnt to cinders. Even the blackened bones were twisted from the intense heat. A pile of charred remains resembled burnt kindling and showed no indication that there ever was a life form in this place.

"You can see the skull has been smashed, Colonel. From the look of it, with obliterating force. All soft tissue has been burnt to the point of disintegration."

The Colonel took a baton from the fireman and poked through the immolated desk, melted metal, roasted plastic, and charred wood. A sagging metal frame flipped over at his touch. It still smoked.

He addressed the coroner.

"The fire burned with a ferocious intensity here at the body but did not spread very far in the apartment. Most curious."

"Accelerant, Comrade. Self-immolation."

"Tell me."

"See this scorch mark? It is a pour pattern. It encircles the body, but the rug, the furniture, and the lamp did not burn at the same rate outside the ring – two different shades of burning."

The investigator signaled to his assistant, who removed samples of the burned materials and placed them in mason jars. They would be analyzed in a laboratory for the presence of hydrocarbon fire accelerants.

"Please observe, Colonel, the ceiling above the corpse and the room walls are soot-stained, but they did not burn."

Thomas Paul Severino

The fire marshal took an unlit cigarette and dredged it on the desk close to the blackened husk of the victim. He smelled the tip and nodded as if his suspicions were confirmed.

The Colonel continued to prod at the remains.

"Wait. That. Right there. I want that."

He turned to a police captain. The officers looked over the shoulder of the army man who spoke through his mouth covering.

"Give it to me at once, Captain."

The fireman picked up the debris item with gloved hands. He brushed it with the palm of one gloved hand. Part of a serial number revealed itself near a set of ports on its side. The police officer placed the object in a container and surrendered it to the Colonel's assistant.

The owner of the penthouse apartment was an enigma. Lieutenant Colonel Katsitsanóron Isapoinhkyaki's name appeared very non-Russian and was never used in any official or social capacity. She was descended from generations of Siberian hunters and explorers. Her late husband, Colonel Michal Leonid Sidorov of the Foreign Intelligence Service, brought her into the Russian Orthodox Church and government service. "Katya Sidorovna" moved upward through the ranks during the Soviet era and became a trusted official in Russian intelligence following the dissolution of the Soviet Union.

Colonel Demitri Malenkov looked around at the burnt-out room. As he left, he gave his final instructions.

"I would like a full report on this incident by morning. This is to be treated as a security level five operation. Make it happen. Do not disappoint me."

***

"Thank you for seeing me, Comrade Secretary."

The officer acknowledged the other officials in the room.

"Well, Malenkov?"

"Staged, Comrade. I am convinced."

The Ivory Knife

The General Secretary looked away through the windows at the blowing snow.

"You're sure of this?"

The Colonel nodded.

"Reconstructing the remains provides evidence that the body in the burned-out flat was killed by blunt trauma to the head and then set on fire. No evidence was found for an instrument of death."

"But it is not her? Why are you convinced of this?"

"The explosion was caused by a state-of-the-art gelignite device timed and strapped to the body. Kerosene was the ignitable liquid used to increase the rate of the body's combustion. The accelerant was poured from behind the body on the desk chair and then detonated. This was confirmed by chemical patterns. No chemical container was found in the apartment."

The colonel turned a page and pointed to a paragraph.

"Interestingly, the detonator was of military design. Russian. The firestorm was intense and localized. The sprinkler system for the apartment had been turned off, but the fire burned itself out without spreading to the other units."

Colonel Demitri Ivanovich Malenkov turned a few more pages. He brought the General Secretary's attention to a specific place in the report.

"Spectral analysis of the remains shows the deceased was younger by ten years. We extracted a small amount of DNA from one obliterated femur. There is no match. Comrade General Sidorovna's DNA contains the sequences found in the Mongol people with some variations of the Indigenous People of the Arctic – Inuit and Tlingit. The genetic profile of the deceased is European, with the sequences found in the Ashkenazi Jews. Comrade Secretary, our minister has staged her own death."

"The list? The Synaxis? Tell me."

"Right now, we are attempting to recover her computer's hard drive. The explosion all but destroyed it. The Securities Ministry has a secure network for its work, as you know. They have a complete record of the Lieutenant Colonel's files, but there is a problem here, Comrade. The list is encoded. We believe that she always carried a hard copy of the Kiviuq Synaxis. Comrade Sidorovna felt it was an insurance policy should she ever need it against the higher-ups."

"If what you are telling me is so, Comrade Colonel. We have a top-level Russian Intelligence officer defecting to the West during defensive military actions against Ukraine. She is carrying with her a list of our operatives throughout the world. The nation's security is in peril, and the outcome of our Ukrainian operation is in the balance."

"Yes, General. Siderovna is running, and she is defecting to the West. We have suspected this for a while."

The General Secretary looked up slowly. Marie Lissemskaia's eyes met those of her operative.

The Colonel put down his glass of tea. He arched an eyebrow at one of the four men seated at the table. The General Secretary slammed the table. The sound resembled a gunshot in the conference room.

"I find your last remark totally incredulous. We suspected one of the key figures in the Russian Foreign Intelligence Service was *about* to defect. About to? What is beyond my understanding, Demitri Ivanovich, is how this got as far as it did. We have spies reporting on everyone in every ministry. We are the most paranoid bureaucracy in the world. Why are we at this point?"

The accusation hung out there with no answer.

"I think we all agree, General Secretary Lissemskaia. The focus of the matter is the missing Lieutenant Colonel. Because she carries too much information, she represents a person of interest for the West. So we must be circumspect."

The distinguished officer with three medals on his dark suit continued. "Quite extraordinary. She is eccentric. I know of no one like her. In her capacity as Minister of International Operations, she makes lists. Extremely Dangerous."

A red-haired operative shook his head. He said, "No more dangerous than emails, flash drives, or coded data dumps. It can all be recovered. Sold. Traded. Used as collateral. Paper burns."

The Ivory Knife

General Secretary Marie Mikhailovna Lissemskaia rose from her desk chair. She stood in the window and watched what was now a blizzard envelop Russia's historic port on the White Sea. The gale of brilliant ice wrapped in a snowy wind seemed to hammer at the windows of the government offices like a polar berserker, slashing and bashing as if demanding human lives.

"Comrades, let us be honest. This is the 21st Century. In this age of cyber warfare, nothing is secure. Nothing. We know everything they know and vice versa. This is not the Cold War, Comrades. Our relations with the West continue to degrade. The integrity of our cyber intelligence must be maintained as a weapon of the highest order. And that weapon is cyber terrorism, the new weapon of global conflict. We Russians are perfecting the West's destruction by the ravaging and wasting of its technological innards."

The General Secretary lit a cigarette and blew out a cloud of steel-gray smoke. Her raven-black hair was parted at the crown of her head and pulled tight to a chignon at the nape of her neck. Her military bearing and blue-black eyes added to the severity of her appearance.

"It is not only the Synaxis, the list of our operatives across the globe, that is important at this point. Our government will be compromised to the full extent if those files fall into the wrong hands. Our agents will be imprisoned or worse. Our intel will be compromised. I am not only talking here about enemy nations. Our trust with our allies, India, Bulgaria, and China, will be irreparably damaged should the identities of those agents be leaked."

Colonel Demitri Ivanovich Malenkov stepped closer as he said, "There is something else. I suspect the defector has something even more dangerous to Russia in her possession. You know what else she carries. Please trust me enough to reveal this, Comrade."

Marie Lissemskaia held her direct report in a slightly hypnotic gaze. She was wagering whether to reveal a very closely kept secret. Ultimately, she simply said, "I underestimate you, Demitri. Yes, there is more – something of monstrous proportions. I will only say its code name is Exquisite Fire."

The storm howled, and the building shuddered. The forces of the Far North broke over the port city and raged in the darkness. The ghosts of

Viking marauders were in the relentless wind, demanding high body counts and blood spoils. Screeching their war cries, their ghostly battle clubs and war axes obliterated the icy landscape as the storm rampaged against the living.

The General Secretary said, "I have briefed the President. He agrees that this operation is a top priority for the Ministry. The woman must be found, the Synaxis destroyed, and the stolen Exquisite Fire files must be returned to the Ministry."

She paused for a moment letting the drama find its apex as she beheld the fury just outside the window.

"At all costs, Operation Exquisite Fire must proceed. Absolutely no one is indispensable in the secret war."

Chapter Fourteen: Square Lights and Prison Bars
Seattle, Washington

From the case files of Kayne J. Sorenson, Ph.D.

"Use your training, Nick. Where the bleeding hell am I? And ... who?"

Right. Nick is not here.

I remember the darkness and the paralysis. Whether my eyes were open or closed, I could not tell at the onset. Gradually I could see glimmers of light that seemed to be in the next room but up on the ceiling. The shafts flickered. I sensed it was daylight because the scant illumination faded to darkness as the hours wore on.

Next, I observed the bars of my containment. The enclosure was inescapable, from a stone countertop to the ceiling of my cell. There were two pass-throughs to either side of a door of iron bars.

Crickey! I am being held captive in a bank.

Definitely an old bank, like in some frontier town. My prison was complete with teller stations and a bloody safe embedded in one wall. Deserted, abandoned, and rotting, the room held a few broken chairs, a decrepit desk, and a heavy table. It was on the table I found myself when I came about. It provided me with an uncluttered sleeping space.

A disgusting lav was tucked behind a broken door at one end of the teller's room. It featured cold water from a drippy rust-stained faucet bent into a fractured sink. There was nothing but bare shelves in the abandoned safe. It appeared the tumblers had been smashed with something heavy. Dirt and dust covered the chamber like a black snowfall.

I spoke into the musty darkness, "I hate bloody rats. Well, I don't exactly hate you, little blokes. Let's just respect each other's boundaries, eh mates?"

On the other side of the cage wall was the bank's lobby. Empty except for an overturned chair and a raised counter with small nooks for paper slips and banking whatnot. A family of mice had staked a claim to one of the cubbies.

There it goes again ... the lights above the space of what would be the sidewalk in front of the bank. I could see through the bank's grimy, almost entirely boarded-up windows. There was a concrete wall where "across the street" should be.

Once, there was a fire here. Not in here but near here. A long time ago. The wreckage, the abandonment – even some ash near the windowsills and doors. The dirty countertops – mostly ash blown in from outside.

A dim shadow passed the exterior windows. Someone was opening the bank's doors. I stepped deeper into the cell's darkness. The figure was tall, dressed in a hoodie and jeans. I concluded he was male by his carriage. His movements further indicated he knew I was awake and hiding. The stranger placed packets on the counter on his side of the bars and left as he had come.

Food.

Recycled paper containers. Asian fare, complete with chopsticks. A Starbucks paper cup of tea. No metal, glass, or rigid plastic.

I looked around my prison again since my eyes had become more accustomed to the darkness. The peeling ceiling and walls held no evidence of electrical wiring. Gas outlets had been broken off in several places, including the interior teller's cage. In the corner of the outer room, a heap of brass, snaking chains, and broken frosted glass suggested a destroyed gas chandelier.

A heap of trash in a corner near the loo on my side of the prison enclosure caught my attention. I picked through the filthy mess in the dim light. Nothing to identify the place or escape-useful. A laundry receipt. Broken tiles. A roll of coarse twine. The brush end of a broken broom. A candle holder with a stub of burned wax.

Wait. The remains of a chimney-less hurricane lamp. No oil and a dried wick. And cheers! A few sheets of paper and a box of antique wooden pencils stamped "The Joseph Dixon Crucible Company."

The Ivory Knife

My head hurt. Reality swirled. I sagged against a broken wall. My brain felt like it was drying up in this dank featureless cellar. I must exercise my cognition. Exercise, exercise – get the brain in gear.

Nick, why are pencils yellow?

That's an easy one, Bossman. In the 1800s, the best graphite came from China. Yellow was the color the Chinese associated with loyalty and respect. China's pencil manufacturers wanted to flag the public that their pencils were the best.

Bring two sharpened #2 yellow pencils for the test.

Good, My love. Now follow the wood, if you please.

Do I get a kiss if I impress you with my investigative knowledge? O.K., here goes. The Dixon Crucible Company, now Dixon Ticonderoga, was one of many manufacturers at the end of the 19th century. Faber-Castell, Eberhard Faber, Eagle Pencil Company (later Berol), and General Pencil Company were the prominent German pencil manufacturers, all headquartered in New York and New Jersey.

But these, Big Man, are made in California. See? That's Incense-cedar. Take a whiff. Best pencils are made from trees cut in California's Sierra Nevada mountains. It has Incense-cedar out the ass. It became the industry's wood of choice.

Hey, did I do the wood for ya? So let's get the fuck out of here, Kayne.

Nick seemed to partially dissolve in the dusty air. He passed through the bars and out through the bank's front door. The hallucinations gave way to the reality of the grungy prison. I took some food and drink, and my head seemed to clear.

Pencils? Bloody hell.

You needed that bit of induction, Kayne boyo. Your intelligence is atrophying in this dank hell. Continue to exercise the synapses, man.

Pencils ....

I turned in a circle while looking up. There was sound above me. Voices. Movement. Muffled indications of the living. In an upper story – a second floor.

Thomas Paul Severino

Climbing, I stood on the teller's counter and held onto the bars like a zoo primate. I stretched. The crumbling ceiling was still a good six feet above my head, but the commotion was coming from above. For a goodly period, I tapped on the bars in Morse Code with a chunk of brick – such an old movie stereotype. Then I just banged away like a caged monkey. I even tried singing. Loud and lusty until I was hoarse. The only change was the light. It grew darker.

Kayne, where are you? I'm looking for you, Boss.

"I am in the buried city, my love. It is so dark. Please come and find me."

Chapter Fifteen: *Le Éminence Grise*
Seattle, Washington

From the Case Files of Kayne J. Sorenson, Ph.D.

"You talk in your sleep, Dr. Sorenson."

I bolted upright on the table into deep darkness. The deep, almost hissing voice came from the outer room, beyond the bars. A light flickered on — a camp light. Strong in the gloom, it illustrated the details of my decrepit incarceration.

"... and you smell."

Two. Two visitors. One seated and one standing in the outer room. They were dressed in black complete with hoodies. Their faces were covered with black masks that ended at the upper lip. That is not entirely accurate. The facial disguise of the seated man was a half mask covering the left side of his face. He was dressing the part of Gaston Leroux's Opera Ghost.

My captors remained just behind the lantern. I was to be the focus of the visuals, it appeared.

"Remove your clothes."

The Phantom's attendant placed a package on the teller's counter and pushed it through the slot. Bar soap, shampoo, and a towel. I stripped.

Deystvitel'no, u nego krasivoye telo, polkovnik.

(Indeed, he has a beautiful body, Colonel.)

Imeyte v vidu, tovarishch, doktor Sorenson ponimayet po-russki.

(Keep in mind, comrade, Doctor Sorenson understands Russian.)

Totally in the nuddy, I said, "Not fluent. A few words, but, yes, I understand some Russian."

I spread my arms a bit and turned around to give them a bit of a show.

Thomas Paul Severino

In the depths of my captivity, Nick, I remain your 'cocky-as-fuck' Bossman.

I did a man package check and said, "Thank you for the compliment, comrades. *Vashe zdorov'ye* – Cheers, ya bloody brogans."

"The water in the lavatory is not hot. We will wait."

Not hot, my bloomin' arse. It was balls-shrinking ice cold. Bloody oath! I scrubbed nonetheless.

As I returned, a stray cat chased something unseen through the bars and into a dark corner. The Colonel was agitated. He spoke to his companion in Russian.

"*Poymayte i ubeyte etogo zverya.* (Have that beast caught and killed)."

Now, there were more gifts on the counter -- another towel and a glass of golden liquid. European style, no ice. I took my time drying off. Hell, if salacious intentions allowed me the opportunity to escape, I was happy to oblige.

The Captain placed a pair of jeans, a tee shirt, a hooded sweatshirt, thick socks, and pair of running shoes up for my grabbing. There were blankets stacked at the other end of the counter.

Upping my accommodation service to the luxury package. I'll take it.

I dressed and sipped the whiskey. My Russian jailers got it right -- my delicious Hibiki.

The Phantom started to speak, but I interrupted.

"Allow me, if you will, Comrade."

Still holding the glass, I pointed with my left index finger.

"You are Colonel Vasily Pavlovich Bounine. Your photos on the Dark Web do not do you justice, Comrade. You are most imposing in the flesh. You, Sir, are a 'power behind the throne.' You have no official sanction by the Russian government and operate with a special entré to the most influential individuals in the Russian Federation. Your accent indicates that your origin is the Republic of Belarus. Minsk or very near the capital."

The Ivory Knife

Bloody yeah. Sorenson brain on fire! Hitting my stride again with these two wankers.

"But, you have recently fallen into disfavor. Your president often changes his henchmen. Oh, how the mighty do fall. Personal indiscretion? A failure to deliver the heads of rivals? You have been relegated to prison duty. So very *tragicheskiy*. I fear for your future.

I pointed to the Captain.

"You are the Colonel's *aide de camp* and have been for some time. You are also his lover – hence few pictures and no name. But my husband, in researching the 'Big Bads,' as he calls them, of the present regime, found you, Captain Sergei Andreivich Sarov."

The brute showed his displeasure by taking a step toward me and punching one fist into the palm of the other hand, but his seated mate placed a restraining hand on the disturbed man's forearm."

"Referring to my nakedness, your racy comment within such a rabidly homophobic culture as Russia's would most likely have resulted in your incarceration. *Ergo*, you are confidantes, i.e., Vasily Pavlovich has interceded to save your bum. The familiarity with which you touch the Colonel belies the intensity of a forbidden relationship. So much energy to remain in the proverbial closet, lads. But, alas, I digress."

I strode the dingy cell as I would pace a classroom during one of my lectures. The exception was the glass of whiskey, which the Captain delicately refilled.

Did he trace a finger over the back of my glass-holding hand, or was I mistaken? *Nick, I am rarely mistaken. Most interesting. Turns out I'm hot.*

Stepping back, I continued the lesson.

"You are both physically powerful men, military-trained. Colonel Bounine, the explosion that took your left hand and a portion of your face was undoubtedly in service to your country. You are a hero."

The Colonel removed his left glove and flexed a somewhat intimidating metallic prosthetic, moving it into the lantern light. He did not remove his mask.

89

"As I said, you are a national hero entrusted with only the most covert operations until recently. I am alive and your prisoner. You need me. Yes, Colonel. The Russian spy games with the West have gone awry, and you want me to fix it. You seek information."

I halted my philosophic stroll and pointed at the Russians.

"Wait. You seek to *recover* information. Someone important is on the loose. A defector with the goods on the oligarchs, no doubt."

"Doctor Sorenson, your reputation does not do you justice. You have uncovered our plan as if you were a mind reader with all your guessing."

Again, I seemed to hear Nick's voice.

Yo, Dick Breath, my man never guesses. He is just that fuckin' smart, Boris.

Alas, I am the Count of Monte Cristo in the Château d'If .... The Prisoner of Zenda ... I shook my head to get the imagined voice clear of my thinking, even though it was like a lifeline conjuring the presence of my love.

The Russian stood and made motions that indicated they were leaving.

"Leave the lamp, Captain, please."

Bounine waved two live fingers signifying assent.

The officer placed the lantern on the counter. Its size prevented its passage to my side of the bars. He removed his heavy winter coat and put it where I could reach it. His smile was lecherous as he whispered, "*Ne szhigay eto mesto dotla, seksual'nyy muzhchina.* Do not burn the place down, sexy man."

Fascinating.

"One last question, if I may, Colonel. How can you possibly coerce me to do your bidding?"

The Phantom replaced his glove and flexed his mechanical hand at the outer door. He turned in the darkness and spoke like a death-dealing wraith.

The Ivory Knife

"Oh, no, Doctor. Not you. You are the bait, you see. The one who will find us the traitor is your husband. It is he who will do my bidding. And quite willingly. Of that, you may be sure."

Thomas Paul Severino

Chapter Sixteen: The Almoner

The Andronikov Monastery of the Theotokos, Abalak, Tyumen Region, Siberia Federal District, Russia

"You are safe. The holy brothers will keep your secret. That is if you are discovered. They are too caught up in their monastic duties, acts of asceticism, and elaborate liturgies to notice anything about worldly matters. Are you warm enough?"

"Yes, Holy Father, even though the train left me at Omsk, I walked the rest of the way like a good monk. Are you …?

The Abbot pulled the mendicant into a passionate embrace. The hood of her monk's robe fell back, revealing a tumble of luxurious hair the color of a Russian caribou, brown shot through with white. Her carnal enthusiasm and kisses matched his ardor.

"Stefan Ivanovich, you are an anomaly. How is a short-bearded, thirty-three-year-old lust-filled man the leader of a Siberian monastery."

The Abbot removed his heavy robes and pulled his subject onto the bed. He wrapped the blankets over both of them.

"Andronikov is my gulag. You know my story, Katya. These many years of our amorous adventures here and elsewhere … I am a prisoner. Indeed, you remember and have the files to make me do your bidding."

"Yes. Your father was in charge of the Abalak internment camp here on the site of the Andronikov Monastery. When the gulags were dissolved, the monks returned and found they had a new Abbot, a mere boy."

"Imprisoned in religious life because I was a degenerate when allowed to live in the secular world."

The woman softly laughed while exploring the priest's naked body.

"Just how many women did you have before taking the oil of Holy Orders?"

She licked and sucked on the muscles of his neck.

"It is the affairs I have had subsequently that will deliver me to Hell, my angel. Also, I seem to remember a few beautiful men somewhere ... at another time ... but I think I was just rebelling. I enjoy women so much more, and it has lately been too long a time."

His mouth and groping raised their play to a more heated level.

"It was the money and the blackmail, correct? Your father paid for the restorations and endowed the monastery. I remember the bargain was to remain silent about the atrocities and that his wayward son would be the Abbot for life. How do you manage your ... ah ... excursions? When you seduced me, you were an adventurous playboy who frequented the brothels of St. Petersburg."

He rolled on top of her and whispered, "Shall we trade sin for sin? You were a married official. I remember the heat and the savagery of our first coupling. You claimed to be investigating some anomaly here at Andronikov. We deceived Michal Leonid for years."

"My husband knew. His own lovers provided too much distraction for him to care about mine."

They did not elaborate on the past but continued their lovemaking, repeated and finished at least three times.

"I will be late for Night Prayers. You should make an appearance in the Church. Stay in the background, bow, and make the holy signs as the other brethren do. We will have food in my apartment. There is much I need to discuss with the monastery's Almoner."

"You did not answer me about ...."

The Abbot turned as he dressed.

"Ahhh... the widows, the mistresses of the fat oligarchs? It takes a lot of rubles to keep this most holy institution running, my sweet Katya. Who better than the Abbot to beg the rich and very beautiful? This holy father gets around, and the rich almost always respond with a warm show of support. Russian guilt and fear of damnation."

He winked, smiled, and left.

Such a bad boy. A very bad boy.

The Ivory Knife

She was glowing as she joined the ranks of the brothers hurrying to chapel.

***

"Why?"

"The state is corrupt. Russia is a total kleptocracy."

"You are just finding this out now?"

The candlelight flickered in the Abbot's chambers. They faced each other across the heavy wooden table. The shutters on the small windows rattled. Another snowstorm was in full fury out on the taiga.

Katya looked at a nearby wall. An icon of the Virgin, Our Lady of Vladimir, was surrounded by hanging oil lamps. The painting's small wooden doors were open. The eyes of the Virgin and the child she held seemed to pierce the evening shadows, following those who crossed in the space before them.

"I have known and been disgusted for some time, Pavel Ivanovich. Our leaders and their cronies are strangling our country, men and women. I had known this long before my husband, Misha, died."

She drew a breath, tore at a piece of fresh bread, and leaned forward with secrets.

"Recently, I became aware of the government's confiscation of funds. This corrupt program was to provide food to feed the many starving comrades in the rural areas of our country. A large part was allocated to Eastern Siberia. While our people died of starvation, the corrupt business leaders enriched themselves -- more yachts, more Manors, and more luxuries. Organized crime is rife in Russia and supported by top government officials. Where are these people who prefer to operate in the shadows? They should be tried and executed."

Sidorovna's eyes flashed in the candlelight.

"Our President and his friends put the state above all else – and the people be damned. They have rigged and postponed plebiscites to make it difficult for opposition parties to focus on essential things. These men have no interest in democracy or in human rights. No, not in a country where the government is allowed to cancel elections, exert total control over the media, and level draconian imprisonment measures on anyone who resists."

The priest said nothing. The Minister spoke again.

"I decided to look into an investigation into money laundering in Germany – the oil and gas pipeline. When certain indelicacies came to light, the government conducted secret trials and forced confessions until finally, last July, the investigators turned up dead under mysterious circumstances. This could not have happened without the full knowledge of our President's propagandistic quasi-investigation.

The Abbot dipped bread in oily herbs and drank a bit of wine. "Katya, surely these matters should be left to the Duma ...."

The candlelight caressed his handsome face. Katya Sidorovna was reminded that sometimes he acted like a spoiled boy.

"Ahhh, my beautiful priest ... monastic detachment has left you naïve in the ways of the world."

The government agent drank from her mug of wine. She continued her excoriation of those who pulled her strings.

"After the division of property following the fall of the Soviet Union, the Yelsinites became richer, fatter, and more powerful. They became billionaires with even more business and a new legitimacy – the oligarchy. The Duma's anticorruption laws that kept greedy Russian companies in check were soon swept away. Doing business Russian-style is filled with paying bribes and receiving kickbacks. The web of deception and this rule by thievery from the people is like opium force-fed on the populace."

Energized, the woman stood up and walked through the room.

"The scale of corruption in Russia is estimated by four international organizations at 30 billion a year. That is ten to twenty percent of our GDP. Our despotic Russian president runs a corrupt state, and woe to those who bring him displeasure. The elimination of political threats is in his DNA."

"There are many rumors of Russia as a failed state. That much I do know."

The Ivory Knife

"Shut up in a monastery in Siberia ... my simple holy man who burns with sexual desire ... Stefan Lebedev, you have no idea. There is even a picture of the president in the monks' refectory."

"Yes. We were told ...."

The Lieutenant Colonel sniffed with disgust.

"The President claims to be committed to the best interests of his country, but he does so with a sharp eye for human weaknesses. He is good at persuading and intimidating people, especially western leaders, with his charm. Stefan, the corruption under the leadership of the man in that portrait has gone beyond the criminal. It is estimated that ninety-four percent of the companies in Russia are owned by the president. The American CIA estimates there is $40 billion under the president's personal control. In 2014, the year he ordered the invasion of Crimea, the president of Russia was one of the richest men in the world."

She paused and gazed into the Abbot's small fireplace. The Russian woman shook her head as she said, "I have looked the other way for too long. So much money has been stolen. So many people have been killed. And now, the war. Something needs to be done."

Sidorovna stopped and stared into the shadows of the monk's cell. The candle flickered in its sconce near the revered icon. She spoke into the warm darkness.

"Yes, now he has his war."

Hegumen Stefan, the Holy Abbot of the Andronikov Monastery of the Theotokos, came behind the government minister.

"What will you do, Lieutenant Colonel?"

She turned into the embrace of her lover. The firelight caught one side of her face setting her cheekbones in high profile.

"There is someone who will help me. However, he is far away, and I must win him over to my way of thinking. I am at odds on how to win him over, but I have had much practice in persuading men."

They stood in silence for a short time, clinging to each other. With her head on his shoulder, Katya said, "I am your poor almoner, Holy Father Abbot. I give from our wealth to the poor. The people depend on me."

Thomas Paul Severino

Lieutenant Colonel Katya Sidorovna pulled the unholy holy man closer. Her voice was a whisper and a flame in his ear.

"I am disappearing. I am going to the North where my people are. I have something for the West. I am melting the ground beneath us. I will ignite the fire that burns it all down."

Chapter Seventeen: Hiding

Amaruq Outpost 3, Gray Wolf Research Center, Nuiquist, North Slope Borough, Alaska.

"Times are very bad in my country. We decided to walk East to the West."

"You walked from Siberia to Alaska in the winter?"

"Almost. Our journey in Siberia led us to the port of Anadyr on the Chukotka Peninsula. You know it sticks out into the Bering Sea. From there, we made it to Vancouver on a tanker."

Jissika prepared her guest a cup of hot tea and said, "Turned around and headed back north? That's odd."

"Marina is of the Inuit people. We were on our way to settle with them somewhere near here. We will make a new life lost among her Arctic people. Where I do not know."

"And you became separated?"

The traveler looked away with a forlorn expression.

"I fear she may be dead."

The snowstorm man was making a slow recovery. He played with his dog rescuers and spoke to the woman scientist in heavily accented English.

"I get the impression someone is trying to send the two of you back to Russia. How 'bout you enlighten me."

"Please do not give me away. I fear I will never see my wife again if I am detained and returned to Belarus. My country does not believe in allowing dissidents to live."

He grew excited as he spoke.

Jissika Pitka Delutuk handed the man a glass of strong tea. She said, "I am pretty much alone up here, especially at this time of the year. We have provisions to last us into the spring. And storms like this are pretty common. How did you come to be way up here?"

The man seemed to ignore the question. He reached for his backpack and removed a flat wooden object.

"In Latvia, Marina and I were very devout. May I place this somewhere special, please? I find it quite comforting.

Jissika cleared a small shelf near a shuttered window. The small space was enough for her 'orphan of the storm' to set up his icon. She placed a scented candle in a Mason Jar next to it. The Virgin took her first look at America.

***

Diary entry for December 15.

The storm continues into its fifth day. Max 6.3°F (-14.3°C) and min -4.4°F (-20.2°C). Fifteen minutes of daylight. Each day less and less light ... colder and colder ... but soon, the Arctic Spring will arrive out of the darkness. It always does.

Still, the dogs and I are all healthy and keeping warm. Anji's babies are getting plump. All eyes open. Sofie is pregnant. Her pups will get here in mid-February. Calendar marked.

The rescued man calls himself Sergi Tal and claims to be a Latvian national living in Belarus. This does not ring true. His accent is deeply Russian, and he lacks knowledge of the Latvian or Belarus football teams. A second-grader in those countries knows this stuff.

It occurs to me that he may be looking to get some state secrets from our Arctic Research facility – WTF? Our studies are ecological and available to just about anyone. We get some weirdos up here, that's for sure.

My Innuit buddy, John Blackjack, also thinks he is a Russian and he is hiding something. No one in the region that John and I have reached out to has heard of the woman, the guy's wife. Our people can read the heart. That is a certainty. I asked him to be on the lookout for a woman who may have followed Mr. Tal here.

Oh well, finally, something interesting.

The Ivory Knife

I uploaded my recent data when I got some web time. Things around here shift and vary. Climate change is a bitch.

Thomas Paul Severino

Chapter Eighteen: The Jock Tease
Pike Place to Virginia Street, Seattle, Washington

Nick Sechi's Journal

"Let's find this man, Nick Boy."

Talking to myself, I dashed out of the Bacon Manor and turned out along the Capitol Hill district along Broadway. At East Madison Street, I switched and headed toward the Pike Place Market and Elliot Bay on the east of the Emerald City.

The hypnotic tattoo of my running shoes on the pavement seemed to underscore my imagining that I could talk to Kayne wherever he was. I went with a conversation in my head as I ran.

Got no idea, Bossman. None. Zero. Zilch. Where the fuck are you? Not smart enough to figure this shit out. But, I know you are here, Kayne – here in Seattle. I sense it.

Nick ... my Nick... let them know you are here, my love. Attract some attention. The Big Bads who have me know that you will come looking. They will be looking for you, my ginger beauty.

How, Boss? Have a parade? Take out an ad?

Remember, you are a stunner, Nick. Use it, Boyo.

That was when I stopped, pulled off my shirt, and tucked it into the waistband of my running shorts. The air was cool and brisk, but the sky was sunny and clear. I ran harder to stay warm. I arrived at the massive marketplace after a kick-ass jog. Despite little sleep and not much food, I powered it down to the lower bay-side streets like a madman.

Pike Place Public Market Center came up like an urban carnival at the end of the street. Even at this early morning hour, it spewed some delicious scents promising delectable eats under neon lights and painted signs of yesteryear. There were iced piles of fresh seafood, advertisements for flying fish, and beautiful flowers in stacked overflowing stalls. Arts and crafts kiosks were slowly coming alive, accompanied by the lazy yawns of slow-moving artisans. A gross gum wall seemed to take the energy out of those who sought tasty eats.

Dodging a friendly couple of cruising jocks -- It's muscle, dudes, I built it, and I love showing it off -- I stepped aside as a street entertainer hauling a spinet piano started his daily setup. A little way along the arcade, a ukulele player was setting out his sign, stool, and open instrument case near Post Alley outside the Pink Door, one of the many restaurants in this heavily touristy site.

I wound along this mash-up of retail, entertainment, and food bazaars. My wanderings toured me through a conglomeration of historic buildings and newer construction that went on for blocks along the Bay. Coming up on an antique fish mart piled with iced offerings from Puget Sound and the nearby waters of British Columbia and Alaska, I decided to make some queries.

Investigate, Nick. That's what you are trained for. What do you observe, boyo?

The stall looked like it had been in the neighborhood for a while and had the markings of popularity. It also had a shady look. Back inside, some pretty rough characters were having a very animated argument. There were few shoppers in the Pike Place Market, and these guys spoke Russian.

I caught the eye, and I mean the *eye* of a vendor. Daddy was rocking a sizeable patch. Channeling the not-so-friendly Captain Ahab, he looked me up and down like I was on the menu or some potential trouble. Another fish guy was carting in fresh catch. I repeated my inquiries, making sure I threw in a bit of an upper-body jock stretch and a hand swipe to the abs to market my own goods.

"Fish? Coffee? What do you want? Make it fast."

Daddy was rough and rude for someone in sales. Last in the class for good customer relations .... maybe it was too early, and Dumb Ass was cranky. And his English was for shit.

"Just looking around, Dude. You hear of anything strange goings-on in this town. Looking for a buddy of mine. Six two and black hair. He has eyes

The Ivory Knife

the color of blue ice. Scar on his forehead's left side. Fit as fuck. Ring a bell, Bluebeard?"

Something about the guy. His face was messed up, and it looked like he was an aging heavy metal rocker. More like a powerful "Scourge of the Seven Seas" type."

I aimed a picture of my man on my iPhone at him.

"Thinking some foul play, if you know what I mean."

"You want to know if anything unusual is going on in one of the most popular tourist attractions in the world? What are you, fucked up?"

He caught me up close in his ungodly gaze.

"Let me ask you. What happens when the fly willingly walks into the spider's web?"

He slammed a massive Chinook salmon onto its bed of ice, followed by three more. Big arms reached for more catch as he threw another dismissal over his shoulder. I got the sense he was hot for but uncomfortable with a half-naked athlete making some convo with him.

"Go away. Go buy some coffee or buy a fucking shirt, braggart boy."

OK, so weird word choice. Did he mean "showboater" or "teaser" or what? English was not his first language, but the accent was unclear. Whatever.

"Come on, Salty Dog. Just have a look. Only take a minute."

He grabbed the phone and took a look. Popeye started to thumb the picture roll. Nuh uhhh. I retrieved my mobile just as his compadre caught a look-see but checked me out silently.

"Hear of anything, send word to the Bacon Manor. Nick is the name."

I attempted to slip Scary Guy some folding money. He looked around like someone who wanted more face time, but something was preventing his full engagement. Eying the bills, he turned his head and spit, then pointed the way out.

"Go."

Thomas Paul Severino

Chapter Nineteen: SkyCity
Seattle Center, Seattle Washington

Nick Sechi's Journal

"You want to go up? We are not open yet, but go ahead, pick up that other pile, and follow me."

"Um, no, Dude. I'm cool. Besides, you don't open until ...."

The young guy with the name tag ID-ing him as "Darren Uralic" repeated his request. "A little help, dude. It's stuff for the kitchen. Let's go."

I pulled on my athletic tee with the Sonics emblazon and gave 'Young and Sexy' a wink. Darren worked in Space Needle's revolving restaurant, SkyCity. The young dude seemed fascinated with me. Was he offering me a guided tour? I know a frisky boy when I see one, folks, but something in his voice and mannerisms suggested a strange urgency. I bent to pick up a stack of kitchen supplies and felt his eyes on my butt.

Kayne was right – flirt a little, and things started to happen.

As I entered the elevator, I remembered.

No, this is gonna work out really well, what with my acrophobia and claustrophobia. Not thinking, Nick.

Up!

The ground fell away at ten miles per hour. We were more than five hundred feet in the sky in less than a minute. I lifted the package pile to cover my face. Darren turned, ran a hand down my back, and said, "Look. Old Downtown. On the edge of a steep hill like the Market. The original city was on two levels – a cliff above the Sound."

There it was, Seattle spreading out from Mt. Rainier to Puget Sound. A large metropolis with buildings, sports arenas, highways, streets, waterways, and parks falling away at my feet at a dizzying speed. Unable to speak, I closed my eyes to stop the spinning as we entered the "flying saucer" at the top of the Space Needle from its underside.

Like he was speaking through water, I heard Darren say, "Welcome to the Emerald Suite, Mr. Sechi."

Holy shit. The restaurant, with its floor-to-ceiling glass panels, was revolving. The floor was transparent. I remember thinking, *This shit should have a warning sign on it for folks like me.* That was just before I hit the floor, unconscious as a terrified possum.

***

"Fold his legs. He will fit. The Olympia Food Services van is at the loading dock. The intel on ginger boy here was dead on."

More darkness. I was stupefied and lethargic but aware that I was being covered up. This kiddo fainted one more time.

When I came to, I discovered I was laid out in the back of a van, and the back doors were opening. Mrs. McCave was saying, "Oh dear, oh dear. It is because he most likely has had nothing to eat this morning. You boys and your physical fitness. Much too strenuous. Easy with him. Benjamin. I will hurry and clean out the Venetian Room."

But, I was not going up into the main house of the Bacon Manor. My tenders took me down a path to the guest house and into the basement.

"There. Put the Sechi on the bed. Yes. Yes. He will stay here and be O.K. Do not touch anything, Sechi. Go to sleep."

The door closed. The lock clicked. Warm darkness descended.

Chapter Twenty: He's There
The Cecil Bacon Manor, 959 Broadway, Seattle, Washington
Nick Sechi's Journal

"The Sechi can come out now. The Once-ler and the Vladikoff are gone."

I flopped on a garden bench and watched the boy plant some begonias along a winding path. Benjamin was immaculate and meticulous in his floriculture. With his carefully laid out tools and flowers, and precisely spaced holes, the landscaper knelt on a pad and worked like a surgeon.

"You read a lot."

Benjamin turned from placing a plant into the soil. There was consternation on his face.

"You did not touch my books, the Sechi."

"No. We are good, dude. I just looked. Would you like me to autograph mine?"

"No. Please do not touch them."

"OK, sure. You like Dr. Suess, too."

There was a copy of L. Frank Baum's "The Wonderful Wizard of Oz" in a conspicuous place. He also had many technology volumes above a very elaborate computer array. Interesting.

Benjamin went back to his work.

"Yes, Sechi."

"You can call me Nick."

He shook his head.

"The Sechi."

Well, he liked my name. That is for sure.

Someone had retrieved my hoodie from the Venetian suite and placed it on the bed in Benjamin's room. I pulled it closer as we talked.

"Ya know, I would have thought a guy like you would not have many books, what with all your technical skills and all. My blog on the Kayne Sorenson Mysteries, for example."

"I like the way books feel."

"Cool. Yeah cool. Hey, listen, kiddo. I have a lot of questions. Can you help me?"

Benjamin looked around like there was danger among the trees and shrubs.

"No."

The boy pointed with his hand trowel to one of the holes and then looked up at me with an expectant expression.

Ms. McCave hustled down the back stairs of the Manor and swept into our space like an overbearing kindergarten teacher.

"Mr. Sechi, I hope you are feeling better. Please come inside. You really do need something to eat."

She so reminded me of my mother, Viola. Food is the ultimate source of well-being.

As I stood, I said, "Thanks for the use of your room. We need to finish this, pal."

I almost touched the boy but drew my hand back like I had tapped a hot fry pan. Mrs. McCave supplied sound effects with a soft gasp.

The gardener spoke to the plantings.

"The Sechi should look there. There."

Benjamin repeated his action of pointing to the potting holes. This time, he looked up and searched my face as if unable to make an important connection.

"There."

The Ivory Knife

Resorting to the kitchen, I thought, *Hell, yes. The kid knows something. If you press him, he will freak, and it will be endgame. This takes patience and some finesse, Nick Boy.*

I was, in fact, famished and dove into the frittata and fried potatoes, washing them down with freshly squeezed orange juice.

"Mrs. McCave. The Space Needle?"

"Yes, you fainted. And that nice young man brought you here."

"Olympia Food Services."

"Yes, that's right."

"Why did you put me down in Benjamin's room?"

"You were in no condition to climb the stairs, Mr. Sechi. Down below was the way to go."

"Mrs. McCave, who are Once-ler and Vladikoff? Did someone come here looking for me?"

My hostess stopped in mid-coffee pour. She looked directly at me and, after a beat, shook her head.

"I am afraid that Benjamin has quite an imagination. Those are villains in some of his Dr. Suess books, his favorites. Also, he reads you."

"Yes, I saw. So no, Big Bads?"

"No."

She stood up. And did her signature smile and hand sweep.

"Everything is well at the Bacon Manor."

Honoria McCave was covering up something critical, some secret. She picked up my plate.

"More?"

"No, thank you. I am good. Delicious, yeah."

Ben came into the dining room. He was slightly upset.

"New blanket, please. The Sechi ... I need a new one."

"Yes, dear. I will show you. Out you go."

Mrs. McCave shooed.

I watched them exit, and my eye caught the guest's travel brochures on the sideboard.

Fuck, no!

Chapter Twenty-One: The Cat in the Hat
Seattle, Washington

The Case Files of Kayne J. Sorenson, Ph.D.

"Meow."

"Listen, mate. They're coming for one of us. I hope for your sake it's me. I'm bigger, and it'll take more energy. That conclusion could be rather premature, I will admit, but we both must have a care."

My sometimes prison buddy had recently begun to lose her standoffishness. She helped herself to some of the scraps of my rations. I managed to do a few leave-behinds for the little mouser. She would sit up high and give herself a wash after eating. I often saw her in the darkness, golden eyes glimmering as she watched me.

As I previously described, the room was divided lengthwise by a chest-high teller's counter that reached the ceiling with jail-like bars. This divider was made of heavy wooden cabinets and stretched wall-to-wall.

Startled by the noise, the lean gray cat hopped up and jumped down on this side. Hair ruffled, she hurried along the floor and into the last cabinet through a broken door. Earlier, she had chased a mouse into the same hole.

I investigated.

The inside partition of the cabinet against the bank's wall had been destroyed. There appeared to be a passageway into the next room. It was about the size of the brim of a ten-gallon hat. Using a foot-long length of pipe I found in the debris lying on the floor, I attempted to probe and then widen the hole.

I squeezed.

The space beyond was just as dark and mysterious as my present lock-up. I thought that perhaps the somewhat enlarged hole would provide an exit to wherever.

Thomas Paul Severino

Stuck.

Chapter Twenty-Two: The City Adjacent
Pioneer Square, Seattle Washington

Nick Sechi's Journal

"The old downtown was built on a mud flat right where we are standing. Everything was wood, buildings -- even the sidewalks. That street behind you, Yesler Way, was a giant log flume. They sent the logs from the upper city on those clifts, straight down here where they were put on the boats for transport, sent out across the bay and into Puget Sound. When the great fire hit, on June 6, 1889, everything in these surrounding blocks, Seattle's business district, burned."

The walking tour director, Amy Simmons, by her nametag, had gathered a group of about 25 tourists. They stood silently for the introduction, iPhones at the ready. She continued her history of the old city.

"After the great fire, Seattle's population swelled during reconstruction to become the largest city in the newly admitted state of Washington. Right now, you will be amazed by the underground passageways and basements which were once the ground level of these buildings when the city was built in the 1850s."

We left Pioneer Square and proceeded up to First and Cherry. The opening to the fabled Seattle Underground Tour reminded me of an old New York Subway entrance—pipe metal railings and worn stone stairs leading to a dark world below.

As we began exploring, I looked into the street we were leaving. Above the entrance, I noted a small billboard for "Seattle's Own: Levitech Systems Inc: Technology From The Ground Up."

We descended.

O.K., Nick Boy. Subways. Think the IRT. You're a New York boy and took the train all the time growing up in "da Bronx." The BART back home in San Francisco ... Don't start the hyperventilation shit now, man.

As we hit the lower level. I said aloud to no one, "Kinda narrow down here."

I could hear Kayne say, *Focus your observations, my love. What is it that you perceive?"*

Long brick and concrete passages linked basements, tumbledown spaces, and mine-like shafts that sent horizontal pipes up into the world of the living. Some very dilapidated areas and creepy-looking abysses were blocked by wooden barricades for the safety of the tourists. Piped conduits ran along some walls, and light bulbs shone from metal cages. This was an eerily fascinating city of darkness and death.

You could hide just about anything down here among the ruins and the secrets. My skin crawled.

After waiting for the photo flashes to calm down, our guide pointed out the features of the sunken metropolis. Volunteer Amy spread her arms wide to encompass the ruins.

"Not too far from where we are standing, on that Thursday, June 6, 1889, someone kicked over a glue pot in a carpenter shop. A fire soon engulfed that building. An attempt to pour water on the blaze only spread the flames down the wooden sidewalks and into other buildings. Soon, entire city blocks were exploding."

She continued to walk backward and tell her tale.

"Seattle's water supply was insufficient, and there were few fire hydrants to fight the giant inferno. The old city was served by a volunteer fire department that could not save the burning of twenty-five city blocks. The conflagration destroyed the entire business district, four of the city's piers, and all its railroad terminals. The Great Fire was the worst in the history of Seattle. Despite the massive destruction of property, few human lives were lost. More than 1 million rodents were killed. The total loss was estimated at $20 million or $576 million in today's dollars."

Amy had the total attention of her guests as she went on.

"We are standing at the street level of Seattle's downtown in the mid-1800s. Everything above us burned in less than a day. The city officials decreed that the rebuild would only be brick and concrete. Fireproof."

The Ivory Knife

She stepped to her left and patted a decrepit brick wall.

"Parallel to the sidewalks, these walls were built. They packed rock, stone, and earth between them to raise the streets anywhere from 12 to 30 feet higher."

She smiled, saying, "In those days, to cross the street, you climbed a ladder, walked across the new build, and took another ladder down to the other side."

Amy turned to the bombed-out storefronts on her right.

"Most of these shops were still in useable condition while their new buildings were being built over them, one to two stories higher. Eventually, shop owners moved their businesses up to the new street level. However, many merchants carried on business on these lowest levels in some cases, and folks continued to use the underground sidewalks to access the stores. So, these sidewalks were arched over."

She pointed to the catacomb-like overhead brick arches that ran perpendicular to the corridors.

"They needed light, and it was before electric lighting. So, that's what these are."

Looking upwards, we had a view of the ceiling of the old sidewalks. They were broken every so often by grids of thick glass squares embedded in concrete.

"Up in the living world, we call them the 'glass skywalks.' The top of the skywalk is walked upon and forms the current sidewalk above us."

One of the old storefronts was open for viewing.

"This was a workroom for a garment factory. More than fifty young women cut and sewed ladies' dresses. Next door, as you can see from the sign, was a dentist's office. Go ahead and step inside."

We entered the dimly lit shop. Some broken chairs and a receptionist's desk were neatly positioned. An open door at the rear revealed a ripped dentist's chair with rotted cushion stuffing erupting through holes in the leather. Vandals would have carried off anything valuable long ago.

The group made its way through the dark labyrinth, entering some shops and wrecked emporia, winding through almost two centuries of broken furnishings, peeling walls, and antique doorways. Interior windows either went nowhere, like blackened jaws enclosing unseen depths, or were boarded up. Inside stairs often led to the new street-level buildings but ended at imposing metal doors. As we walked, the sounds of the businesses above us filtered through into these neglected dungeons.

Along the tour route, certain passageways branched off at right angles. I figured they led to other buried streets in the destroyed 25 blocks hidden beneath modern Seattle. All of these were closed to the public. The intention was to keep tourists on one safe path. I purposely lagged to the group's rear and stepped into an alcove to watch them round the bend that was just ahead.

If you are down here, Bossman, you are damn sure not on the tourist parade route. I need to go off-circuit.

There. An accordion-like metal barrier stood off to my right. It had a big lock, but the hasp was not closed. Someone was neglectful, possibly leaving in a hurry. I pulled it partly open, went through, and closed it behind me. I reached into my backpack and retrieved my military tactical flashlight. You know, the kind they advertise them on TV every 20 minutes with some no-nonsense militia hunk claiming you can drop them into the core of a nuclear reactor, and they will still work.

Only 19.95. And, if you act right now, we'll send you a second Macho Light. You pay only shipping and handling.

Please, Mary. Seriously?

Mine was a SureFire E2D LED Defender. With a price tag of two hundred, this baby pierced the darkness with 1000 lumens, and you know that much glam glam will fuck up the night-adapted vision of any attacker.

The way through to the other side of the Underground was in super rough shape. I needed to avoid collapsed beams and some pretty heavy wreckage. This side showed a lot of damage from the fire but the foundations and walls of the buried establishments still held.

I said out loud, "O.K., Benjamin. I'm looking in the hole. Where the hell is he?"

The Ivory Knife

Tracks in the dirt and across the broken wooden pathways led to one particular entranceway adjacent to an overhead glass skywalk. The structure had once been a bank.

Strange. The door looked somewhat newer than the shop. Its padlock was definitely modern. Someone was keeping folks out or was keeping something or someone in. I used my SureFire and ran a beam from an ideally located windowpane across the interior. It looked like a trashed bank interior from reruns of "Gunsmoke."

Open the safe and put the money in the saddlebags, and no one gets hurt.

Holy shit. Those white carry-out Chinese food containers -- those were recent additions. A family of mice had climbed to the top of the counter, proceeded through the teller's bars, and enjoyed some Far Eastern fare. They blinked into the light with long tails twitching, annoyed that I interrupted their dinner.

This shit's coming together for me fast. I looked for a chunk of cement with which I could smash a window. I set down my backpack, put the tac light in my mouth, and stooped for a sizeable rock.

It was then that I saw the cat.

Thomas Paul Severino

Chapter Twenty-Three: Unplugged
221 Baker Street, San Francisco California

Notes to the file by Andi Rodriguez

"Ms. Rodriguez, I conclude that Mr. Sechi's mobile is off and that he turned Dr. Sorenson's off because the antagonists, in this case, are tracking them via these devices – an effortless way to spy on your opponent."

"Yeah, Mycroft. My first instinct was to assume that they had been captured or worse."

"Regardless, do you have any other way of making contact? I was surprised to find out that the Cecil Bacon Manor has no record of Mr. Sechi. Is he there under another name? It is odd that on the date he arrived, no other …. "

Eric Sorenson was shaking his head. He reached for an electric cord to the side of my office credenza.

"Does this lead disconnect this bleeding wanker?"

"Commander Sorenson, I would advise you not to do as you intend. The current uses of artificial intelligence are essential to human-run agencies. Furthermore …."

"Die, bitch."

Eric pulled the plug. He looked at me with that intense gaze that indicated, "pay very close attention." As one of the identical Sorenson triplets, Eric bore a striking resemblance to his younger-by minutes brother, the internationally famous Kayne J. Sorenson, Ph.D. His features were a smudged version of Kayne's – more raw and rugged. Kick, the baby triplet, had a slightly lighter tone to his coloring, but the high cheekbones, the clear blue eyes, and the sensual mouth were all "in da haus." Wrap all that in three muscled jock physiques, and you got the boys from 'Straya - - a whole lotta lotta.

"When Kristof gets here …."

I heard the sound of bounding steps on the stairs.

"The Kris is here, folks."

"Lad, we need you to go down into the house and disconnect Alexa everywhere she is. Folks can turn their own bloody lights on."

"Pop, the security cameras, The program is also IA. It records, notifies, and summarizes activity."

I was typing and searching.

"There is an option for our security system that substitutes a local network for the web. Bingo. Changeover."

I checked the feeds and verified that all were delivering clear pictures of the surroundings of 221 Baker Street, front, sides, and back.

Eric looked over at the pups.

"You'd better up your game, dog, or you're on the street. *Yoi banken ni narimashou, Chouko-san.*"

Chouko sat up from snoozing with Alice and said, "Woof," indicating he accepted the assignment and would indeed be a good guard dog.

I addressed the Commander, "Remind me why we are doing this. I have an inkling, but tell it to me like I am in the first grade."

Eric lit up, ignoring Sorenson and Sechi's no-smoking policy.

"My brother has been kidnapped. He and Nick have many enemies. There are too many electronic portals for these 'Big Bads,' as Nick calls them, to have access to our little band of whatever we are. Take it from me, Ms. Andi. Take to the darkness where no one can find you."

He pointed to my PC.

"That being one of them."

"Impossible to be without, Mr. Sorenson. I keep practically nothing on the cloud despite firewalls. I keep the sensitive stuff on flash drives and in the safe."

"Good lass."

The Ivory Knife

"Uncle Nick has got this thing by the balls if I know him. We cannot give them the way into his whereabouts."

"Kris, my email to my Bosses has stopped. No way I am communicating anything to anyone regarding their current activities."

"That bleeding shit, Mycroft knows. Our men are in Seattle and have accommodations at the Bacon place. Bloody hell."

Eric turned to Kris. "No offense to your butt boy, Jack Ishida …."

"Whose butt boy?"

Enter Matt Crowley with a very puzzled look.

"Kris, I thought …. are you back with Jack?"

"It's cool, dude. Dad is ragging some ancient history."

Kris smooched his man – his current man, anyway -- was that too bitchy? -- and put an arm around Matt's shoulder.

"Hey, lad. I was saying that piece of techno shit has turned, as sure as hell. He's working for the other side, the bugger."

Enter Oscar.

"Can I use my iPhone yet?"

Simultaneously, four voices said, "No!"

He took in the room but focused on Eric.

"Do you know how hard it is to close on a fixer-upper without a cell phone? But we did it, Eric. The property in the Mission … the deal is completed."

He hugged the Commander and said, "Tonight we celebrate with *Poronkäristys*. You all must come. Andi, Raul too. Getting reindeer meat in San Francisco is very difficult, by the way."

I shook my head at the Finnish doctor.

"I cannot believe you are cooking Rudolph and serving him up."

Kris said, "Come on, Matthew. We have to put Alexa out the door."

Thomas Paul Severino

He did a matinee idol hand to his forehead as he added, "It continues to be a jungle of a day for the Kris. I believe a disco nap is quite in order. Trasker keeps my old room ready for such contingencies. Ahh, the worry, the pressure ... how am I possible? Wherever shall I find relief from all this ungodly stress?"

The big ham began his exit with his renewed love mate.

Matt backed out with a raised eyebrow, indicating they might be late for dinner.

Chapter Twenty-Four Recovering
Ft. Lauderdale, Florida

"Myanmar, my ass, Micah. Mark is in Kyiv. I am sure of it. CBN is posting his reports of the Russian invasion. 'An anonymous source on the ground,' bullshit. I recognize his reports."

"Ms. Quinto, try and concentrate on your physical therapy. Mark has been up against tougher outfits than this. He will come out of all of this and come home soon."

"Tell Eris to get him this message: The water in the building has been turned off. The timetable for the completion of repairs is yet unknown."

Rebecca used the parallel bars to make her way from one end of the therapy room to the other. They were alone.

"No internet, Ms. Quinto."

"You'd think so, right? Elon Musk is lately his good bud. Since Mark got the Pulitzer, he hobnobs with the stars. What can I tell ya? I am willing to bet Musk hooked him up with a Starlink so he could access the net. Get Eris on this. Email bullshit makes me think I need to find a more secure way to communicate with him."

"Will Mark's IA let me communicate with her?"

"Interesting. Eris can be a real bitch, as you know. She is rabid about protecting Mark, which is a good thing. My password for Eris is in the safe, as you know. I would do this myself, but, to be honest, I would rather not make contact with her from this hospital. The firewalls at the museum are far more trustworthy."

Rebecca wobbled a bit as she did a turn and started back the other way.

"Wait one hour for a response, and then come back to me here, please."

"You got it."

Thomas Paul Severino

"Please arrange for the three assistant curators assigned to Borealis to be with you when you Zoom me at 2 PM. Have Security join us at 3."

Micah nodded. He looked at his Boss as she continued her somewhat grueling regimen of getting from the waist down back in operation. As if reading his mind, she said, "I'll be damned if I will miss the opening of this new exhibit, and be assured, darling, I will be dancing at the gala."

As she pulled and shuffled along for another "lap," Rebecca added a private thought.

... hopefully with Mark.

Chapter Twenty-Five: Boots and Saddles
Seattle, Washington

Nick Sechi's Journal

"What's up, cat? You look like you're up to something."

The feline meowed in an almost song-like expression, drawing out her yowl. Her tail twitched with excitement, and she locked her golden eyes on my face.

"Nasty place for a pretty gal like you. Been eating mouse lo mein in the bank over here?"

I stepped closer, and the creature jumped up on a hitching post to get a better look at me. My eyes were caught by the shop that stood next to the bank as I reached out to her. A rectangular sign hung by one corner, dropping across the double doors and smashed windows of "J. Douglas and Sons Outfitters: Boots and Saddlery, est. 1843."

The cat swatted my backpack as it dangled from my shoulder. I unzipped a large pocket and retrieved a power bar. Breaking off a crumbly piece, I shared.

"Guess I should have opted for tuna flavor, huh? Say, you look like you know some stuff. Who has been visiting you down here, kiddo?"

Purring like an idling lawnmower, my new little buddy took the corner of the supplement bar and did an about-face. Hopping down, she went into the outfitter's shop through a space between the double doors and the cracked lintel. I followed, but I had to swing the sign out into the passage and push hard on the door. It came off its rusted hinges and crashed into the shop.

The place was a ruin. Wrecked furniture and crates were scattered throughout. I played the flashlight beam over empty and broken shelves, open display counters, and racks for merchandise. Three sawhorses without newly crafted saddles stood against one wall, separated by a table-height bench. My entrance was further obstructed by a partially fallen beam. When I tried to move it aside. It also crashed into the gloom, but the ceiling stayed up.

I was quite startled by the voice that came out of the darkness.

"Have a care, my love. The place is already about to cave in on us."

***

"Kayne! Holy fuck, am I glad to ... hey, are you alright?"

I shone the tac light below a built-in bench on the wall that this place shared with the bank next door. One arm, part of a shoulder, and most of Kayne's head emerged through a hole in the crumbling brickwork.

They fuckin' walled him up, man.

"One would suppose that I have put on weight during my unfortunate captivity, but, truth be told, the back of my shirt and part of my pants are hooked by some supporting metal folderol."

"Pushing from the other side ...?"

"Useless. The bars are quite prohibitive."

The cat positioned herself to watch the humans and their predicament with further tail-swishing fascination. She had placed the morsel before her prison buddy, but he seemed indisposed.

"Stay right there ... I will get help."

What an idiotic thing to say.

"Nick, my jailors will most likely return momentarily. We must act quickly."

I raced into the depths of the shop in search of tools. A workroom at the back was being used for storage. Levitech Systems Inc, apparently on the floors above, was storing old equipment down here. Far to the back, I found some leather working tools. Quick to return, I dragged the bench away from Kayne's confinement. I placed the flashlight on a pile of bricks and aimed for the dude in the wall.

The Ivory Knife

The mortar and brickwork came away easily, and I could loosen the hooks that hung up his clothes – some ripping but so much for modesty in the chambers of Hell. Soon he was out and in my arms.

"Bossman, I ... oh, shit Kayne, I don't know what ... are you hurt?"

Kayne stretched and dusted off as best he could. Walking the room a bit, he was puzzled at what to do about the rip in his pants and shirt, trying to pull together torn gaps.

"Surprisingly, despite my damaged couture, I am uninjured. Nick, where are we?"

"Seattle. Or at least in the ass end of it. Fuckin' dungeon and garbage pit."

"Ahh, the fabled Seattle Underground. I have never been here, but I always wanted to see it, though not this way. In my younger days, I was in a bar called the 'Seattle Underground.' It would appear the establishment and this place share a decorator."

We both tried to laugh but clung to each other on the brink of exhaustive tears. Our cat would have none of this display of sentimentality. Something startled the feline, and she sprang up onto a shelf, turning her gaze to the shop door. An arched back and a hiss announced intruders.

"Mr. Sechi. How wonderful to see you again. Dr. Sorenson has been quite resourceful but very rude. About to leave without saying goodbye? No, no. We cannot have this. Not at all."

There were two of them. Thick accents like I had heard when we were in Odesa last year. Russians. Black stalker garb for cruising the underground ... gunpoint from the Beta Guy. Alpha Dude was hiding half of his face.

"Yo, Boris. The tryouts for 'Phantom' are one block further over. If you and Zorro here hurry, ya just may make it. Mention my name and give it your best."

Then recognition took hold. I waved an index finger and said, "Wait a second – the Market. You're the rude bastard selling fish with this ugly dumb ass there. What's up, the salmon all go bad? Sure smells like it.

Guess your play going down at Pike's Place would have attracted too much attention, huh, *tovarich*?"

Kayne was sizing up the odds and edging slightly to my left. The air in the shop was fraught with danger. Between the fishmongers and me, our tac light beams played a bit of chicken with each other. The moving beams made the room spin. It was getting close to "go" time.

Yeah, but have to play along a bit because of the gun. Things are about to get nasty.

I waited for a signal from Kayne. However, when it came, it was from a surprising source.

The cat sprang off her perch on the shelf just over my right shoulder. She glided like a flying squirrel and landed, claws outstretched on the head of the main thug. He screeched like a maniac whose face was on fire and tried to pull her off, shaking back and forth and rocking in the darkness.

Illuminated only by the dim glow of the glass skywalk in the alley beyond, a shadow was barely visible as it crept through the open door. Bent over, our silent intruder positioned himself like a high school joker behind the now very astonished gunman.

Before Villian #2 could make sense of his Boss' hysterics, I did a spin kick and knocked him backward over the human barrier. The gun went off as he flipped and smacked his head.

At the explosion, Rescue Cat jumped back from making face tartar. She disappeared into the darkness. The Phantom was still whirling and pawing at his face as Kayne made an exquisite series of moves on the panicked Russian.

He took the dude at the hips from behind and rocked his panic dance so that the jerkwad's thrashing head made a skull-cracking impact with a hanging ceiling beam. The bitch was out cold on the floor.

Simultaneously, I vaulted over my mysterious wingman and kicked the gun from the hand of the dazed and prone Beta Boy. A third kick right to his jaw, and he joined his boss in Russian Mafia Nap Time.

The shadow stood up.

The Ivory Knife

"Not passing out on me this time, Sexy Man. We need to get the fuck out. Leave the gun, take the cannoli – I mean the backpack."

Well, WTF? Turns out, Our Godfather-quoting-ally was none other than Darren Urlaic from the Space Needle.

Kayne joined us and said, "Pleased to meet you, and thanks for your brilliant assistance, mate."

"Dr. Sorenson, these two have compatriots, no doubt somewhere down here. Let's hustle the hell out of this shithole. Please follow me."

I snagged my backpack as we made our exit from J. Douglas and Sons Outfitters. It wiggled.

"Looks like we'll be four to go, men."

The cat pushed her head out of one of the satchel's compartments.

Hey, don't jostle so much. Taking a nap here, fellas. Saving your collective asses is hard work.

Thomas Paul Severino

Chapter Twenty-Six: The Cabal
Cherry Street and First Avenue and The Cecil Bacon Manor, Seattle, Washington

Nick Sechi's Journal

"Push."

"Ooof. Stuck."

"One more time, muscles. Put that big back to work."

Darren had led us further into the ruinous subterrestrial warren. Behind us, we could hear the arrival of another group. Since the noise was coming from this side of the barriers, I could tell the advancing troops were not another group of tourists.

We were in a back corner, just about where the labyrinth deadends when our 'Virgil' pointed to a ladder.

Now on the upper rungs, I struggled with the exit. Darren clasped me around my legs to keep me from falling down the chute and landing on my ass. I sent the manhole cover rattling into the street above. The three of us and my backpack emerged as traffic swerved around us.

Kayne and I replaced the cover as Darren tapped his phone for an Uber.

***

"We must get you on your way and quickly. You are in grave danger here."

We were in the Venetian Room with Darren and Mrs. McCave. Benjamin knocked, came in, and closed the door behind him. His hands went out to the cat, who was winding her way between human legs, rubbing and sniffing.

"Kitty, kitty, kitty. Your kitty, the Sechi?"

"Yep, kiddo. She is a real Avenger."

"Looks like my cat, Rocco. Rocco, Rocco the cat."

He stooped, but Christine, named for the heroine in The Phantom of the Opera, was playing it coy. She lashed her tail excitedly and pranced away.

Kayne was freshly showered and in a white terrycloth robe. He observed our friends with his usual acuity. He pushed back his wet bangs and shared his thoughts.

"Please let me express our combined gratitude for your assistance and hospitality. I conclude that your group is some sort of clandestine society. You, the boy, and young Darren here. The Manor is a safe house. You are CIA, I perceive."

Mrs. McCave did not respond. Placing an envelope in my hands, she addressed her words to Benjamin.

"Please go down and wait for Dr. Inokapti. Please bring her up here when she arrives. Listen to me, please. If anyone else approaches the house, call the emergency number. You know where I keep it. Go."

After the boy left, our hostess turned to Kayne. She remained silent and mysterious.

He said, "He is indeed a technology systems genius, your group's connection to all things data and internet related. Benjamin tracked the plane from Ft Lauderdale, which got me to SeaTac Airport, unconscious and restrained. Was it Ben who placed the clue box for Nick in the post office box in San Francisco and left the key at 221 Baker Street? The G.I. Joe with my sartorial markings?"

"That was me, Dr. Sorenson," Darren confessed. "Benjamin and I worked out our little scheme. Benjamin loves that you guys interpret case details and solves puzzles. He is a bit of a riddle master. But the kid is not a flier. He totally freaks. P.S. That's some awesome place you guys have there in the City by the Bay."

Kayne countered, "He did, however, arrange travel accommodations on our business associate's computer so that Nick stayed here."

I broke in with, "How did he know where you were being held captive, Boss? Could have been anywhere in this town."

The Ivory Knife

"Levitech Systems. Their world headquarters are in the building above my imprisoning bank. They use the outfitter shop for storage. Benjamin Waska is an excellent investigator, my love. He became aware of my imprisonment by using the connecting stair and listening through Christine's wall hole."

Mrs. McCave said, "After you are seen by Dr. Inokapti, please do as directed."

She pointed to the envelope in my hand.

"The world is in great danger caused by the clash of superpowers at this time. The balance has been disturbed -- thrown off. We are now on the brink of a great Armageddon. I am not exaggerating, gentlemen. The situation is dire. The free world needs your assistance."

Saving the universe? I thought we did that a few cases ago. The bitch is in trouble again? Ohhh, man.

"The people of the north ...."

Kayne snapped his fingers, "That's it. You all are Inuit. The features are blurred by other genetic strains, but you are of the indigenous Arctic Tribes."

"Just so, Doctor. We are many. And we are quite efficiently connected. I believe I hear Benjamen and the Doctor. You need to be cleared physically for the next part of this adventure."

"Madam, may I impose on your graciousness again?"

Knowingly, I picked up Christine. Kayne petted her, and she licked his hand.

"To abandon one of my saviors at this point would be very disingenuous and rude."

"I'll take care of it, Doctor. There is a vet just five blocks down on Broadway. I will see that she is in perfect health for her trip to San Francisco. To whose attention?"

"Ms. Andi S. Rodriguez, Executive Business Partner, Sorenson, and Sechi. You have our address."

"Come, Christine. At least one of these gentlemen will be indisposed very soon. I bet you'd love some of Rocco's Wild Salmon Surprise."

As she passed me with our new bud, Honoria McCave said, "You must hurry."

***

Dr. Pauline Inokapti was a bit younger than Kayne, small, and very business-like. Her features bore the beauty of an ancient northern Asian people. She took his vitals, entered data on her tablet (patient name: Theodor Geisel – one more Benjamin touch), palpated his abdomen, felt for swollen glands, and removed a few vials and a syringe. Darren stood in the window, watching the street below with occasional glances at my husband's physical examination.

Kayne asked, "Well, Doctor. How fares this old body?"

"I must say, Dr. Sorenson, you are in excellent shape given the biological risks of the Seattle Underground. A few scrapes and you are slightly dehydrated."

I asked. "Biological risks? Such as?"

"Bubonic plague – although that was some time ago."

She handed me two containers of pills.

"Directions are on the label."

She pointed to my jeans.

"Drop'em and bend over."

I did a full-body blush and complied.

"Ouch. Why did you give Kayne his in his arm."

"Doing a friend a favor, my bucko."

She winked at Darren. The dude was grinning like a Cheshire Cat. Kayne chuckled as he dressed. Our friends had guessed his size – Ben again, no doubt.

The medic packed up her supplies.

The Ivory Knife

"Let's roll, Sorenson and Sechi."

Kayne said, "Thank you, Dr. Inokapti. Please take care."

"*Tavvauvusi*, Doctor Sorenson. I wish good luck to you both."

Darren scooped up satchels. I grabbed the backpack while rubbing my sore butt. Downstairs, I could see Christine through the swinging door chowing down. Benjamin handed me a canvas bag of delectables from the Cecil Bacon Manor Kitchen in the entrance hall.

"Thanks for everything, bud. We owe you big time."

Benjamin smiled and looked away. He hurried back into the house.

Thomas Paul Severino

Chapter Twenty-Seven: The Cascades Regional
King Street Railroad Station, Seattle Washington

Nick Sechi's Journal

"The first train out. Track seven. We'll arrive at our destination in about four hours. I sent our bags ahead."

"Vancouver."

Darren smiled. "Excellent, Dr. Sorenson."

"Elementary. You had asked about our passports."

The King Street Railroad Station was an Italianate edifice near Pioneer Square. The early morning light painted the bricks and marble of its impressive clock tower a sunflower yellow on its eastern side. We hurried beneath a massive multi-globe chandelier above a navigational star compass laid out in hand-cut marble tiles in the center of the waiting room floor.

As we made our way to the train that would take us along the coast of Puget Sound to the largest metropolis in British Columbia, Kayne suddenly called a switch to our progress.

"Follow me quickly. I will explain."

We bounded down the platform and vaulted onto the train on track six going to Portland and Eugene, just as the southbound train began to leave the station. A conductor pulled us into the moving car just before closing the doors. Darren was mystified, but positioning him between Kayne and me allowed us to navigate him into the wrong train. Kayne continued our sprint toward the back of the car jostling between passengers who were settling themselves and their carry-ons. The squeeze was tight, but we made the platform between the next car as the train picked up speed.

Kayne opened the door on the side opposite, turned, and said, "Time for drop and roll, lads."

We were out on our asses on a strip of grass. I looked back to see the train accelerating out of the station, our conductor hanging out of our abandoned car looking mystified, and two security guards hurrying to meet us.

Kayne brushed off dirt and leaves and opened his arms to the guards to admit his stupidity.

"So sorry, gentlemen. Wrong train. American rapid transport is so bloody complicated."

"Do you know where you should be going, Sir?"

Kayne pointed to a train on track seven as it started to inch away.

"There."

We ran across tracks and jumped.

***

"There."

Kayne had pulled the sunshade on the window of our compartment. It was transparent but tinted dark. He pointed to three men moving through the corridor of the train we had recently quit. They looked big and aggressive, pulling past commuters searching for something or someone. The northbound and the southbound train shared parallel tracks for about a mile. Our pursuers' Super Chief picked up speed for the south at the diversion point as our Cascade Regional headed north.

"Dr. Sorenson ...."

"You were about to ask when I realized we were being followed. The answer is quite simple: as we left the Manor, Darren. They never investigated our lodgings because Mrs. McCave has her own muscle on the sidewalk outside 959 Broadway. A cabal is, after all, a cabal. Security is tantamount.

"The Underground thugs followed our Uber to the station. Have you boyos never jumped from a moving train before? I have a lot of experience in the sport of train hopping. When I was in grad school in the EU, I almost had my Eurail Pass revoked in Budapest. *Les liaisons dangereuses* as the French would say. Sometimes one just needs to escape."

The Ivory Knife

I looked at Darren and said, "Let's go, dude. We need some answers. I got a whole bunch of 'whys' that need some reasons and solutions. Time to turn states evidence."

"Two weeks ago in Arkhangelsk, Russia, a high-level information officer faked her death and disappeared. Lieutenant Colonel Katsitsanóron Isapoinhkyaki, aka Katya Sidorovna, of the Russian Foreign Intelligence Service is carrying vital information believed to be important to the western democracies."

Kayne asked, "Back up, lad. Who are you, and who are your friends back in Seattle?"

"You asked that question back at the Bacon Manor."

"And I received no answer. I conclude you and your fellow Inuit superheroes are some kind of intelligence cell concerned with national security. You work in support of the West, as evidenced by your opposition to my Russian captors. The rest is — I apologize. My cognition has been thrown off as of late. Dungeon imprisonment will do that."

I settled next to him and took his hand in mine. There had been little time to show him how grateful I was for his release.

Darren paced our compartment. He raised the shade and watched the passing scene. The early morning sun, breaching the Cascade Range to the east, poured intense light over Puget Sound, turning the blues and greens to ethereal jeweled tones.

"We are an agency of ordinary people, laborers, managers, executives, trained in certain aspects of government intelligence science. We move out in the community and are known only to our superiors and sometimes to one another. Government security is our goal. Counterintelligence information is secured, relayed, and used to neutralize foreign agents undermining national interests.

"Every so often, you hear of a family from the suburbs who lead ordinary lives. Turns out they have been trading secrets with a rogue state on the United States weapon systems. We are the ones who see the traces of espionage, set the traps, and facilitate the workings of the CIA, the FBI, and our Judicial System."

I said, "It takes ordinary to catch ordinary."

Darren nodded. "We are literally at ground level. There is no such thing as useless information, Nick."

Kayne was fascinated. He remarked, "An innkeeper, a restauranteur, a landscapist ... a motley shadow network working to combat foreign terrorism and intrigue."

"We have had our successes, to be sure. Last fall, we helped eliminate a domestic group that planned to interfere with Washington, Alaska, and Oregon elections. They were a group of hackers operating out of a bakery in Boise."

Kayne said, "Election interference? Come on, lad. They had ties ...."

"Yes, Doctor. The group was filled to the gills with foreign connections. I am speaking of criminals from despicable rogue nations who want our democracy to tumble and use our own citizens to accomplish the deed."

"Darren, the Inuits," I asked. "What's the connection? You guys are like secret Native American mercenaries or what?"

"Seriously, Nick? The circumpolar world is set as the stage for the next battleground of an all-out conflict between east and west. The world of my ancestors is literally melting away, and the superpowers are money-blind to stopping carbon emissions that are destroying the planet. Advocates? Yes. Mercenaries? It may lead to that. The missiles that will fly will cross the skies above the Arctic Circle. Many will be intercepted and brought down."

The young man leaned forward in his seat, elbows on his knees.

"Hunters -- the *piniartoq* living at the top. That is who we are. That is who we have always been. My people have a sense of community that goes back 4,000 years. The Inuit people and our cousins stretch across three continents. The center of our world is not the equator but the pole – all lands are to the south. And it is the south we watch. It is from there that the destruction comes.

"The danger within must be seen with a hunter's eyes. We look for the signs in the *aglu* – the holes in the ice and the breath of espionage that arises. Our sleeper agents, like the one in Seattle, follow with the skills of an expert trapper. We can dispatch with knives to the throat. Blood on the ice ...."

The Ivory Knife

The door to our compartment opened, and a middle-aged woman in a business suit entered. She extended a hand as Darren moved back. The choreography of our orientation session onboard the Cascade Regional moved on to the next act.

"Gentlemen, I am pleased to make your acquaintance. I am Regina Netsilik. I am the CEO of Levitech Systems Inc. I am a leader in the field of business tech...."

Kayne shook his head as he stood and took her hand. "No, madam, you are not."

"I beg your pardon." The woman quizzically smiled as she said. "Why then did I go to all the bother to have all those business cards printed."

"If Levitech has a division of technology that is open for public commerce, it is a cover for more covert operations," Kayne said. "Your company neutralizes the effects of foreign interference in the technology that runs this country. Foreign hackers are your prey, and, given the right resources, your many divisions and branches are doing a passable job in building impregnable firewalls and outing hackers by the score."

The woman's smile became more genuine as if previous concerns about our eligibility to assist in this mission had just vanished. Regina Netsilik confirmed Darren's choice of allies with a single look.

"Yes. We have facilities up and down the west coast of the United States and Canada. My company specializes in enterprise IT environments for protecting the underlying networking infrastructure by installing preventative measures to deny unauthorized access, modification, deletion, and theft of resources and data. Busy little signal jammers, keeping the bad guys out of our shit, to put it simply."

She sat.

"Everyone wants to bugger us in our technological asses these days. Sometimes it seems like Levitech is in the prophylactic business."

Out on the sound, a family of sea lions, a mother, and three pups emerged from a morning swim to find a napping spot on some sunny rocks. A group of common loons dipped ass-end up, hoping to spear some breakfast in the shallows. I returned my attention to our train's interior and the elegant businesswoman who had joined us.

"I have recently been in touch with my superior, the President's National Security Advisor. She wants this operation regarding the missing Russian to be carefully handled by confederates who operate below ground level."

Kayne and I both chuckled at the imagery.

Regina continued, "The world is run by massive technological infrastructures — transportation, communication, healthcare, economic enterprises, energy grids — foundational technology services, software, equipment, facilities and structures upon which the capabilities of nations, cities, and organizations are built."

I said, "Sounds like you want us to find this Russian woman without much international attention to our game plan. What is she carrying?"

Now the head of one of the country's most essential techno-security agencies stood and reflected on the view of the passing landscape.

"Katya Sidorovna left the Russian Foreign Intelligence Service ten days ago with hand-written codes for viruses that were supposed to be passed on to Russian agents in seven western countries. This is ransomware within a Trojan Horse intended to be inserted into the computer systems that regulate the operation of ...."

Regina turned to take us in. Kayne filled in the blank.

"Nuclear power plants."

Chapter Twenty-Eight: *Pysanka*
Bidwell and Davie Street, Vancouver, British Columbia

Nick Sechi's Journal

"Kayne Sorenson, you man-whore! What are you doing in the Saltwater City? Did they throw you out of the U.S. as they did in so many other European countries?"

The man hugging my husband was a tall blond in his early forties. He was genuinely glad to see Kayne. It was apparent they had a past.

He held Kayne at arm's length and continued razzing him in a voice that could be heard throughout the restaurant. The Easter Egg colors were the main design features of the bistro/restaurant/bar, intricate and jewel-like.

"The Hungarian. What a fuckin' shitstorm that was. And you at the center, the boy who lost his pants. Sex Bomb Sorenson – on the loose and naughty."

"Aleksei, this is my husband, Nick Sechi. Nick, Aleksei Volkov, an … um … an old friend. Yes, that would best describe it."

The affable man raised his arms as he approached me. His palms connected with each side of my face.

"But, Kayne-ya. This boy is beautiful. A red-haired Italian." He pulled me in for a triple kiss with a full-body hug-up. Solid male. Dude works out.

"Nick is Nicholas?"

"Close. Nicola."

"Ahhh. Then you are 'Kolya,' as we Ukrainians say."

He motioned to the bartender as we made our way to three stools at one end of the bar.

"Grisha, three."

Nemiroff Honey Pepper Vodka – the dude left the bottle.

"Ypa!"

He kissed Kayne again after the first shot. And before refills.

"Crimea?"

"Wait. Grisha, is Tim in the back?"

Aleksei made another hand motion that translated as, "get him out here."

The bartender set down another glass and went through a rear door.

"Yes. 2014. I left the company in Sevastopol, and my Timofey left the team. We fled. Putin's government does not like gays. The horror stories from Russia and places like Chechnya ... we were both done. Canada took us in, and Pysanka is our home and our business."

We were joined by a tall man emerging from the kitchen at the back.

"Ahh, my own beautiful man. Tim Chernoff. This is Kayne Sorenson and Nick Sechi."

He poured his husband a drink. We slammed the empty shot glasses on the bar with a lusty clamor.

Tim Chernoff also had a striking Slavic look — mid-length black hair and blue-green eyes. As he smiled broadly and stood with one arm over his man's shoulder, I considered they made a remarkable-looking couple — a pairing of the fair and the dark men of the Slavic race, a Cossak and a Tartar.

Kayne looked closely at the man's face.

"Sbornaya Rossii po khokkeyu s shayboy."

"Tak, tak, tak. But Alyosha must have told you, *da*?"

The Slavic name diminutives were hard enough to figure out. So, add more vodka to the mix, and the result was even more confusing. "Kayne-ya" for Kayne, "Kolya" for me, "Aloysha" is Aleksei, and "Timofey" is the nickname for Tim — go figure.

Alyosha did a palms-up and a shoulder shrug.

The Ivory Knife

"Your husband indicated you were a jock. Your teeth indicate your sport is hockey. Russia's Men's National Hockey Team is the logical conclusion."

Chernoff and Volkov laughed heartily.

"My Timofey, you see? I told you about this one, yes. *Paren's* mind is clockwork. Tic. Tic. Tic. And his body is sin. Yes?"

Another pet name (*paren* = boyfriend) and a stare from the jock that mentally undressed Kayne ... I poured the next one.

"*L'chaim!*"

The jock in question tapped his upper front teeth.

"Yes. These are ill-fitting. I am replacing them very soon."

Kayne patted the chest of his old friend and remembered former times.

"This bloke, Nick. La Bayadère. The bloody lead dancer, Nick. I believe it was in 2000 that the Kirov/Mariinsky Ballet created a new production of Petipa's masterpiece. When he reprised the role for the Australian Ballet, the critics praised his *Grand Pas d'action* with the highest accolades. The dance critic for the Melbourne Herald Sun made a fool of himself over this brogan's spectacular arse and legs. Cheers, mate."

I could see where this was going fast, fueled with some delicious Ukrainian vodka. I tried to rescue our investigation, and Kayne slipped into the Australian slang that signaled he was "on his face."

I said and did not even slur, "So Tim, my man, word on Granville street is that this is the place for meeting up with Russian ex-pats in Vancouver."

Chernoff moved closer and indicated the patrons. "Tourists, bah. But at night, Kolya. At night the Rus – they come out of the darkness to hear the strains of the balalaika and morn the plight of Mother Russia."

He raised his arms in an inviting gesture and sang.

Vokrug nas spokoyno; Kholmy pokryty tumanom,

Vnezapno luna svetit skvoz' tuchi,

Mogily sokhranyayut spokoystviye.

Thomas Paul Severino

Beloye siyaniye krestov – geroi spyat.

Teni proshlogo kruzhat vokrug,

Vspominaya zhertv boyev

Tim closed his eyes and swayed to the exotic and melancholy song. Kayne translated line by line, softly speaking under the mournful crooning.

Around us, it is calm; Hills are covered by mist,

Suddenly, the moon shines through the clouds,

Graves hold their calm.

The white glow of the crosses – heroes are asleep.

The shadows of the past circle around,

Recalling the victims of battles.

A few customers stood with glasses raised and joined in the Russian lyric.

Kayne's buddy, Aleksei, he of the unbelievable ass and legs, jumped up on a barstool. Grisha added support as the pair attempted to drown out the lament with a patriotic and rousing anthem. Grisha called out, "Those Russians... always crying... be a man, *tovarysh.*"

My narodylysya u velyku hodynu,

Vid vohnyu viyny I polum'ya postriliv,

Nas plekav bil' vtraty Ukrayiny,

My hoduvalysya hnivom I zloboyu do nashykh vorohiv.

We were born in a great hour,

From the fires of war, and the flames of gunshots,

We were nurtured by the pain of losing Ukraine,

We were fed by anger and malice to our enemies.

The Ivory Knife

Now, the second set of patriots, Ukrainians, took up the lusty pean. Vodka flowed for both groups of partisans. The joy in the club was getting freakier. Secret soldiers with hearts aflame for the motherland attempted to drown out the foe in a battle of songs and vodka.

Kayne pointed to each of the proprietors. "Rival nations, especially with this terrible war. The heart breaks for the people."

Aleksei pointed to a boarded-up window.

"Two nights ago."

He did a hug-up on his Timofey and yelled. "We stand with Zelenski."

Chernof yelled back.

"*Da zdravstvuyet Ukraina*. Long live Ukraine!"

They kissed like porn stars. The patrons roared their approval.

***

"She was here three nights ago with a man. They sat in the back and talked to another couple. Big plans, from what I could tell. Grisha, come, please."

The bartender served another customer and then approached us. I showed him the picture of Katya Sidorovna.

"Yes, yes."

He tapped the phone.

"This woman and her companion, a man ... they were speaking with the Shatralevs. They are trying to disappear. You know, new identities, fake passports, and someplace where only horseradish knows them."

Kayne asked, "How do you know this?"

"I asked their server, Misha. He is excellent at overhearing."

"Grisha," I asked. "where can we find the Shatralevs?"

"Like I said. Only horseradish knows. If this one had the money, that couple would take them out. You want to talk to them?"

Kayne said, "Yes. It is most urgent."

Grisha wiped his hands on a bar towel and started to walk away.

"Dress warmly and *Udachi, druzi* – good luck, it is a big country."

He began to fill another drink order but whispered one word our way.

"Alaska."

Chapter Twenty-Nine: In the Hero City
Mariupol, Ukraine

"Comrade Captain, you do not want this war. These people are innocent. They are shopkeepers and their wives, school children, teachers, and factory workers – three generations, comrade. The blood they share is Slavic, like yours."

Mark Gadarn pleaded with a Russian officer behind the Orthodox Church of the Holy Mother of God in Mariupol, the Donetsk Oblast of Ukraine. Around them, tanks roared, and buildings fell. The refugees, people from the parish surrounding the church, huddled in the basement of the church's crypt. Down the street, soldiers and townspeople huddled in the steel factory, the frontline of the doomed city.

"The streets are already crowded with the bodies of the dead. Let me have them. I will take them to the west. Please allow them to enjoy the safety a family should have, Comrade. Your parents, wife, and children are safe tonight in Russia, no? Your friends, also? How will you be able to return to them with the blood of these innocent people on your hands?"

"You will leave personal matters out of this. Reporter. You and your kind are the worst."

"There is nothing more personal than war, Comrade Captain. Nothing."

A mortar shell struck somewhere close and lit up the night sky, full of white snow and the black dust of war. The once beautiful city, Ukraine's gateway to the east through the Sea of Azov, was shrouded in an apocalyptic haze of death and destruction.

The captain barked a command, "Take this man back to the rest of the prisoners. Those tanks will advance on the steelworks. Our orders are to level those factories and storage facilities."

Mark shook off the arms which reached for him. Defiantly, he faced the Russian commander once more. He wanted the other soldiers to be aware of his intent to take their prisoners to safety. The conscience of a soldier was a critical factor in war.

"Captain Korolenko, the city is yours. Russian forces occupy the entire Oblast. The whole region is under Russian control. What happens now is critical. It will change this war and its aftermath. You and your command risk the world's judgment if you violate the international laws of war."

With passion in his voice, Mark pointed to the Church's undercroft.

"You stand on the brink, Captain. Do not turn the crypt of the Church of the Holy Mother of God into a killing field. The world will remember and hunt you down. These are people, not dirt to be cleansed."

The Russian spoke into the darkness like a man filled with disgust.

"In Buca, they shot everyone they saw. Orders, supposedly ... I know .... in Moscow, members of the Duma are demanding capital punishment for Ukrainian captives. I have my orders, Gadarn."

"Comrade Korolenko ... the Nuremberg Trials... 1949 ... the 'I only followed orders' defense was condemned by the international tribunal, as were the men who obeyed those orders. Captain ... The Soviets concurred with the proceedings and the verdicts."

The captain was about to order the return of Mark to the holding area when shots rang out. Russian soldiers under Korolenko's command cut seven men in half as they rushed into the darkness. The slicing fire of their Kalashnikovs dropped the black-clad men onto the debris of a destroyed building. Behind the slaughtered, a dark cloud of companions screamed and dropped to their knees with hands in the air.

"A bomb, Comrade Captain. That one is carrying a bomb. They were rushing here from the destroyed Cheremushki Synagogue down the street. They are terrorists. Nazis like the rest."

Mark leaped free from his captors. Guns took aim as he scrambled to the figure crawling aimlessly in the dirt. He dropped and pulled the dying man to him. The stovepipe, wide-brimmed hat had fallen to the side. The man's long white beard was blood-spattered, and his blank eyes looked at death. As Mark lifted the dying man, the rabbi's long black coat opened, and the "bomb" fell out.

The Ivory Knife

Mark looked up at Captain Ivan Illyich Korolenko above the blood-stained scroll of the Torah.

Thomas Paul Severino

Chapter Thirty: The Mermaid
Coal Harbour Quay, Vancouver, BC V6G 3E7, Canada

Nick Sechi's Journal

"We needed a break anyway. Grisha is delighted to handle Pysanka for a few days. We will accompany you as far as Ketchikan. The crew will see to your continued journey from there. There she is. Isn't she a beauty?"

Aleksei pointed to a trawler riding the calm harbor waters tied to her berth. Coal Harbour Marina sparkled with white yachts and pleasure crafts. Seabirds spiraled overhead in the bright morning air.

"That is the 'Rusalka,' our Marlow Explorer 61E. This little mermaid cost us a small fortune, but the business has been good. We took her out last weekend up to Port Edward. The Mermaid is outfitted as befits a queen, and she can take the Inside Passage even in winter."

The moderately sized yacht featured a covered cockpit and side decks. Tim caught me checking her out as he boarded with supplies.

He said, "Lots of rain here in the Pacific Northwest, especially in spring."

He gestured to the covered decks and added, "Good protection for the crew when it pours. Aleksei is headed to the pilothouse, Nick. Go on up. Looks like Kayne is on a call."

He headed in the direction of the galley. My Bossman was down on the pier, phone to his head, talking and pacing. I am glad we brought warm clothing. The sea air was brisk. A salty breeze tossed his longish black hair so that he had to use his right hand to clear it away from his face between gesturing to someone at the other end of the line.

I investigated our pleasure craft with the notion that she needed to be built to catch a spy.

The crew of the Rusalka consisted of a Captain, Michael McDowd, a Cook/First Mate, Eva Nakoyak, and a Steward/Cabin Boy, Cameron Jakobs.

Thomas Paul Severino

The three came from an agency our buddies had used before. Part of their contract included storage and maintenance of the boat at the Marina.

The Captain was a short man of military bearing. Cook was all business, also. The young dude was apparently a college kid. He reminded me something of Kris, only dark-complected. I did a 'Kayne' and drew some conclusions from my observations. The boyo was another hockey jock.

Kayne ended the call but did not come aboard. He punched in another number. Waved to me as he waited for pick up.

Captain McDowd explained, "The Rusalka's separate pilothouse with this open plan allows us to cruise in the darkness. Not much traffic in the Inside Passage at night. Logs in the water – hazardous. Remember, up here, winter nights are up to 21 hours. With the galley just aft of the pilothouse, this design is a very practical situation. Even the galley crew can keep an eye out for logs. In warm weather, we use the flying bridge for navigation. Just up that stairway there."

"Designed for maneuvering the dangers?"

"Aye, lad. Ya, like boats, I see."

"Yes, Sir. Our work takes us on the high seas from time to time."

I hesitated to add specifics. It wasn't like we crewed or anything. And the submarine – too cramped and claustrophobic for this sailor boy – best be forgetting that case, lemme tell ya.

The Captain showed me a design plan for the yacht.

"The Rusalka has a special hull design with two prominent, strut-type keels ahead of the props and rudders, an excellent feature where shit in the water threatens. She almost always hits something. This gal has additional protection that helps avoid major damage when collisions happen.

"How fast will you run her, Captain?"

"You wanna cruise and see the landscape, lad? Ten knots or so. Leisurely and relaxing. Up ahead, we will be crossing a stretch of big water that's open to the ocean."

He pointed to a sizeable nautical chart.

The Ivory Knife

"Entrances here ... Port Hardy to Moresby Island. Full seas to our west. Also, here ... Masset to Ketchikan. And we'll come out here near Juneau. There to Valdez, the Rusalka is in the rough waters of the Gulf of Alaska. Fourteen, fifteen knots ... a good and safe pace."

"Nice. Speedy and compact."

"Aye, mate. The owner lads like to take her out a lot in the nice weather. All the way up, ya see. At 65 feet, the Rusalka just makes the limit of the marinas along the way."

I looked down at the gangway.

What was taking Kayne so long?

***

"Rebecca, from what Eris tells us, I conclude he is in the middle of the conflagration in the southeast. Your man has a habit of being ass to balls with the enemy. He is apparently trying to get out. You and I know he is not coming out of a war zone alone, my girl."

"Yes. That last time in Yemen, Kayne, seems to have set a pattern. Mark is a one-person Red fucking Cross."

"Easy, my girl. We need to call in some markers, and I have an idea of who can help. Get Eris to be more specific on Mark's location. Rebecca, is your man chipped?"

"Like a Labrador Retriever. Subcutaneous. Right forearm."

"That will make it easier. I will check in with you as I know something. We will have to consider the time differences."

"Call anytime, darling."

"Glad you're walking, my girl. I will claim a dance at the opening gala."

"I am just glad you are found. Love to Nick."

***

"Andi."

"Kayne. Good to hear your voice. Thank you for the cat. She is a beautiful baby. Cleared by the vet this morning. Alice and Chouko are figuring her out, but she kinda rules."

"Good to hear. Sorry to rush, but we are about to get underway here. I would like to speak to the entire Sorenson and Sechi team. No Mycroft. I agree with your suspicions. We need to get him rehabilitated. Please ask Oscar to join. We can zoom. Just text me the time. Also, please let Eric know I need to speak to him for a meeting after the meeting."

"You got it. Some case requests came through. Nothing that can't wait."

"Good. I will review your emails as soon as I can on those. Take care."

***

Kayne walked to the foot of the gangway and looked up its length.

"Permission to come aboard, Sir."

Aleksei said, "Get that sexy Australian arse up here, Sorenson."

Chapter Thirty-One: *Arvik*
The Inside Passage

Nick Sechi's Journal

"Oscar just needs to think about it. You can understand his reluctance. He is a process-oriented person. He will come around. It is a good plan. It is what needs to be done."

"No reservations?"

"None."

I re-aligned the laptop for the zoom meeting so that Kayne and Eric would have a better perspective. The others had left Kayne's conference table in our San Francisco office.

There was a momentary pause, and Eric continued.

"I am pleased Nick found you, and you are without injury."

Kayne said, "There is something else."

"You want information on the Shatralevs, Vadim, and Livinia. They are members of the Moldova underworld, my brother. They specialize in refugees seeking to come to America illegally. These are dangerous people, and their allegiance varies depending on who pays the most. Two days ago, they were in Ketchikan with what appears to be a couple — new clients. Your mark, my brother. Sidorovna and her companion ... this is certain."

"I am appreciative, brother dear, but I fear we are pulling you back into the game."

Eric took a drag on his cigarette and blew the smoke just to the left of the no-smoking sign on the console. He grinned in that creepy way that only involved the lower half of his face.

"Since our dear father last took me out to the woodshed to provide me with some behavioral correction, I have been aware that I am one dangerous bugger who can well take care of himself."

Yeah, really. The wounds that never heal... ever.

The Commander reached for the keyboard to sign off.

"We can share a victory when you two return. Nick, remember, you cocky little ...."

Kayne spoke over the sure-to-be raunchy utterances of the Mayor of Crazytown.

"Quite right and all that, brother dear. Keep the home fires burning and everyone safe. Cheers."

The signoff image Eric got was my resting brat face, sticking my tongue out at the Lord of Darkness of Pacific Heights.

***

"On deck, hurry."

Tim's knock brought us up to the flying bridge, trailing parkas and caps. We struggled into our gear. Aleksei was snuggling with his man against the port side rail. The moon was full on the cold, choppy waters of the Passage. There was no wind. Overhead, the Milky Way looked like a giant had thrown a handful of diamonds across a cloudless sky.

Aleksei spoke in the semi-darkness like an all-knowing Arctic Sea sprite. He pulled Tim next to him on the rail, entwining their cocktails and parka-wrapped bodies. He gestured out over the water, which balanced the full moon's white disc on the western horizon's edge.

"Welcome to Alaska, where frozen wonders await."

Eva Nakoyak had prepared some smoked whiskey old fashions and a tray full of small bites on a table at the back of the bridge. As we mounted the stairs, she pointed forward on the port side. The mute officer added a sign in ASL.

Kayne said, "*Arvik*. Whale."

The pod of humpbacks was swimming and breaching in the midnight blue waters shot through with moonlight. As they leaped up into the night sky, the water streamed from their spiraling bodies like a net of white lace strewn with shiny black pearls. Here and there, a calf would scurry to circle around a descending parent whose balletic leap brought them down on their back, sending a spray across the water's surface like an arc of crystals reaching across the rolling sea.

We were awe-struck.

"They have the largest brains of any creature on the planet, my love. Brilliant incredible beings of moonlight and water."

Aleksei cried out as a massive Leviathan seemed to soar up to the full moon, wanting it for a snack.

"Un grande Jeté d'Alaska. Magnifique!"

Tim explained in a soft voice.

"They usually feed in the northern reaches of the Passage during this season. Their migration patterns are changing. These days, more families are seen in this part of the Alexander Archipelago."

What appeared to be the rolling dark surface of the Passage suddenly was broken by a shot of air and water like a blast from a firehose breaking into the atmosphere. The moving humps ended in a lifted fluke, broad and waving before slipping underwater.

"The adults slap their tails on the water to signal delicious fish schools to their family members. See there, their cousins, the Orcas, and the dolphins. It is dinner time in the icy deep."

He raised a glass to the curving blue-black bodies of these diving marine mammals. The dorsal fins of the black and white killer whales crested like tall sentries patrolling the night seas. Waves glittered and danced on all sides like millions of dark sapphires reflecting starlight.

I felt Kayne hug me close as we looked at the panorama of nature's beauty. He whispered, "Listen, Nick."

Groans, grunts, whistles, and whoops competed with clicks as the pod danced off into the waters off the port side. Whalesong – hypnotic and exotic.

Kayne took Eva Nakoyak's hand and lightly tapped it for each click and murmur. His lips formed the pucker of a whistler and switched to an open-mouth expression to match the sounds of the passing whales. Sometimes he put her fingers to the side of his throat and softly imitated the sound. The woman nodded and smiled.

She made a "W" with three fingers of her right hand and extended her other forearm in front of her. She bobbed the "W" up and down, over and under – "Whale."

Kayne moved his right hand to cross his body at chest level. Then he moved his left hand back and forth above his right as if conducting an orchestra –"Song.".

The water next to the Rusalka suddenly was shot through with iridescence as schools of small fish swam near the surface. Another whale sounded next to the boat, its blue-black form rising like a submerged pillar of mass and wonder. As we beheld this incredible beauty, she seemed to pause – not lifting or settling but suspended alongside us. She appeared to scope me out in the darkness with her enormous eye. In the creature's magnificent orb, I could see a world of wonder and profound mystery.

As the whale lowered, Eva Nakoyak signed excitedly.

Kayne chuckled and translated, "Our First Mate is explaining that whales love the color red."

He tousled my hair.

Chapter Thirty-Two: *Kichx̱áan*
Ketchikan, Alaska

"What did you expect? You are hiding. Accommodations at a five-star luxury hotel, *tovarich*? That would be the first place your enemies would look. This is a cannery. It is clean. Livinia has gone into town for food."

Katya Sidorovna stood at the window, looking at the boats. Salmon fishers were heading out and returning into the rainy waters of the Tongass Narrows. Dark rain clouds sat on the hill of Betton Island, directly across the channel. A small ferry boat was docking in the cove where they were sheltered. The cannery was only accessible by water.

When the former Russian agent spoke, it was with a reserved authority.

"This place smells. Do you know who I am?"

Vadim Shatralev blew smoke into the cold room.

"I know who you *were*. Now, you are a woman of no country, a traitor to Mother Russia with a price on your head. We are talking about a considerable amount, so my sources tell me. This brings me to an essential point in your plan to escape. Expenses have increased beyond anticipated amounts. You will need to pay us eighty thousand USD more."

He tapped out ash on the wooden floor, looked at Stefan, and added, "Humph. No one is interested in a spoiled priest. There is no money for the likes of you. You carry no secrets. Not even that stupid icon. It is worthless. Not gold."

Stefan Lebedev was not a man to be taken lightly. He clenched his fists and said, "You promised safe passage and American passports. Where is what you promised?"

He reached for his backpack and threatened. "You will keep your filthy hands off what does not belong to you. You commit sacrilege with your greed."

Sidorovna spun into the mix and rummaged in the backpack. She stood up, glaring at Shatralev.

"What have you done with it, thief?"

As she advanced on the fearless man, Livina Shatralev came through the door of the small studio. She carried a shopping bag. A large shoulder satchel was looped around her neck, the strap crossing to her hip.

"Fuckin' Rain City – the wettest damn city in the world. I am drenched. The ferryman is a lecher if anyone wants to know. Well, it seems there is something amiss. What?"

The woman put down her parcels and shoulder bag. She slipped off her parka and gloves. The irritated woman unwound her scarf and hung her outerwear on a peg.

Lavinia walked to her husband and took a drag on his cigarette. Without returning it, she asked, "Did you tell them?"

Vadim nodded as their eyes met.

The angry Russian said, "Give me the knife."

Lavina stepped back to her shoulder bag and removed the *ulu*. The artifact was six inches from end to end. The handle arched across its top, and the blade was attached below this like a chunk of sharp stone. It was an excellent example of a knife used by the Inuit for skinning and cleaning animals. The handle was carved Walrus ivory, and the blade was honed slate.

She turned it with both hands and said, "One hundred and no more. The pawnbroker said only the handle made it worth anything. Alaskan tourist shops are overflowing with native scrimshaw. And by the way, people are asking for you in the city. Dangerous people."

Katya Sidorovna lifted the tool from the Moldovan woman's hands and turned her back to their escorts. After a minute, she turned around and nodded to Lebedev. He walked to the door and set the lock.

Livinia lit her own cigarette.

"You will give us more money, Comrade. You must understand we have a problem here and cannot continue this project."

The Ivory Knife

"I see, but I believe I have the solution, Comrade."

***

"The man and the woman have had their throats cut with a jagged and somewhat dull blade. He was murdered first, on this side of the room. The woman attempted to flee, but before she could unlock the door, the killer sliced her neck, and she fell where you see her. Observe the bloody footprints and the scratch marks on the wood. Wood slivers are present under the fingernails of the dead woman's right hand."

Kayne looked up from his place kneeling near the second corpse. Detective Hyder from the Ketchikan Gateway Borough and the Coast Guard Captain Marjorie Silverman. When the Rusalka docked in the Harbor, we were taken off the yacht and immediately placed aboard a Coast Guard Cutter. The Captain explained that the Borough was in dire need of our investigative services. She dropped the name "Mary Chance." Connections and more connections – the chase was on.

"The killer is a woman. She wears a size six snow boot. The manufacturer is Russian – Valenki. She stands five foot five."

Standing up, Kayne pointed to the stride length indicated by the footprints

He continued.

"The murderer -- she knows how to dispatch a human, but there is a particular hint of more depth to her crime. As well as an assassin's experience, our murderer kills like a hunter. The slice is precise – carotid artery to carotid artery – exactly the same on both victims. But the weapon is primitive. These are raw and jagged slashes."

He held up a sliver of something in a small glassine bag.

"Slate. From the man's hyoid bone – just superior to the thyroid cartilage."

"There is no ceremonial evidence to the blood bath other than our murderer kills with an ancient weapon. One more important detail, there was another person in the room. Next to the woman, you will see two bloody knee prints and a man's footprint. Someone, not the killer, knelt alongside her as she lay dying. I suspect prayer was the intent for nothing by way of medical aid would have assisted either victim."

Captain Silverman handed Kayne the photo IDs of the dead couple. He shared them with me as he turned for another look at the deceased.

Kayne again surveyed the mutilated corpses and the extensive splashes of blood. He muttered softly.

"Ahhh ... there you are, Lieutenant Colonel Katsitsanóron Isapoinhkyaki. Yes, there you are. We have been looking for you."

Chapter Thirty-Three: The Butcher Approaches
Mariupol, Ukraine

"They are not our jets, Sir. They are advising we fall back to the east and the north."

The pastor's office served as the command center for the 16th Machine Gun Artillery Division. On the walls, blank, lightened patches hinted at removed icons. One large crucifix hung behind the pastor's desk. The Russian flag and a division banner stood to either side.

"A renewed attack will follow, no doubt, Comrade Corporal. We will regain this territory for the Motherland in a matter of days. Give the order to move my units out."

"The Ukrainians and those Jews in the crypt? Five guards and enough ammunition ... I need to think!"

The explosions of the bombardment rocked the rectory. The Russian commander covered his face with both hands.

A voice from a dark corner said, "They are coming for you, Comrade Captain. Accountability time, Korolenko."

Mark was tied to a chair. The Russian was in the midst of planning for his ransom or exchange when the news came of the nearing Ukrainian army. The captain tapped his keyboard.

"Perhaps a waste of arms. I see no escape route in the direction you suggest, Comrade. The Air Defense System given to Kyiv by those blasted Slovakians is up and operating. What is here?"

"Out troop carriers in the Sea of Azov. The 5th Division Command Center is here."

He pointed to the map.

Captain Korolenko rechecked the area's Movement Tracking System. The Division's real-time integrated GPS technology brought war into the

21st century by providing communication with armored vehicles. He searched for information on unit location change.

Korolenko stopped tapping his laptop. He looked up at his Number One.

"We go to the port. Make an arrangement on that end. We fall back to Taganrog."

"The civilians? The hostages? Him?"

"All. We are leaving. The prisoners go with us. Put this American in the crypt. Food and water as much as you can. We are not animals."

Mark uttered in English, "All evidence to the contrary notwithstanding."

"Get it done, Comrade."

The Corporal saluted, released Mark, and steered him into the underground chamber with its wounded, injured, and terrified prisoners.

As he descended, he heard the cries of the most recent captives pleading with their guards. The members of the Synagogue community were begging the guards to allow them to bury their dead. One old rabbi was scratching at the broken concrete and dirt with a stone. A weeping woman assisted him. They would not be deterred from digging a grave in the crypt.

"Three days. Sir. Internment. Cannot be delayed. We must be allowed to bury them. It is our way."

Amid the crowd of detainees, Mark secretly eased back into the crypt and found the gravestone of one of the nineteenth-century archimandrites. He wiggled the loose stone and removed the cell phone.

Chapter Thirty-Four: The Sentry
Ranger Bar, Newtown, Ketchikan, Alaska

Nick Sechi's Journal

"What about this case do you find unusual, my love."

"Where do I start, Boss? O.K., so we are taken to the scene of a double murder – by the United States Coast Guard, no less. Seriously? You pretty much wrap it up for them, except for the fact that the murderer, Kat Woman, and her accomplice, Priest Guy, have escaped."

"Yes. Please continue."

"Borough police and the Lady Coast Guard Captain, just send us on our way? WTF is up with that, Kayne? No post-crime scene consultation? It was like we said the wrong thing at the wrong time. No one wants to bring the killers to justice? Hello?"

"I believe we said the *right* thing, Nick, and added to a tense situation that predates the murder. In addition, now they know what we know, and we know they know it. Another beer?"

"Sure. Thank you."

He raised a hand, and a server made his way to us. The kid reminded me of Kris. Or didn't, really. Totally different coloring and a whisper of First Nationers features. Just been thinking of our super self-assured nephew lately. (My Spidey Sense was tingling – Kristof in trouble again?)

Perhaps, it was the bit of a cocky jock swagger on Server Boy. He was rocking a ballsy approach to having the moon on a string. Are all twenty-year-olds this energetic? His name tag said "Cleatus."

"Two more?"

Kayne nodded and put some folded money on the boy's tray. Outside, the rain poured down like Noah's Deluge in the Book of Genesis. The western windows of Ranger Bar provided a spectacular view across a harbor-side covered patio and into the misty fiords carved into the mountainous islands that bordered the Inland Passage waters. Everything was blurred by the curtain of a gray downpour.

"The whole thing is like a spy novel, Boss. I mean, nothing is what it seems. Irony seems to be everywhere. Where is she heading? How do we find her? Fucking clueless."

"Your puns are showing, my love."

"You are rockin' your Cheshire Cat face, Bossman. What is it that you know that you are not telling?"

I pointed at my husband as he smiled wickedly and tossed back his pesky bang – like Christine's swishing tail, the movement was a signature "tell," indicating Kayne was excited about some shit.

He looked out at the harbor.

"Searching for the parade of animals, Dr. Sorenson? Two-by-two?"

Cleatus Lee put down our drinks. His face said, "Go ahead, ask me."

"My love, our server, young Cleatus, is a fan."

"Oh shit, yes. You guys are way hot. Read every one of your blog entries. You get into some sexy doings – fuckin' bad-assed bad boys."

He pulled up a stool like servers do when they ingratiate way too much.

"Saw you guys pulled off the Rusalka. Captain 'Large Marge' is one to be avoided, dudes. Big Christian and doesn't like us. Which reminds me, tell me that your nephew, the jock prince, is here somewhere. Make my fuckin' day."

The kid was super excited. I took a swig, shook my head, and said. "Home."

"Bummed, Nick. Way bummed. So, what are you two working on? Like you're gonna tell a barback, right?"

Kayne opened his phone.

"Ever see any of these individuals, lad?"

Cleatus scrolled.

The Ivory Knife

"These two, yes, and this other woman ... I think so, but she wasn't alone."

The young man explained.

"See that deck? Given that we are about fifteen minutes of daylight each day and it's been raining since 1950 ... seems like anyway."

He straightened up, hands behind his back, and recited like a schoolboy.

"Rainfall in the Borough averages 153 inches or 3,893 mm per year, falling more heavily in autumn and winter."

Kayne tapped the cell phone's screen.

Cleatus continued, "It's just that not many people are coming to the bar, so I sit out there and ... and ... well, you know."

He winked at Kayne.

"... observe. Got a pair of night visions. How cool is that?"

I corrected him. "Cruise, you mean."

"Nick. This is Alaska, Bronx Boy. Hot men in a cold climate. Yes, yes, yes. Make mine a double. This boy is looking to net one smoking hot Royal Mountie Daddy. You know, the type with a ... they got the big where it counts."

"Cleatus," Kayne said. He tapped the phone again.

"Sorry. Three days ago. Off the Frontier Queen from Vancouver and points to the south. Real 'not touristy' -- you know what I mean? Not locals, but they've been here before. Kinda smug/judgey. Know what I mean?"

Our new friend looked over to the main bar to check on his status. His bartender was making drinks and chatting up the few customers that were in the place.

"Princess Pain in the Ass did some shopping this morning at the Salmon Landing Market and the Mining Company. What can I tell ya? Ketchikan is a small town. Also stopped in at the Sockeye Pawn Shoppe. You can see it there on Water Street. The totem pole with the bear on top."

He pointed through the window wall into the rain. He then came back to the phone.

"That one ... nah, I got nothing. Wait ... hold on."

He dashed to the bar and spoke to the bartender. The man looked at Kayne's phone.

"Kayne, Cleatus the Sex Bomb is missing the man candy right under his nose. Did you check out Dudley Do-Right behind the bar? Muscles for days on that Bull. My, my my, my my."

"No, my love. As I have said many times. You are all the man I require and the only man for whom my longing gaze lingers."

I choked on a beer swallow and touched his nose with my index finger.

"Bullshit. We need to deconstruct the Aleksei thing. There is a story there, and I want it for the record."

"Perhaps the Mounted Policeman making boilermakers is not a member of our tribe. Not a poofter. Eh?"

"The fuck you say, Doctor. When we walked away, he so checked out your ass. Thought I was gonna have ta bitch slap the gurl."

Our frisky buddy returned.

"Léo said she was a bit spooky. Determined but rigid-like. Military like 'Large Marge.' Her companion was a priest. Younger. Léo can make a priest at five hundred paces. Jesuit High School in Calgary ... there is a lot there, dudes.

He handed Kayne back his phone.

"So yeah, so. Léo saw them at the ferry terminal around noon. The boat to Juneau."

"Dude, this is great. Thanks."

"Cleatus!"

The bartender sounded a warning that our guy was neglecting someone, I don't know exactly who, in the practically empty bar.

"Yep! Got it covered."

The Ivory Knife

He gave each of us a hug up. As he pulled away, he grinned and muttered. "Ohhh, yes. Un-huh."

A little too much grab-hold for a first hug. Just saying.

"You guys should stick around. Karaoke Night. Then we could ..."

"Sorry, mate. We need to head on over to the Sockeye."

Kayne pointed to me.

"I need to pimp him."

I tossed my watch cap at my goofy husband.

Turning to the nearly swooning Cleatus, I corrected.

"He means 'pawn' me."

Kayne chuckled.

"Yes, yes, 'pawn.' Pimp is when one ... quite. I do remember what a pimp is."

I retrieved and swatted him again with my watch cap.

As we passed the bar, Kayne left some bills for Léo.

"Au revoir et merci, Léo."

In a tank top, tight jeans, and sporting a scruffy square jaw and matching raven hair, the beauty nodded and said, *"J'espère te voir plus tard, homme sexy."*

Thomas Paul Severino

Chapter Thirty-Five: *Gyáa'aang*
Sockeye Pawn Shoppe, Newtown, Ketchikan, Alaska

Nick Sechi's Journal

"Just like this one, only different."

"Would you be more precise, please? What exactly do you mean, Sir?"

The pawnbroker, Orville McGinty, looked for a moment at Kayne. My man looked like a local – trapper, adventure, lumberjack, just all rough and rugged. With his Siberian husky eyes, slightly almond-shaped, big build, and long black hair (Loving the scruff, Boss. A really sexy visual.), he was the image of a crude frontiersman. That is until he opened his mouth. Kayne spoke like a university professor with a slight Australian accent.

McGinty handed Kayne the curious object.

"Her's was older than this one. More primitive -- like it belonged in a museum or something. Who's gonna buy something like that, I ask you? The tourists want trinkets, not old hunting tools. Souvenirs and crap. I keep telling 'em this is a pawn shop. Try the damn Emporium across the street."

He gestured to a case along the wall.

"Got another one with a metal blade. Not antique, however."

The proprietor turned the strange knife in Kayne's hands. My detective said, "Authenticity is a matter of history and geography. Metalworking came much later to the Inuit. Tools made with stone and bone indicate communities of the far north in the circumpolar regions. Clans in the southern reaches of Canada and Greenland would have learned to mine, smelt, and fashion metal tools."

The pawnbroker said, "So, on the *ulu* she wanted to pawn, this part wasn't caribou antler. It was walrus ivory. Markings all over it. Pretty good scrimshaw, I will say. A whale, a walrus, I think ... and oh yeah, a wolf."

"Ivory, did you say, Mr. McGinty? Definitely the northern clans. Their carvings invoke the spirits of the animals. The woman was trying to sell a sacred object, one that was important to a community of First Nations People. An *ulu* was used to kill food animals and prepare skins for clothing, shelter, kayaks, and sleds. The Inuit in the far north have also used knives like this for thousands of years to cut the ice blocks to make their igloos."

"Why do you feel like I need a lesson on this shit? You want to buy it or what?"

"Just a small demonstration, Mr. McGinty."

Kayne hefted the instrument and stepped up behind me.

"If you please, my love."

I slipped out of my parka, and he made as if to cut me ear to ear from behind. He enacted the murder three times, each very slowly, making a mental note of about a thousand details – the position of the blade, the stance of the two combatants, the contours of my neck, how I raised my arms when attacked – that sort of thing. Then, using the pawnbroker's mounted, lighted magnifier, Kayne examined the edge of the stone blade.

"How much?"

"Two-fifty."

"Visa?"

"Of course."

The deal was done. I slipped the parcel into my backpack and made to leave – back into the rain. The pawnbroker looked at the card before handing it to Kayne.

One more thing, Mister ... ahh ... Sorenson. The *ulu* that the lady tried to sell ... yeah, its handle was hollow. The end twisted off like one of those sword canes. There was something inside, that ivory handle, but I don't think she was aware of it."

"Mr. McGinty, did you happen you see what it was?"

"No."

"Thank you. You have been most helpful."

***

The Ivory Knife

We came across Aleksei, Tim, and Eva under the shop's awning. The cook was signing rapidly and making distressed facial expressions. Some passers-by were looking on.

"Hey, sexy boys," Aleksei called out. "We have been shopping to replenish the Rusalka's stores."

Kayne began speaking while watching Eva Nakoyak.

"Ms. Nakoyak tells us that this is number four – " It is a desecration of something sacred. They have no right to defame my people. We are First Nationers. The Gyáa'aang is sacred to my people."

The somewhat outraged woman pointed to the totem pole a few yards from the pawnshop.

Tim explained, "Eva is of the Haisla people. They are said to have originated the totem pole as a monument to represent and commemorate ancestry, the past, people, or events. Some of the oldest poles in the North are up along Ketchikan Creek and Totem Drive. They tell stories of the ancient people."

The Cook/First Mate nodded and pointed to the hills southeast of town. Kayne read more of Eva's signs.

"Ketchikan has more totem poles than elsewhere in the Pacific Northwest."

More Tim: "Totem poles are carved from red cedar, a wood relatively abundant in the Pacific Northwest, and would be erected to be visible within a community. Most totem poles display beings, or crest animals, marking a family's lineage and validating the powerful rights and privileges held by the family. Totem poles tell stories and the history of the clan."

Kayne examined the totem after pulling up the hood of his parka. Eva nodded throughout his lesson. He pointed to the top and worked his way down. He signed as she spoke.

"This clan is represented by the thunderbird. Its wings are outstretched, and its beak is curved. This top figure is different from the straight-beaked raven – the third one down. See there? Between them, the eagle perches on a wolf's head, the clan's second fetish animal."

Thomas Paul Severino

Eva signed the following figures, a grizzly bear, a killer whale with frog inserts, and a raven with salmon carved into her feathers. She explained that the images at the bottom were the most important, bearing the weight of all the other figures.

I said, "I guess the line 'low man on the totem pole' is misleading."

The woman frowned and made the sign for "white people."

Kayne said, "Mainstream parlance inserted by the European settlers, my love. The grizzly bear with her cub on her lap at this pole's bottom is at eye level with the viewer. That heightens her significance."

Eva led us to another totem just across the street. Eva related its story in ASL with beautiful gestures that reminded me of a dance.

"This pole tells the story of murder over a debt, an unpleasant occurrence about which the Native Americans in the community prefer to remain silent. It is, however, a widely known tale. The large figures tell of the heroic exploits of the Cedar Man, who married the Bear Woman. He was killed by the Frog King. See how the artist has included killer whales, salmon, and birds in the open spaces of the feathers and fins of the creatures."

A wild menagerie of the totemic wildlife of the people on the monument told the story. Two snakes wound their way between the head of the bear and the human above her. A salmon and three of her offspring slid down the open spaces on the back of a beaver, just above the owl who was nestled in the toothy mammal's paddle-like tail.

The piece was painted in reds, greens, yellows, and browns. All of the creatures had black eyes edged and highlighted in white. They looked mysterious and wise as if joined in a spiritual bond to the earth, sky, and sea.

Our Haisla friend bent to rub at the stylized human figure at the bottom with her wet gloves. Peeking over the head and shoulders of the mysterious figure at the base of the totem pole were the heads of five other humans. One was painted a contrasting bright red, different from the more maroon colors in the towering art piece.

The angry woman signed her frustration again.

The Ivory Knife

Eva signed, "These figures are additions. They are not original. In my explorations around Ketchikan, this defacement has been repeated many times. It is an insult."

Kayne turned to me and said, "Someone here in the Borough is sending a message. Secrets — most curious. Most curious indeed."

Thomas Paul Severino

Chapter Thirty-Six: Secrets
Douglas Island, Alaska

"They reached Ketchikan but have disappeared—the defector and her priest."

General Secretary Marie Mikhailovna sat in semi-darkness. Outside the cabin, the winter night was pock-marked with a few village lights and the illumination of the Juneau-Douglas Bridge. Colonel Malenkov stood just beyond her desk.

She asked, "Our operatives?"

"No contact in the last eighteen hours. Reported dead."

"You know this to be true, Demitri Ivanovich?"

"Yes, Comrade. Our agent in that city used a consulting detective to confirm her suspicions. The Lieutenant Colonel and her companion, the priest, Stefan Lebedev, assassinated them."

"Tell me how they were killed."

"Sidorovna sliced their throats from behind with a knife. Comrade Silverman reports that the weapon was ...."

"A native hunting tool. I am sure it was. Carved ivory handle and stone blade ... Katya had it in a glass case on her desk. I have seen it many times. Not found in the remains of the fire, of course."

"That is correct, my General."

"Who, Colonel? Who were the detectives?"

"Kayne Sorenson, Comrade. And his partner, Nicola Sechi."

The General Secretary made no indication that those names meant anything but a slight spasm ticked in the muscles of her left eye. Malenkov knew this information was troublesome.

"Send in the Belarusian."

Thomas Paul Severino

The agent stood before the General Secretary. The light on his one good eye seemed fiery red. His attitude was somewhat defiant as he adjusted his face covering.

"Seattle?"

The man in the half-mask shook his head.

"Let me understand you, Vasily Pavlovich. Your brilliant idea was to hold Dr. Sorenson for ransom while his number one, this former police officer — Sechi, I believe, located Lieutenant Colonel Katsitsanóron Isapoinhkyaki and the Synaxis. To put it another way, you convinced me to let this hotshot do your work. Now you tell me you have failed. Arlovski, you leave me no alternative ... none."

"No. You are mistaken. Despite the escape of Dr. Sorenson, they are hunting for your precious Colonel. The American traitor, Silverman, brought them to the murder scene herself. Sidorovna eluded her and them. Find the detectives, and you will find the spy. They make quite a wake wherever they go, Comrade. That should be easy for you and your, ah ... sycophants."

"I am up to my ass in filthy *khuyesosy* and spies, but none who can do a job correctly. I hope what you say is true, Comrade."

She waved Arlovski away with his escort. Turning to Colonel Malenkov, Marie Mikhailovna said softly, "I understand the glacier crevasses to the northeast on the big mountain are very treacherous. Should an accident befall a hiker, the body would never be found. Please see to it. "

She lit a cigarette and said to no one in particular, "It would appear that our prey has increased to four."

***

By the full moon's light, three figures crossed the rugged terrain of the glacier. One used a flashlight to maneuver the ice and rocks. A large opening filled the illuminated spot with a deep darkness like a scar soaked with black blood. There appeared to be no bottom to the ice gorge.

Behind them, the land groaned like an awakening night spirit ready to destroy all in its path. The air was suddenly filled with the sound of

The Ivory Knife

exploding water as pieces of the glacier fell into the shadowy sea. One of the men knocked the man in the middle to the ice with a blow to the head.

As the thugs stopped to pick up the unconscious man, four suppressed shots sounded like the strikes of a deadly bullwhip. Somewhere close by, a shelf of ice and snow collapsed, rumbled, and the scattered snow hissed across the ice. The two would-be killers spiraled to the ground, and the light beam and its source disappeared into the chasm.

Lit only by the moon, a solitary figure approached the three bodies. He tossed the murdered men into the glacier's dark belly. As he moved the unconscious man, a stray moonbeam glinted across the metal of his left arm, outstretched in the snow.

The gunman lifted the other across his shoulders and headed down the mountain's heights. The metallic arm dangled down the back and legs of the rescuer.

Thomas Paul Severino

Chapter Thirty-Seven: An Unexpected Passenger
Gastineau Channel, Alaska

Nick Sechi's Journal

"The fisherman appears to be in trouble. I am bringing him aboard."

The moonlight on the black waters of the channel revealed a single local dude in a canoe. A spear, a lantern, and some nets were the only equipment in the boat. In the endless night, whale sounds could be heard over the waters near Douglas Island. Somewhere a crash ... ("One of the glaciers is calving, my love. Unfortunately, we cannot see it.") The lights of Juneau glittered in the darkness to our starboard.

Captain McDowd assisted the new passenger into the yacht's warm lounge after ensuring that the Ship's Steward, Cameron Jakobs, secured the man's canoe to the Rusalka.

Kayne approached the native man who was seated on a couch and tossed a remark over his shoulder, never removing his eyes from the hunter.

"Thank you, Captain. I assure you our friend here is quite well. May we have the room?"

McDowd and the boy left the cabin.

"Lieutenant Colonel Sidorovna, you have indeed come very far. I conclude you wish to tell us something."

The woman lowered the hood of her parka, removed her gloves, and fished in her jacket pocket for her cigarettes. Kayne took her lighter and did the honors before returning it to her. I passed an ashtray.

Her hair was black and straight, and her features were definitely the strong facial characteristics of the Arctic people. Her eyes were the color of midnight. She passed a hand through her straight black hair, loosening its tightness, and smiled, but it was more ironic than a friendly grin.

Breathing smoke, she said, "This is where you tell me how you deduced my identity with tiny details pulled together by your superhuman brain. My movements are feminine with a *soupçon* of the military, etc., etc., etc. The incidental reveals the hidden. I know you. Dr. Sorenson. You and your party games. I anticipate utter boredom. But, please, do continue."

She glanced in my direction, and then, pointing with her cigarette back to Kayne, the woman continued.

"Indeed, I know you."

"Yes, you know me. I live with a price on my head. Indeed, I am flattered by the time spent by those who work for the Spider, the Dragon, and the many others who would bring about the destruction of my family and me. Those who work for the death of justice and freedom .... just review my husband's journals of our cases ... our sworn enemies are there, and they feed on vendetta. But they underestimate my husband, my friends, and my allies, I assure you, Lieutenant Colonel. But, in one respect, we share a renegade status. And that, Comrade, is where our similarities end."

Kayne turned his back and studied the woman's reflection in the lounge's windows against the Alaskan darkness outside. Despite all evidence to the contrary, she was indeed a woman of evil intent.

After a moment, Kayne turned around and shrugged. He said, "Identifying you tonight was child's play, ma'am, to be honest. Your picture, Comrade. On Google. You are most recognizable. Russian intelligence, for all its covert operations, should have at least hacked this file."

This brought a somewhat hearty laugh as I flashed my phone. Siderovna flashed me a deadly glance like a scanner – laser light moving from the top of my head to my feet. When she spoke, it was to Kayne.

"Elementary then, Dr. Sorenson."

"That and the fact that not even the most experienced First Nationers fish for salmon at night in the late winter. If you fell overboard, you would freeze in a matter of minutes. No, you are hunting *us*, Comrade."

The Russian nodded and added, "And I am perhaps the most wanted of us all. But, perhaps you will understand."

The Ivory Knife

She blew smoke and got right to the point.

"You know of the alliance of the Arctic States, *Da*? The Arctic Council ... of course you do."

Kayne studied our visitor as I rattled off, "Russia, Canada, Denmark, Sweden, Norway, Finland, the United States, and Iceland."

"You are only partially correct, Mr. Sechi."

The Russian intelligence officer added, "Aleut, Alutiiq, Yup'ik, Iñupiaq, Athabaskan, Tlingit, and Haida. Why are these nations always left out when powerful states discuss one of the most strategic areas of the globe? Is the conversation never to include the original custodians of their ancestral homeland? Why? The U.S. state you see out there, Alaska, is approximately eighteen percent Indigenous."

Kayne was not impressed.

"Stop, Lieutenant Colonel, you are no advocate for the First Nationers. You have pledged your allegiance to a country that is at the top of the list of their exploiters. Enough with the hypocrisy. Russia loves oil."

Sidorovna interrupted, "Ha! And the West does not?"

Kayne continued, "The circumpolar world is abundant with this black gold. NATO and the democracies on the Council hope to keep Russia from dominating the Arctic, exploiting its resources, and exterminating its people. Russia does not play well with others. Totalitarian regimes never do.""

I inserted, "Point of fact – what your country is doing in Ukraine."

The woman shrugged.

"So many political animals. You ... him ... me ... most impressive and deadly tragic."

She went on.

"Russia's war on Ukraine isn't the first conflict an Arctic-rim state has engaged in, nor will it be the last."

"If the Council partners marginalize a member who claims more than half of the Arctic lands," Kayne said, "the alliance's work essentially suspends all capability to deal with *any* issue inside the Arctic."

"Such as?"

I went for it. Spooky Sister was working my last nerve.

"You want the list, Tatiana? Human health, including telemedicine and disease surveillance, climate change effects in the Arctic, sustainable tourism development, Arctic safety, security, and stewardship, including search and rescue cooperation, oil pollution preparedness and response, marine protection, maritime shipping, and ocean acidification monitoring. Am I getting through to you?"

"Nick."

"No, Boss, I'm on a roll with Miss Thang here."

I continued.

"What do you and your country folk have against diplomacy, Ludmilla? Huh? You speak of the Indigenous. The Council has worked to improve economic and living conditions in the Arctic, including pursuing innovative technologies, advancing mental wellness research, and addressing telecommunications infrastructure."

Sidorovna looked at me with eyes that would melt a glacier. She held up the non-cigarette hand.

"Your journals speak of how flushed you get when irritated. I am seeing this firsthand, and it undermines your desired superiority. Let us start with this little bit of diplomacy. You will refer to me as 'Lieutenant Colonel' and nothing else."

She blew smoke in my face.

"Consider, Mr. Sechi, the choice of the liberal-western Arctic states to 'freeze' all Arctic engagement ignores exactly what the region is in for. Please understand that Russia's invasion of Ukraine should *not* be followed by impotent political dialogue. I have been and remain a critic of the war and its atrocities, much to the frustration of my superiors. My position is that the neutrality of the Arctic must remain a region of the

The Ivory Knife

globe without tension. How's that for an endorsement of diplomacy, Mr. Sechi?"

I asked, "Global warming has opened the Arctic Seas and created shipping lanes, Lieutenant Colonel, the Northern Sea Route. We have an expression in the West, 'Follow the money.' Do you understand?"

"Moscow will not be outplayed by NATO's expansion," Kayne said. "With their interest in the alliance, Finland, Sweden, and Ukraine threaten the world dominance of the Russian Bear. Her response will be to bring additional partners into the theater. China, India, Southeast Asia, and the United Arab Emirates -- the would-be stakeholder nations are scrambling for a seat at the Arctic table. Greed for economic riches will crowd the negotiations for long-term resource control. The nations that refuse to condemn Russia's aggressive behavior do so with questionable motives."

"Russia will never stop in Eastern Europe. You may rest assured," said Katya Sidorovna. "She desires to win the war at all costs – and the price continues to be great. She holds the world by the throat."

Kayne took a step closer and met the Russian agent eye-to-eye. He said, "And you have the knife."

"Yes, Doctor. I have the knife."

The Lieutenant Colonel could not hold his gaze. She walked away and stared into the night.

"Or I did have it."

"Where is he?"

"The priest? His reaction to my little acts of murder was hysterical. Talk about hypocrisy ... has not the holy church – and what other religion, for that matter, destroyed countless lives in the blood-soaked human-divine partnership?"

She shrugged.

"Dr. Sorenson, I thought we might somehow have similar views over these matters. Leaving my country and getting in bed with her enemies brings me no joy, especially when the alternative to Russian sinfulness is just as corrupt. Perhaps my true homeland of ice and snow calls to my errant spirit. Burn it...burn it all down. Eviscerate the evil and spill the blood. Allow the phoenix to rise."

"Lieutenant Colonel, you must come in. You are wedged between nuclear superpowers – a dangerous place for the sensible. Bloodsport is that which has gotten us to this point. The intel you possess is invaluable for those who desire peace. The Bear must be brought to heel. Her current course will bring only death."

"Truthfully ...."

She laughed at the word and started again.

"You have failed to convince me. East ... West ... who speaks for the disenfranchised? Who? Was it not Hamlet who said, 'The rest is silence'?"

The Russian ended her chain smoking, stubbing out in the ashtray. Looking up, she anticipated Kayne's thoughts.

"I do not know where he is but believe me when I say this, the Ivory Knife is the ultimate weapon, Dr. Sorenson. The ancient tool becomes the final destroyer. I intended to turn it over to the West and castrate Russia's war efforts in Ukraine. That remains to be seen. Regardless, my Stepan must be found."

Katya Sidorovna replaced her parka and gloves and made for the door. I blocked her exit, ready to take her down.

She stepped back, bent to her cigarette butts, and shot me a look of sardonic humor.

"Mr. Sechi, as much as I respect you and your husband, please be advised that having killed two people in the last 24 hours. You are no threat to me. I am a soldier trained in Systema, the martial arts of the Soviet Red Army. Kindly remove your hand and step aside."

She turned to Kayne.

"You will please give my best to your brother – another of my well-respected adversaries. Please tell him I said he was right all along, it seems. Good night, gentlemen."

The Ivory Knife

Katya Sidorovna disappeared over the side and into the night.

Thomas Paul Severino

Chapter Thirty-Eight: The Base of the Flounder's River
Juneau, Alaska

Nick Sechi's Journal

"This case has some interesting features, my love. We are in one of the world's largest wildernesses, in highly challenging climatic conditions, searching for two people and an ivory knife."

We were kicking back in our cabin aboard the Rusalka – me in briefs and Kayne in silk boxers. I made sure the heat was comfortable in our quarters. Through the windows of our quarters, we could see our approach northward in the Gastineau Channel between Douglas Island and the capital, Juneau.

"The number of players in this one, Boss, reads like a list of characters in a Dickens novel. In the pursuit, we have the Russians, the two major freaks from the Underground – they want their intelligence files back, not to mention the heads of the two defectors."

"We have yet to know who Bounine and Sarov report to. I am convinced it is very high up the chain of Russian Intelligence. And, it is clear, they are close by, my love."

"The Phantom and his butt boy ... love to throw down with those punks again. Kremlin mafia, to be sure. And whoever pulls their strings can kiss my ass."

Kayne sorta chuckled. I continued my list.

"Then there is our home-spun Native American network, Mrs. McCave and Company. Those goofy kids just kept coming out of the woodwork, Benjamin, Darren, the doc who stuck my fine gay ass."

"Connections to the CIA, of that there is no doubt, Nick. Our own sleeper cells. Regina Netsilik is the keeper. Of that, there is no doubt."

"Yeah, she activates the network. Gotta be."

"Do not forget the Moldovians, my love. Shatralev and Shatralev. Eric's sources make them as big operators in Transnistria."

"Missed that one on my Google Maps, Big Man. Please bring me up to speed."

"Transnistria – a breakaway region of eastern Moldova. Russian troops are all over it. The EU has described the region as rife with organized crime. Our entrepreneurial friends are denizens of a black hole known for illegal trade in arms, the trafficking in human beings, and money laundering for the global criminal underworld."

"Bigtime dirty business, Boss. They will not be missed by us, the forces of light."

"Nick, the knife. I fear it is the key to a perilous strategy or that it is a doomsday weapon. So far, two murders and an attack on our woman in Ft. Lauderdale."

"Seriously, Boss? The falling chandelier?"

"An absolute certainty, my love. That piece of deadly theater was Bounine and Sarov. Very melodramatic, and their purpose was to secure our entrance into the game of finding Katya Sidorovna. You were to be the pawn, and I was to be the hostage."

"Oh well ... guess not, fuckwads. Oh, wait. We *are* after Miss Ice Queen and her Fallen Priest. That is what the Russians wanted in the long game. Smart of us to let her find us, huh, Boss?"

"In addition to your very sexy abs, your irony is showing, my lad."

I leaned in for Smooch City.

Kayne pulled back in a bit and said, "You continue to be a very well-enjoyed distraction, but I do you an injustice. You are not just any himbo, I believe is the expression. I will add that you are my himbo and a very intelligent beauty at that."

"Blah, blah, blah ... you are so cognitive/sexy and a hunky doofus, Kayne. Just truthin'. But, Rebecca. Makes me think of Mark. Shall we call Eric to see how the plan is going?"

The Ivory Knife

"I fear we will bring the ever-present listeners, aka hackers, into the mix, Nick. All evidence to the contrary notwithstanding, there is much to be said for trusting my brother at this time."

"Yeah, and Kris has his school, athletics, and theater auditions, so he is well out of the turmoil, thankfully."

"I wonder, my love. I do wonder. That lad is ...."

He was interrupted by a knock on the cabin door.

Ship's Steward Cameron Jakobs entered with a tray of nightcaps.

"To welcome you to The Base of the Flounder's River."

He pointed to the dock and its surroundings growing more prominent in our cabin window as the Rusalka made port.

"Juneau."

"Bollocks, lad, you are up to something."

I joked, "Looking to check us out in our skivies?"

The kid flashed his bad-boy eyes as he handed out the drinks. He raised a glass and spoke.

"I can help you find her."

Thomas Paul Severino

Chapter Thirty-Nine: St. Nicholas
Juneau, Alaska

Nick Sechi's Journal

"I cheated."

Kayne and Cameron huddled with me over my laptop. I was doing my best shit-eating grin.

"You tagged her, Nick."

"Yep. Just as our Russian Doll was leaving – all about how bad-assed she was -- I got close. Her parka has many pockets. One of them now has this in it."

I held up a tracker disc slightly smaller than I dime. I pointed to a red blip on the map.

"That's her there. She took the ferry to Skagway."

"From the Lieutenant Colonel's remarks last night, she intends to blend into the Inuit community above the Arctic Circle. She has sent her traveling companion, the priest, ahead. She is in a hurry but is reluctant to use air travel as she most likely sees it as a risk to her anonymity. Skagway is a most puzzling choice. Except for the highway into British Columbia, it is a dead end. This is wilderness in its roughest form."

"The Inuits are Canadian also. Perhaps that is where ... yeah, Boss. This is a big-assed country."

Cameron shook his head.

"Get into your gear, guys. I told you I could help. I want to show you something."

***

We disembarked at the Juneau Harbor and, with Eva Nakoyak, made our way on foot through the city to the warren of streets in the shadow of the State Capitol Building. Juneau is a mixture of modern buildings and the historic wooden structures of its gold rush mining town past. Many totems and murals evoked the original culture of the Auke and Taku tribes who inhabited the surrounding area for thousands of years, harvesting herring and other sea life.

As we explored, our journey took us closer to the backdrop of this unique American capital. Away to the northeast and looming against the horizon, the gigantic Mount Juneau seemed to wrap around the edges of the city's downtown. The light was just enough to make out the features of this unique wilderness. The rain had stopped, and the branches of the many lodgepole pines glistened with moisture. As they proceeded up the mountain's lower slopes, their yellowish-green needles turned dark green on the higher slopes while their orange bark faded to gray.

Cameron and Kayne would sign as we spoke. Eva pointed up. And Kayne translated.

"See that scar on the mountain? The 1962 avalanche ... major damage. So much so that they ended up moving the entire neighborhood. That big white mass there is the Juneau Icefield. Over one hundred and forty glaciers. The Mendenhall glacier is one of them."

Cameron continued as we walked, "Juneau is the 'Island City.' She has no roads to anywhere else in North America. They just end in the wilderness. Everything in or out goes by plane or boat. The Juneau Borough Municipality is bigger than Rhode Island, bigger than Delaware, and the only U.S. capital on an international border."

As the Native American public art seemed to dominate more and more of the old city sites, Kayne took up the lesson by saying, "Tlingit, Haida, (he pointed to Eva), and Tsimshian of Southeast Alaska. Which are you, lad?"

"I am Athabascan. My native name is Yakecen – Sky Song. We are *Dena* or 'the people.' Everyone else is 'not the people.' My tribe comes from the interior of Alaska."

We came upon our destination, the Russian Orthodox Church of Saint Nicholas. The blue and white wooden building was a high-quality example of the "Russian Colonial" style of architecture. A golden onion dome capped by an Orthodox cross with three horizontal crossbeams, the lowest one slanting downwards, rose against the nearby mountains

The Ivory Knife

"The Russians were the first Europeans to come to this area," Cameron said. "They were fur traders with the Alaskan Natives, not settlers. As more whites came here, the Tinglit appealed to the Russian Orthodox Church for support against the thievery of their land. Hundreds were baptized, and the Russian priests had the scriptures translated into the Tinglit language. Many believe the ancient sacred burial grounds are beneath this church's precincts. The markers contain many Natives as well as Europeans."

We entered the church grounds through a gate in a white picket fence. A grove of blue-green mountain hemlocks shaded a crumbling cemetery. Eva pointed out and communicated that the conifers were more than eight hundred years old. As the first mate signed, a large back bird emerged from the branches and swooped directly overhead. Raising a cawing ruckus, she perched on a gravestone and eyed us suspiciously, turning her head from side to side and cackling.

Cameron brought our attention to some recent carvings on the wooden grave markers. The graffiti-like markings were animals and symbols, and they were recent.

Kayne said, "The five totemic figures from the totem poles in Ketchikan – very clear. The tale continues and is monitored by the elders here. Observe, my friends, the five watchers."

Eva nodded excitedly, signing, "See? I told you."

Cameron traced his hand along the markings carved in a series of crosses.

"The People are conversing in the old language. See the Raven-Woman. She flies across the land ... there ... do you see? The great war spear thrown by the powerful chief of the *Dena* – the Athabascan people .... and that icon is the mighty dome built from its flight."

Cameron Yakecen Jakobs looked first at Eva Nakoyak and then at Kayne and me with eyes filled with age-old wisdom. He continued to sign as he spoke. Eva finger-spelled a six-letter word.

"Your Lieutenant Colonel is on her way to Denali."

Thomas Paul Severino

Chapter Forty: The White Thunder
Disenchantment Bay, Alaska

Nick Sechi's Journal

"Do you still have her, my love?"

I checked my tablet.

"Actually, Boss. 'The Spy Who Hates Me' is hauling ass just over those mountains, moving north toward Whitehorse in the Canadian Yukon. Just like you said. I'll wager a hitch on an ice trucker's rig will bring her to the interior somewhere near Anchorage."

We were on the fo'c'stle – the Rusulka's foredeck, kicking back with some heavy blankets and golden whiskey concoctions in cut crystal glasses. Cameron had played bartender – brandy, slightly warmed, and without accompaniment. The yacht cruised into Disenchantment Bay at the northern end of the Inside Passage.

Kayne swirled and took a taste. He said, "Katya Sidorovna has 'gone bush' as we say in 'Stralia. The madwoman is in a race with destiny. We must head her off in the interior and gain possession of the Ivory Knife. I grow more apprehensive as this case proceeds."

He pulled closer to me for warmth, but our attention focused on Wrangell—St. Elias National Park and Preserve as we entered the inlet to Disenchantment Bay. More than thirteen million acres, the protected areas stretched before us are the largest single wilderness area in the United States – mountains, rainforests, and fjords.

"Man, look at that, Boss. Our Kris would see this, and his theatrical side would go into high gear."

"It is indeed wondrous, my love, but I'm not getting the reference."

I kissed his brandy-soaked mouth and teased, "Your problem, Dr. Sorenson is you see, but you do not observe."

"Ahhh, ever the Holmesian. Please elaborate."

"Check it out, Kayne."

I extended my arm across the entire panorama and waxed eloquently.

"It looks like a stage set for a spectacular theater of ice and snow. See there, across the far distance and on both the starboard and port side, snow-covered mountains seem to hold up lowering curtains of clouds above the dark stage of the bay's crystal clear waters. And there, reigning above and behind it all like a giant puppet master, is the divine-like presence of Mount Saint Elias, spreading her mountainous skirts on the misty western horizon."

"Your visual sense is masterful, Nick, as is your descriptive prose. And yes, our nephew is gifted with the same imaginative sight. He gets it from you. It is quite breathtaking."

Our buddy Cameron joined us on deck as the Rusalka made her way further into the bay. He pointed to a rock cliff on the starboard as he refilled our drinks.

"The welcoming committee."

Chubby masses of tawny and reddish-yellow beasties raised their sleepy heads to inspect the cruising visitors from their rookery among the tide-soaked rocks. One large bull scratched his snout with his hind flipper claws. Several black pups connected snout first to their moms. Noses sniffed, and ears wiggled. Three young adults slipped into the sea at the sight of the Rusalka and its nosey inhabitants. Two dove out of sight. One stuck her head up to watch the funny-looking humans a bit more.

As Kayne stood up, the adults and the adolescents proceeded to bark excitedly. "Arf, arf, arf," ... their chorus echoed off the rocks, ice, and water like theater music.

"Arf, arf arf, ya selves, ya beautiful mugs. Crikey, lads. Those are Stellar's Sea Lions, *Eumetopias jubatus*. I'm bloody dashed! They are a threatened species and the largest eared seals. Brilliant!"

Cameron again pointed and said, "See there, my friends. Not one, but two. Just there is the junction of *two* glaciers, the Valerie to the left and

The Ivory Knife

the very fuckin' massive Hubbard. That big mother is the largest tidewater glacier in North America."

He raised a glass to the towering glacier massifs that rose like a barrier wall sealing off the inland end of Disenchantment Bay. The body of the Hubbard Glacier wound its way back up into the Saint Elias Mountains, Like the tail and body of a smoldering ice dragon wedged between insurmountable inclines.

"Hubbard is seventy-six miles long, seven miles wide," Cameron explained. "And as tall as a 30-story building. Her façade is 360 feet from bottom to top, with another 250 below the frigid surface. It always takes my breath away. What do you think?"

Kayne, somewhat glassy-eyed, said, "Bloody gobsmacked, mate. Astounding."

I said nothing – words failed. As a writer, I can only say that we were in a place of hope and sanctuary, inspiration and history, amid a land of dynamic change. Yeah, this was indeed a once-in-a-lifetime experience.

"Fuck me dead, mate."

Interestingly, when Kayne gets tipsy, he lapses into Australian slang. I have become an expert in "Strine." He also gets even hotter than he is, with his wild hair blowing in the Arctic sea breeze and his Siberian Husky blue eyes.

O.K., so I was out to impress, and I had scrolled Google. I admit it entirely. Not just another muscled-up ginger, dudes. I *do* got me some brains. I jumped in like the over-achieving honor student with this tidbit of Believe It Or Not.

"I'll wager that you guys didn't know that it takes about 400 years for ice to travel that glacier's length. That ice shit you are looking at right there, boys, left the source somewhere around 1622 CE."

As we drew closer to the glacier's lofty massif, it became apparent that ice isn't white. It's a variety of colors ranging from a glacial blue to a filthy grey-brown. Cameron pointed off to the starboard.

"That peninsula was the connection between the Russell Fiord and Disenchantment. See that barrier of rock and mud? Hubbard created that with its moraine – boulders and soil pushed down from the mountains by the creeping ice. Took a decade, but Hubbard totally sealed off the inlet a few years back. It is a lake for now, but things change – a very high drama place."

The Captain slowed the Rusalka to a silent cruise, carefully avoiding what revealed themselves in the smoky midst as a litter of icebergs surrounding the tidewater edge of the glacier. Standing against the rail, I gave them a voice saying, "Puny humans beware. There is more to me than meets the eye."

Kayne dropped an arm over the shoulder of our Steward and did some refills. The sound of our clinking ice-ice cubes cut through the strange stillness as we faced the glacier. The temperature dropped on the fo'c'stle. I noticed a pod of barnacle-covered gray whales, each the size of a school bus, swimming into the deeper water of the bay. They slipped in and out of the clear dark-blue water in absolute silence. The theater of ice and snow seemed to be waiting for a spectacular moment of climax.

When it came, it sounded like a rifle shot, echoing across the Bay in full surround sound as it sped across the water and landmasses. My police reflexes kicked in. I yelled, "Shooter! Everybody down!" I dove on top of Kayne and pulled Cameron into the heap. His face was inches from mine.

"No, Nick, look."

Gonna say an ice mass the size of a ten-story building folded in its place on the glacier's ice wall. A sonic boom rang out as the monstrous ice cliff crashed into the sea. A horizontal plume of ice and snow shot from the jagged gap out to the Rusalka's port side. Our deck caught the white barrage as if someone had fired a gigantic canon of ice at the yacht. The Captain heaved to and turned across the blast as a flock of ten-foot waves reached for our craft -- newly-calved icebergs like an Armada of white warships seeking destruction.

Cameron was almost breathless as he explained, "The People call it the White Thunder."

As our ship rolled, we saw the most enormous mass sink to unknown depths in the cold bay waters before re-emerging. Its uppermost part was visible, while the majority remained hidden, and threatening, below the water's surface.

The Ivory Knife

And now, as the waters smoothed out, an icy peacefulness descended. Captain Michael McDowd on the bridge could be seen doing his best shit-eating grin as we wiped the snowpack off each other.

His voice came over the deck's small speaker as he headed the Rusalka back to the inlet of Disenchantment Bay.

"At least you saved that good French Brandy, boys."

Thomas Paul Severino

Chapter Forty-One: Yahoo
The Bay of Alaska

Nick Sechi's Journal

Stories have a unique power ... the Inuit believe they can capture souls.
-- Chris d'Lacey

"Long before Denali was created, an Indian named Yahoo lived in Alaska. He possessed great power but had no woman. Yahoo built a canoe and paddled west to find a suitable wife."

The boy was naked, sitting cross-legged at the edge of our bed and creating a unique afterglow speech using First Nations people's legends. At twenty-one, he possessed the magnificent body of someone who did a lot of kayaking, hiking, and seafaring. His jet-black hair, brown eyes, and exotic cheekbones set off a handsome face with tender and sensual lips. His enthusiasm for a frisky sex-up matched ours as we explored the hot ways of the flesh with a savage flavoring.

The cabin was warm with the scent of some rather acrobatic sexin'. Kayne was propped against some pillows, bare-chested in long John bottoms, a partial post-play cover-up. I stood naked near the cabin windows and watched the dark night sea coast roll by, rocks, waves, and mountains bordering our path through the Gulf of Alaska.

Cameron continued in a sing-song voice, filled with the character of storytellers around ancient campfires.

"As he approached the Raven Chief's village, the brave Yahoo began singing a song that explained his quest. Fog Woman, the Raven Chief's wife, spoke softly. 'Take my daughter, but do so and go quickly. Kutkh, the Raven Chief, my husband, is preparing to kill you.' This was very disturbing to the young brave."

O.K. So, Cameron was young but a real charmer and quite worldly. Kayne and I sometimes added others to our intimate play, ensuring all was consensual, safe, and recreational. This proved to be a bit of fun on the journey north.

The young Athabascan, Cameron/Yakecen, the "Sky Song," now added gestures to dramatize the tale's events. The story got exciting as his singing filled the warm cabin.

"As Yahoo began to paddle away with the young woman, the Great Kutkh pursued them. In desperation, the Raven Chief caused a great storm with surging sea waters. A tidal wave threatened to sink the escaping couple's canoe. Just then, Yahoo took out a powerful stone and threw it ahead of him, calming the seas, but the giant green waves continued to roll behind him."

The kid stood on the bed, legs wide and arms spread in a spear-throwing gesture. Kayne was mesmerized by the reenactment and tipped his whiskey glass for a sip. He reached up to caress the flanks of the young *angakok*, the shaman who dances the stories.

"Next, Kutkh threw his great spear at Yahoo, but Yahoo, using the medicine of a trained spirit lord, changed the large wave behind him into a mountain of stone just in time. Kutkh's great spear glanced off the crest of the stone mountain. When Raven's spear hit the top of the peak, there was a crash of breaking rock, and the great weapon flew off into the sky.

"Then, the angry Raven Chief sent a second tremendous sea wave that was even larger than the first. Yahoo used his medicine to turn this wave into another massive stone mountain. Two stone mountains were now between them."

One could almost hear the drums as he swayed to the rhythm of his song.

"Kutkh paddled so quickly that his canoe struck the second great stone mountain. Great Kutkh, the Powerful Chief, was thrown onto the rocks. There he changed instantly into a raven and flapped to the top of the peak. Exhausted, Yahoo fell asleep. When he awoke, he was home with his new wife at his side."

Our Cameron collapsed onto Kayne's side and was pulled into a muscular two-arm hug. But through all those embracing muscles, the saga continued.

"Gazing around, Yahoo saw that he had created two mountains. There was a smaller one off to the west. This peak he now called 'Foraker.' The

The Ivory Knife

larger one, the peak on which the great war spear ricocheted before shooting into the stars, that mighty dome would be called 'Denali,' whose name means 'The Great One.' Yahoo looked at the sky to see the great raven. The Bird God was happy to be back with his people, dancing his approval in the wind."

As Kayne reached for me to join the heated action, I stepped forward and retrieved my husband's empty glass. Anticipating another round of frisky play, I snapped off the bedside lamp. It was then that the arcs of light filled the skies beyond the Rusalka – the saga come to life in the magical reflections dancing in our cabin.

Kayne released Cameron and me and sprinted out of the cabin to our deck.

In the freezing cold, my half-naked man cheered, "Bloody brilliant! A fucking masterpiece! Nick!"

Cameron grabbed the down comforter and wrapped himself. I scooped up two parkas and followed Kayne beneath the glowing skies. We huddled up, sharing the thick warmth.

Across the sky, beneath the mountains and the waters of the bay, curtains of red, green, and blue descended in a rich and breathtaking luminosity. Near the lower reaches, the swirl of the arcs slowly tipped in yellow and orange in the cold night sky.

Kayne advised, "Listen."

It was soft and almost imperceptible, but we could hear a faint crackling in the glowing spirals above us. From the folds of the duvet, Cameron produced the whiskey bottle and passed it.

"For fortification, my friends."

The light display continued as we shivered, hugged up, and sloshed the golden liquid. Finally, Kayne led the way back to bed. In the dark cabin, the *Aurora Polaris* would illuminate our next very athletic and very hot play.

But, before things got seriously savage, Sky Song Boy waved at the outdoor bands of light through the cabin windows.

"The Raven is pleased."

Thomas Paul Severino

Chapter Forty-Two: The Simulacrum
221 Baker Street, San Francisco, California

Notes to the file by Andi Rodriguez

"Dad, Cousin Pesho is in Brussels. He's the go-to guy on this. I'm so there."

Eric and Oscar were ready with the first objection but said nothing as Kris held up one hand and continued.

"Before you guys give me the rab-jab. The University has canceled classes from tomorrow to Monday because of Holy Week. I can get a replacement to handle the services at the church. We can make this happen."

We were huddled in the kitchen of 221. Oscar had finished repairing a stopped-up drain for Mrs. Trasker. Dinner was being prepared, and the kitchen smelled of the rich aromas of coq au vin á la Trasker.

Oscar said, "Kristof, can you not just call your cousin and ask for his help?"

"Nahhh, this has to be a face-to-face, Doc. Bulgarians don't conduct important business over the phone, not in my family, anyway. This is a super big deal."

Eric held up a hand as he said, "Kris is right, Oscar. Too many lives are at stake not to make this a real conversation between equals."

Oscar continued to play devil's advocate.

"I understand that this is a crucial intervention. I suggest we think this through on all sides. You are not a prince of the blood, my son. Your connection to the Tsar's family is one through marriage. How can you be sure they will not simply brush this aside?"

"My grandmother's second husband was third in line to the throne. That's pretty right up there."

"A throne that is a revered memory of the past -- a titular imperial family. The Kohárys were made figureheads after World War II. The House of Saxe-Coburg and Gotha is a patriotic simulacrum."

"And that is a word I will have to Google, but I get the idea, Doc – image but no substance. No power. Except, you need to know that members of the Koháry family have been elected to the National Assembly, and the late Tsar was Prime Minister for a while. So there's that."

"The Royals loved my mother and this boy wonder," Eric said. "I can assure you that they will seriously consider any request he will make. Right now, it is our only option."

I asked the former spy, "Asgard? The mercenary network that has helped us before."

Eric shook his head but said nothing. I took this to mean that either operation by that secret organization ran in conflict with the proposed rescue of the Ukrainian civilians or there was some domestic friction. The guiding business/family principle was to keep Commander Eric Sorenson free of the deadly world of espionage. Oscar was the guardian at the dark gates on this one.

Kris added, "Prince Petar Stoyanov Ivanov is a member of the Council of Ministers. The dude has big pull, I can tell you. The talk in Sofia is Cousin Pesho will be sitting in the Prime Minister's seat real soon."

Eric started to pace. He reached into his jeans for his smokes. Mrs. Trasker did an interception from across her culinary kingdom, holding a wooden spoon that just begged for some action.

"Commander Sorenson, do not even think …."

Surrendering, Eric raised both hands, one with an unlit cigarette between his fingers. He pivoted as he stepped to the kitchen door and backed out onto the porch. Just before the door closed, he waved at us to follow him.

The back entrance to the kitchen was screened-in and provided access to the house's flagstone patio, gardens, pool, and parkour course. The covered structure allowed protection from San Francisco's frequent rains. I snagged a jacket as I joined the men and chose a spot out of the way of any secondary smoke.

The Ivory Knife

Christine lifted her head from a nap on the small café table to inspect the humans trespassing on her newly claimed territory. Her attitude was one of feline tolerance but imperious disdain. Trasker had given her one of Kayne's old sweatshirts, and Christine made it her table-top day bed. I imagined that as the cat examined Eric, she was thinking. *You're not him. A pretty good copy, but ... yeah, no.*

Kris stepped onto the mist-covered patio and lobbed a tennis ball far across the yard. Alice and Chuoko dashed after it.

Eric spoke between drags, and Kris remained in the conversation between toss and fetch.

"NATO or Moscow. Bulgaria is torn to shit over Russia's aggressive war against Ukraine. Sanctions? Military aid to Ukraine? There is even an internal fuck storm regarding banning Russian state media within the Bulgarian Republic."

"This might not be as easy as I thought," Kris said through the screen.

"Not easy by any means, lad. Recently, a spy ring was uncovered in the Bulgarian Defense Ministry. An army general was arrested for spying for Russia. But, the pro-Russia stance meets with broad approval in the populace. Our Prince Minister has been maneuvering all this while dealing with NATO's condemnation of the war."

Oscar muttered, "So much for keeping you away from international affairs."

The dogs were fussing about something near the side gate, most likely a passer-by, and Kris stepped away.

Eric blew smoke and shook his head as he stared at his son.

"He sees this as a chance to man up with some vital responsibilities. Kris has a fire in his gut for this."

I offered, "Kris doesn't want to be the hot jock sex bomb he sees himself continuing to be. This is a growing thing for him."

"I should go with him. Alone is not good."

I heard Trasker answering the front doorbell.

Thomas Paul Severino

Eric looked at Oscar, whose hackles continued to rise. He acquiesced as he said, "Yes, yes. I get it, Oscar. That would be disastrous all around. I need to continue to lay low. Still... I am concerned for his safety."

Oscar sighed and attempted to pet the cat. She allowed. Kris and the dogs were returned to the steps of the porch.

"Andi is right. This is part of the lad's journey to the authenticity of self. Wow. Did I really say that? I am rather good."

As Kris came inside. His expression was one of shock. The dogs were in a barking frenzy.

"An Uber... luggage ... we have a visitor. Does anyone know what's going on?"

As he spoke, a very familiar woman walking with a fashionable cane stepped through the kitchen door. She carried herself regally and smiled like a screen star behind large sunglasses.

"Hello, darlings. I hear we're going to Brussels."

Chapter Forty-Three: The Face in the Ice
The Sagavanirktok River, Prudhoe Bay, Alaska

"The Arctic char is the opposite of its cousin, the salmon."

The old fisherman was wrapped in a heavy parka made from animal hide and fur. Thick mittens and seal hide pants tucked into rubber boots completed his outfit. Not too far off, his wife was dressed similarly. Her ice-fishing couture gave some concession to a bit of fringe, some simple beaded work, and an oversized knit cap under her parka hood.

"It spawns in freshwater rivers and returns to the ocean in the springtime. There, see. You can see them through the ice."

Stefan Lebedev removed his snowshoes. He kicked and hand-pushed a patch of snow off the ice at his feet. The abbot saw only an aqua icy crust.

The fisherman grunted as he stood up from his ice hole. He flattened face down on the cleared space and placed his tongue on the ice. As he returned to his seat, the fisherman said, "Look again."

The priest pressed his face to the salivated wet spot at his feet. The white and silver char were plentiful, swimming downriver in the blue-green crystal clear waters to the Arctic Sea. Righting himself, he watched the woman use a long-poled ice chisel to make her fishing hole. He reflected --- the Inuit were practical in everything. The chisel, a willow twig with 12 feet of twine, a pronged spear made from caribou antler, lures made from walrus ivory – no modern equipment or technological assistance for miles.

Cabin fever brought the holy man out of his seclusion to the fishing grounds of the Sagavanirktok River. Jissika Delutukl, having some business at a remote station to the east of Prudhoe, encouraged him to explore some Indigenous communities. He followed a group of anglers onto the river ice. The Arctic Sea rolled within a thick fog of frost and sleet on the far horizon. Inuit hunters ventured out in kayaks or on foot, searching for small whales, seals, and otters.

Thomas Paul Severino

The old fisherman sat on a shelf above his ice hole. He patiently jiggled a carved whitish lure into the porthole and down into the water. After a moment, he stood up and sent the spear into the opening. When he retrieved it, a good-sized char flapped within its prongs. He flipped it onto the ice.

The woman was talking in a language Stefan did not understand, seemingly to herself. When he approached, she switched to English. She waved a dismissing hand at her husband.

"Yesterday, I caught twenty-seven. My husband got ten. Bah! Kid's stuff. This is the only way to do it. Keep back. I do not want to hit you with all the fish I catch."

She knelt next to her ice hole and leaned over it, blocking the light.

"Shadow," she explained. "The char can see the opening and stay away."

The woman angler twitched the lure up and down while blowing the ice chips to one side of the water's surface.

"Very clear. I can see right to the bottom. I am making my lure dance for the char."

She coaxed her prey.

"Come, come, pretty one. Play with the toy. See how it gleams. Yes, yes, go for it, my beauty ... yah!"

She set the hook and yanked. A flapping char flew up into the air as the woman yanked her catch down onto the ice.

"Big one. You see. That's the way. More. Yes, more to come."

She looked at the Russian with a broad grin.

"You keep counting. I will win."

She went back to her ice hole.

Stefan was fascinated by the clarity of the ice surface. He scraped at another portion to see more of the fish school below. As he looked into the mirrored surface, the reflection of a face took form in the white wind over his left shoulder.

The Ivory Knife

Simultaneously, the fisherwoman flipped up another catch, and he looked up at her. Looking just beyond the kneeling priest, she cursed and said, "Ugh. Him. Nasty Ice trucker."

***

The large black man wrapped in layers of protective gear didn't say much. His green goggles made him look like a monstrous alien – The Thing from Another World.

"I picked her up near Destruction Bay in British Columbia. Sidorovna used the Synaxis to make contact. I'm on the list. She had doings, she said, in Anchorage. She told me to give you this."

The trucker handed Stefan a quarter. It was one of the America The Beautiful Quarters series, dated 2012. The reverse featured a Dall sheep with the peak of Denali in the background.

"Oh yeah. She said to remember to bring the Virgin."

Thomas Paul Severino

Chapter Forty-Four: Portugal and the United Kingdom

NATO/OTAN Headquarters. Avenue Leopold III, 1110 Brussels, Belgium

Notes to the file by Rebecca Quinto

"My dear cousin, what you are asking me is extraordinarily impossible. The political climate right now in Bulgaria is almost Orwellian. Our country is very divided by this war. The prevailing sentiments are to move carefully like a cat and watch what the Russian Bear will do next."

The Bulgarian diplomat reconsidered the request but shook his head.

We have been taking large numbers of refugees. Even in Pomorie – our "Little Moscow" with its many Russians. Ukraine wants weapons to fight this Russian aggression. The Parliament is a tenuous political coalition of four parties. Each with divergent views on the war. The Socialists threatened to break with the government should Bulgaria send weapons to Ukraine, while the democrats warned of similar consequences if the country does not."

I said, "Our request is not for weapons, Pesho. We need an escape plan for non-combatants. We need an Exodus, cuz."

Ambassador Gotha looked like he was carved from cream cheese, darling. We are talking filmstar good looks and a drop-dead smile. His immaculately coiffed gold-brown hair was gently ruffled by the spring breezes and set off his dashing appearance.

I thought back to our recent introduction. *No formalities, please, Ms. Quinto. We are family. I am Pesho. And I am delighted to meet you.*

Honestly, my darling, this family has the genes for gorgeousness, and while I know that Kris is not blood, it's just that – hunky Slavic posse for days and from what I have seen of the women – some real beauties.

Reluctant as I am to make light of the matter that brought us to Brussels, I will borrow from Nick's fabulous style when I tell you that "the Dude was Dior-ed out the ass, bro." And, darling, this woman knows her couture. Prince Sexy's handcrafted wool suit was navy blue and featured a two-button, notched lapel jacket. The coat's cut set off his broad athletic shoulders. As entranced as I am over a spectacular man ass, I practiced custody of the eyes. Suffice it to say the pants did his jock ass good. (So, I sneaked a look or three.) Pesho was also sporting some expensive Dior footwear.

We met at the Headquarters of the NATO Alliance, a curious building. It was designed as eight glass wedges that, for some reason, reminded me of biscotti, lined up so that the largest end of each wedge intersected with the ones to either side. The grounds were well fortified behind large fences and sentry stations.

The Bulgarian Ambassador suggested we enjoy the beautiful day. So, under the watchful eyes of campus security, we strolled outside.

Carefully manicured emerald lawns swathed the approaches to the buildings. There were sculptures evoking peace, strength, solidarity, and progress throughout the park. A large circle of the members' flags in a paved courtyard was surrounded by two grassy stretches.

Kris almost did the bro-shoulder-clutch, but the shifting uneasiness of the security soldiers made him think twice. They fist pounded, and all that male wiggly-hand jive.

"Pesho, we are talking men, women, and children. Innocent civilians. Many of whom are Jews, and the Bear eats Jews for lunch, bro. You know the deal, cuz. The Russians say they will allow the refugees a safe passage corridor. Still, you and I know that *if* they are telling the truth, those folks in Mariupol are going to Russian-occupied territories and most likely labor camps."

I broke in with, "There is a strong feeling that the massacres, tortures, and sexual assaults on the people of Bucha will be repeated in the south. It is genocide, Prince. People have been imprisoned in basements without food and without water. When the Ukrainians take territory back, the mass graves are revealed."

"And your young man is one of those trapped by the aggressors, Rebecca. I am very sorry to hear that. Mark Gadarn is an extraordinary journalist and a very brave man."

The Ivory Knife

"Thank you."

"There was some talk among my colleagues regarding the suspected war crimes. The European Court of Human Rights and other international courts are looking into conflict-related cases with the cooperation of Ukraine. What is essential is the documentation of the crime for future prosecution. Having said this, I realize that this is of no help to Mr. Gadarn and the people in the crypt of that church. I sympathize."

The Prince swiped his hair off his face and looked into the eastern stretches of the campus. He shrugged.

"As I started to say, the Russians shut off the gas, and polled support for Russia dropped to 25 percent. In addition, most of my country's folk support Bulgaria's membership in the European Union and NATO. "

Kris held up a hand.

"Cousin, the question for the Bulgarian Parliament is, are you folks willing to allow these atrocities or step in with rescue? Gas or children. Do it as a private citizen, Pesho. The Tsar is sympathetic to the cause of the Ukrainians. I heard he is urging your government to accept even more refugees. Some of our cousins have gone there to fight."

"True, Kristof. I do not know if you know that your cousin and my brother, Krassimir Saxe-Coburg Gotha, the titular Duke of Varna, and his husband, Major Yordan Sasselov, are fighting for Zelensky somewhere in the south. But there is nothing more we can do. If they come west, then ... seems like all we can do right now."

"They can't escape, cousin. They are trapped in the East."

The Prince shrugged. He tried to control his frustration.

"Then what you are proposing is impossible, my dear cousin. You remind me so much of your grandmother. Stubborn and so self-assured. The Dowager Countess Margarita would latch onto something and never let go, often charming her adversaries to get her own way."

He shot me a glance that seemed to imply that women, collectively and individually, were quite a handful.

"Halt! You are trespassing! Remain where you are."

Close by, a guard chased after a group of children, retrieving their soccer ball. Kris took up an expression that was somewhere between mischief and daring. He pointed at his cousin.

"You're a diplomat, right? Well, here's a negotiation especially designed for your ass."

Kris did a two-finger whistle and jogged towards the boys and the guard. I saw him squat down and talk to the kids. First, he showed them his phone. They looked from the screen to him with mouths agape. Then, he pulled some bills from his pocket. The guard removed his hat and scratched his head. Pesho waved, "It's O.K."

From the other side, a well-dressed staffer approached the Ambassador. Before the aide connected with Pesho, Kris returned dribbling the soccer ball – kicking it before him in a light run.

The Bulgarian smirked.

"I see where this is going. My assistant, Mihail – Ms. Rebecca Quinto and my quite mad cousin, Kristof – from America."

Kris lingered a bit, scoping out the staffer, then got back into it.

"Sudden death. You win. We get back on the plane. But, if I score. We come up with a rescue plan. Deal?"

He pointed to the flags.

"Portugal. The United Kingdom."

Pesho started to say something, but Kris undressed the Ambassador, pulling at his jacket and tie while unbuttoning his shirt. Pesho laughed.

"Mikey, you hold "The Flea's" jacket and shirt. Careful, dude. Expensive. Cufflinks even ... here, one, two. Got them. And the watch, here. Cartier, Rebecca. Smooth, Pesho. Very smooth."

My jock co-conspirator dashed over to me, still possessing the ball, and started to strip. It was to be undershirts and rolled-cuff slacks. The competitors went barefoot, with Mihail and me also watching their shoes.

As the kids, a few guards, and some potentates moved in, I thought I heard, "Gotha is at it again. Amazing."

The Ivory Knife

Kris grabbed his cousin by the arm and showed me the five colored rings tattooed inside his right bicep.

"Tokyo, 2020. The Flea is a former midfielder for the Bulgarian National Football team. The Lions brought home the Balkans Cup three times under his captainship. Lemme show you the lion tat on his ass."

The Royals tumbled to the grass in an impromptu grapple.

"Maĭnata mu! Prokletata ti bolka e zadnika."

"No, *you're* the pain in the ass, bitch, and don't say 'fuck,' Flea. You are supposed to be high-class – three hundred Euro haircut, Cartier, and shit ...yellow card here, ref. Here. Right here. Foul language on the Flea. Very Bad."

Kris made an exaggerated pointing motion at his cousin, who could not help laughing.

"You are great fun, my cousin, but very nutso as the Americans say. How do they keep you under control in San Francisco?"

Kris grinned, "They don't."

I said, "Grass stains on Dior. Such a tragedy."

"Do not fear, Miss. The Minister has an excellent dry cleaner."

"Send me the bill, Mihail darling."

They went far out on the lawn. Coin toss and a diplomat friend of Pesho did the ball drop. Other ambassadors and staffers stepped behind the flagpoles to catch shots on Portugal and the United Kingdom.

Kris took the drop and went backfield before he turned and charged. Pesho dropped him quickly with an excellent sliding tackle. They went up and down the lawn, and the crowd got thicker and pretty noisy.

"Bŭlkhata! Bŭlkhata! Bŭlkhata!

Two superb athletes, well-matched, the cousins ran, kicked, trapped, juggled, dribbled, and shot, sweating in the Belgian sunshine.

"What are they saying, Mihail?"

The assistant chuckled.

"*Bŭlkhata* is the Bulgarian word for 'flea,' Miss."

Kids and guards served as linesmen and ball retrievers. Pesho made a spectacular fake and then a shot, but it went wide -between the Netherlands and Norway flags.

It was athletic. It was balletic. It was fuckin' hot, darling. The onlookers were joyous over this splendid lunchtime distraction from the affairs of the Alliance. Of course, you know "The Kris" pulled off his tee shirt and showed his magnificent upper body. It was a celebratory gesture at blocking an unbelievable shot by Prince Charming.

The crowd went wild. I expected cell phones would be snapping pics. No, no, no. Not at NATO headquarters, darling.

And then, my marvelous nephew yelled, "*Tova e za teb, baba! This one's for you, Gran!*"

Kris' flying scissors sent the ball curving high. Pesho leaped into the air as he tried to stop it with his head and missed. The ball sailed between Portugal and the United Kingdom for a sudden-death win. The place went nuts. Pesho raised his arms and approached his victorious cousin. Kris was seated on his heels, laughing like a hyena. As the NATO Ambassador got close. Kris reached up and pantsed the Prince.

And there it was. The Lion made its appearance on one breathtaking man-ass.

***

"How are you not in custody? How are *we* not in custody?"

"Relax, Aunt Rebecca. Bare-assed soccer players are a common sight in Europe. I intend to do a lot of that at USF. Some prime muscle there."

Back at our hotel, Kris slapped his towel-clad butt and poured me a vodka neat. Freshly showered, he poured himself some carrot juice and kicked back in the other club chair.

"Well, you did it, darling. The devil's in the details, but Pesho will help us devise a plan. And I think it is all gonna come out all right despite all of this flying by the seat of our pants. But with all of these international complications, there is no other way."

The Ivory Knife

"Your resources and influence are an excellent addition, Aunt Rebecca. We'll get Mark and those folks out, sure thing."

I raise my glass. "Your dad will be very proud."

The lad thought and then grinned. "You know, I think he would have pulled some crazy-ass shit like that himself."

He suddenly stood up with a horrified look on his face.

"What was I thinking? Uncle Kayne is gonna bust a gut when he finds out – one shirtless, one bare-assed – and in front of NATO headquarters. FUCKKKK!

"Oh my darling, your Uncle Kayne and Nick, for that matter, have been caught with their pants down around their ankles in much more auspicious venues than NATO. Believe me when I say it."

Thomas Paul Severino

Chapter Forty-Five: Underneath
Whittier to Anchorage, Alaska

Nick Sechi's Journal

"She's headed into the Yukon, Boss. She took a right turn to the east. See?"

The blip flashed on the Canadian wilderness portion of the map.

"It's total wilderness up that way. No roads, just mountains, ice, and snow. See, she crossed the Yukon River there. Our conclusions about her final destination were wrong, it appears."

As the Rusalka pulled into Whittier's deep-water harbor, she docked near a tanker, the "Siberia," emblazoned with the Alaska Marine Highway logo. I checked the position of our fugitive Russian spy on my laptop. Kayne was distracted by the larger ship for some reason.

He turned his attention to my screen.

"Do the history, Nick."

I tapped the app's feature, and the screen changed to a display of the tracker's whereabouts for the last 24 hours.

Kayne touched the display. "Beaver Creek, yesterday on Canada Highway 1. But what does that tell you?"

The blue line did indeed turn into the wilderness, but the trail was squiggly and often turned back on itself. On the banks of the Yukon, it traveled back and forth before fording the waters and allowing it to be carried with the current.

"Fuck! She found the tracker."

"A human, even a fugitive, does not travel like that. There in that bog, the moose foraged for over an hour before moving on."

"She fed the thing to a moose! Son of a bitch."

"Most likely. Lieutenant Corporal Sidorovna embedded the tracker in some food, and *Alces alces* had it for lunch."

"Who?"

"A moose. A cow, in this case, with at least one calf no older than 18 months."

I was lost, as usual, and my man read my mind.

"The grazing and fording indications reveal a slow-moving solitary species – no herds like their deer cousins, with an offspring. See where she chooses to cross the river – shallow waters. Mother can swim deep rivers but chooses to keep her baby or babies out of harm's way in the deeper torrents. Calves remain with their mothers until their eighteenth month. She will pass the small device very soon."

"And Spy Woman?"

His gaze drifted back to the "Siberia," but he said, "Let's see what we can find out in Anchorage. The woman is too dramatic not to stage her defiance in a lesser venue. Sidorovna is headed to the top of the world."

***

Whittier is a small and very rustic Alaskan frontier town on the northeast shore of the Kenai Peninsula. The small city stands at the head of Passage Canal, a well-traveled waterway on the west side of Prince William Sound. With a population of about three hundred permanent residents on a strip between the mountains and the sea, the small city has an economy based on transportation – goods in and out. Whittier is the seaside connection between the Alaskan Panhandle and Inner Alaska. Vital highways and seaways converge on this very rustic town. The town is popular with tourists, outdoor sports enthusiasts, and naturalists because of the area's abundance of wildlife and natural beauty.

It was snowing as we disembarked and piled into the black SUV driven by Cameron. A train loaded with containers traveled alongside us as we hit the highway.

"Anchorage is just the other side of those mountains, men. We'll be there soon."

The Ivory Knife

"What's up, Kayne? You're looking at me like I'm about five years old and about to create a load of trou... ohhh, shit! Seriously?"

The roadside sign said, "Anton Anderson Memorial Tunnel."

I could feel the panic rising and started to wiggle in my seat.

"Cam, do the switchback — mountain roads, just not this. Is there a ferry?"

With what seemed to be the Voice of Doom, our driver said, "Sorry, bud, the tunnel is the only way in. We'll clear it in thirty minutes or slightly more, depending on traffic. The Anderson Memorial is a mixed-use road and rail tunnel. See those traffic lights? Trains first and then north and south-bound traffic alternate. Once we get through, it's an hour to Anchorage."

The scratching claustrophobia bugs in my bloodstream were multiplying and racing up through my viscera and into my brain. I began to hyperventilate as the large A-frame entrance to the passage came up in front of us. We were going into this gigantic mountain at its base.

"You gotta be fucking kidding me."

I fiddled with my seatbelt.

"How bad would it be if I wait for you guys on this side?"

Kayne stopped my exit. He said, "Have some water, Nick."

I swallowed half of the bottle in furtive gulps. He removed a bandana from around his neck, folded it, and tied it around my head, obstructing my vision. I could hear the train enter the tunnel as Kayne pulled me against him, saying, "Have a snooze, my love. I got you."

***

"You slipped me a Mickey."

"You sound like a page of dialogue in a Dashiell Hammett novel. A Mickey? It was Dramamine — safe and reliable. We are coming up to Anchorage. The next chapter in our case begins."

Thomas Paul Severino

A state police cruiser pulled us off the road. The woman officer, D. Kowtok, asked for our identification. Cameron had no explanation as to why.

Behind mirrored sunglasses, the trooper said, "Lotsa shit comes through that tunnel. Hope you don't mind if I ... whoa, hold on."

She stepped away and spoke to her shoulder mic. I stretched in an attempt to overhear but could not. Kayne read her lips.

He said softly, "Right here, as a matter of fact ... roger that. We are on our way."

He pushed off his floppy bang and said, "We are about to be conscripted again, my love."

The trooper motioned to our driver. Cameron murmured, "Flashing lights, sirens -- hot shit. The fuckin' case!"

Chapter Forty-Six: The City of Lights and Flowers
Anchorage, Alaska

Nick Sechi's Journal

"My people, the Athabaskans, came down through the mountain passes and displaced the Chugach Alutiiq about two thousand years ago, Cameron said. "Then Captain Cook and the Europeans came seeking the Northwest Passage. His ship, the HMS Resolution, explored out there in the inlet that bears his name. But neither the Cook Inlet nor the Turnagain Inlet led to the fabled Northwest Passage. They searched for a shorter means of reaching the Pacific from Europe than sailing east around Asia or south around South America."

Kayne said, "Russians."

"Oh hell, yes, Dr. Sorenson. Their trading posts were all along the inlets along there. We gave them furs, gold, and seafood. They gave us smallpox which killed half of the Native population."

The panorama of the largest city in the state, built on treacherous mudflats and against the backdrop of the misty Glen Alps, passed by outside the SUV's windows. Cameron pointed to the turning State trooper.

"Looks like they want us at the Port."

***

It was a small, gray-green outbuilding with metal siding and a steep roof. The locale was a storage area for jet fuel for both the Ted Stevens International Airport and Joint Base Elmendorf–Richardson, a United States military facility in Anchorage. The place was surrounded by vehicles with flashing roof lights out the ass – police, military, state troopers, and Port Authority security. No one was near the crime scene. Everyone had been held back. Blood seeped from under the closed door of the shed.

"Thank you, Captain Farrell. I see you know my methods."

Thomas Paul Severino

Captain Ciarán David Farrell of U.S. Coast Guard Intelligence nodded to us, saying, "Good to see you again, Dr. Sorenson. It has been a long time. Berlin, I remember. The lost briefcase, right?"

"I remember it well and you quite fondly, Sir. My husband and colleague, Nick Sechi, and our steward and guide, Cameron Jakobs, of the H.M.C.S. Rusalka out of Vancouver."

The Air Force man shook hands and said, "The Rusalka? Not Aleksei and Tim's tug ... Pysanka. Many good times there,"

As we shook, he continued, "Huge fan, Mr. Sechi. I have read all of your adventures. Wildest of all is how you ended up with this catastrophe."

He smiled slightly.

O.K., big Irish Fly Boy plays on our team and may have played closely with half of our squad – oh, man, Kayne. We need to deconstruct when we get alone. You got some past, my man.

Kayne and I donned nitrile gloves, tossed a pair to Mr. Jakobs, approached the shed, and opened the door while carefully stepping around the blood.

There were two sprawled on the floor just inside the door.

Kayne went no further. He turned to the Captain and said, "They were murdered less than two hours ago, right where they lay. There was a struggle wherein the two victims, and the murderer used extreme martial arts. The dead men are Colonel Vasily Pavlovich Bounine and Captain Sergei Andreivich Sarov of the Federal'naya Sluzhba Bezopasnosti Rossiyskoy Federatsii, the Federal Security Service of the Russian Federation and the main successor agency to the Soviet Union's KGB. – the FSB."

He added after a moment. "They were intimate partners and fellow soldiers. They arrived in Whittier two days ago on board the Siberia."

He stooped to examine the prosthetic arm and lacerated face mask of the fallen Bounine. He spoke as if to the dead men.

"The assassin is Lieutenant Colonel Katsitsanóron Isapoinhkyaki, aka Katya Sidorovna, of the Russian Foreign Intelligence Service. She is quite insane. With this kill, she sends a message to their superiors to stay away."

The Ivory Knife

He tipped the head of the dead captain.

"Sidorovna slit their throats forcefully and fatally using an *ulu*."

Kayne looked up at the gathered officers. He clarified.

"An ice knife."

Thomas Paul Severino

Chapter Forty-Seven: Orso
Anchorage, Alaska

Nick Sechi's Journal

"Your table is ready, Captain Farrell. If you and your party will follow me."

"Thank you, Courtney."

The interiors of Orso, an upscale restaurant on the campus of the Alaska Center for the Performing Arts on West Fifth Avenue in Anchorage, were elegant shades of rust and red with warm wood appointments. It was a very romantic venue in which to discuss murder.

The hostess brought us to a small, open room at the back of the mezzanine section of the restaurant. It was private but allowed a view of the floor below and the elegant stairway.

We did cocktails with Antipasto Orso served with golden olive oil, coal-black balsamic vinegar, and thick slices of rosemary potato bread. Criminals and assorted badasses make one hungry ... yeah, and apparently, crimefighting makes some dudes frisky. The body language between US Coast Guard studly and sexy cabin boy was a case in point. I see this stuff instantly. Kayne is always oblivious.

The petite young woman passed small plates and said, "With our compliments, Captain. I will be back."

CPT Ciarán Farrell, aka "Ray," again expressed his thanks, and the young woman left us. Kayne began.

"There is no honor among thieves, and in this case, spies. I need to remind myself of that from time to time."

"Have you turned into a disappointed optimist, old buddy? Since we last ... ah, saw each other, quite a few narrow escapes and evil geniuses have plagued your ass."

He winked at me and raised his glass.

The soldier was about Kayne's age, a bit shorter, and built like a tough warrior. His shaved head accentuated some solid and masculine features highlighted by a sensual mouth and sparkling green-grey eyes.

Kayne turned into the conversation.

"How is your family, Ray-Ray?"

Farrell grinned and chuckled.

"You remember everything, Kayne."

The Captain turned his left forearm and rolled up his sleeve. A circle held three spirals in dark ink.

It's the Celtic Triquetra, the Trinity knot."

He showed Cameron and me the design.

"You can see one continuous line interweaving around itself, symbolizing the eternal trinity of soul, heart, and mind. Mine signifies the unity of the family."

Kayne proceeded to bust balls. He cocked an eyebrow and flipped back his floppy bang. His index finger pointed at the dude, but I was unsure where. Cameron was fascinated, and it showed.

"And?"

"Yeah. My family's all good. My little brother, Ros – 'little,' ha! He's twenty-seven and sturdy as an ox. A real pain-in-the-ass lady killer. Up for a part in a series. Nude scene and everything. The kid is in hog heaven."

"Teaghlach ar dtús – "family first." You are about as fanatically loyal to your clan as I am to the Sorenson brood. Blood and ... ink."

Captain Ciarán blushed, lowered his head, came for a sip of Redbeast Irish whiskey, and laughed.

Kayne ran an index finger over the back of the man's upper arms.

"When we were hellions at Notre Dame and a bit on our faces, this brogran, "Ray-Ray the Irish Warrior," had that legend tattooed on his triceps. I remember the questions he used to get on the soccer field and in the gym. Some stuffy blokes have no appreciation for the Celtic."

The Ivory Knife

Cameron ran a hand over the arm closest to him and cooed, "That must look amazing."

Farrell turned to look into the kid's smiling face and gave him a wink and a pat.

"Yep, got me a few dates back at uni, some too hot to mention."

"Ya blighter. Mitch is doing very well. Married Kick, and they live in Colorado—lords of the land."

"Mmm, the Archangel -- pride of the Sorensons. Our whatever it was was over too fast."

I explained, "Cam, Kayne is a triplet, and Mitchell is an adopted brother."

"Wow. All these hot men. Hotties this far north are few and far between."

"Hey you, the Sockeye here is incredible. They do it Niçoise. Unforgettable."

Ciarán took the young man's menu and playfully gripped Cam's trapezius. Daddy is way interested, kiddo.

"What say I order for you, cabin boy? Sound good?"

"I'm in your hands, Captain."

Holy shit. Before this turned totally porno, I said, "The case ... two homicides ... Kayne?"

"The detectives at the scene are testing my conclusions as we speak. They will find out I am correct. Additionally, I stand by my previous surmisings regarding honor among spies and the like."

'What do you mean, Boss?'

"Colonel Vasily Pavlovich Bounine and Captain Sergei Andreivich Sarov were killed in cold blood. Cam, that means ruthlessly and without feeling. They posed no violent threat to Sidorovna. No weapons were found at the scene. They approached the Master Spy intending to come over to her side. Before their fatal rendezvous, Bounine was attacked. His handlers tried to do away with him, and I am reluctant to say this was punishment for his failure to use me as bait. However, the pair escaped only to meet death at the hands of Lieutenant Colonel Sidorovna. The cabal of Russian agents so avidly pursuing the Lieutenant Colonel is outraged because they do not have the Ivory Knife and its secrets."

"Back up, Kayne. I don't understand the motive."

"Difficult, Ray, because the murderer is insane. But, recall the body of the dead Colonel. There was an old head wound that he brought to the party. Someone was doing payback for failed performance, and the two of them escaped."

The Irish American looked around and leaned in. He said, "What does the defector have, Kayne?"

Kayne sipped his Hibiki and said, "The only thing worth turning traitor for -- information vital to the security of Russia."

"The Synaxis."

"Overrated, my friend. This is not the Cold War. The West and Russians know the identity of almost every agent on the planet. My brother Eric could rattle off the names and aliases of the brothers and sisters of espionage in any significant capital. But, yes, she does have the infernal list of the spy networks and is using it to secure allies for her covert journey. Her comrades see that Sidorovna is getting to her destination and remaining undetected."

I asked, "Kayne, why then are her own military after her?"

Kayne spread his hands, indicating the answer was elementary.

"She went rogue, my love. Unheard of in the spy game. The Ivory Knife holds the key to some sort of weapon that Russia needs in that country's aspirations to dominate Europe and other nations. The agents of the Motherland cannot allow that information to be jeopardized."

"A superweapon?"

"No, Master Jacobs. Again, please let me state that we are in the Post-Post-Cold War era. The ultimate superweapon these days is technology. The global warfare of East against West, in which we are up to our bloody asses, is a War of the Machines -- computers. Don't let anyone tell you differently."

The Ivory Knife

Kayne turned away from us and stretched out an arm at a figure against the opposite wall.

"Especially not her!"

I bolted and chased the woman in the black overcoat down the stairs, nearly toppling our ascending servers.

Out into the street – she was gone.

***

"The fuckers are jumping out of the woodwork, Boss. Can't believe she got clean away."

"Actually, it was not a woman, Nick. Our nosey friend was a man in drag and not trans -- a man doing bad drag – prominent Adam's apple, but we'll allow that to pass. The three of you were unaware of his presence. First, because of the furtive romancing between the randy US officer who was putting some very experienced moves on the very willing and highly sexual cabin boy. You were oblivious because you are always in the "frisky zone' when we are close and getting stretcher cased with the grog."

I continued to pull off his clothes in the warm hotel room. He returned with complimentary stripping.

"Pretty full of ya self, Bossman. What if I was edging for a four-way with your old boyfriend, Muscles O'Brian? Watch the zipper, Boss. Going commando and ... ouch...."

"Because you are with me, boyo. To paraphrase the late great Paul Newman, "I have steak at home, why should I go out for hamburger?"

"Your eyes and body are better than his, which is saying a lot, bruh. I so loved watching his movies."

I did some hot-mouth preliminaries. Naked and gorgeous, Kayne tasted of Hibiki and his own natural *oishii* – deliciousness."

He breathed, "Well, we have seen to it that Cameron Jakobs is out of harm's way. If I know CPT Ciarán Farrell, this *affaire de coeur,* will last the weekend or perhaps longer. Tell me, Nick, do folks hook up sexually so easily these days? You need to do that again, lad. Ohhh, yes ... you hot... I am going to... yes, brilliant move, boyo."

Thomas Paul Severino

I came off a very intimate and smoking hot maneuver, looked him in his half-closed eyes, and said, "That was not a hook-up, my sexy man. That was the thunderbolt."

I went back to things that mattered.

Chapter Forty-Eight: The Gateway
Talkeetna, Alaska

Nick Sechi's Journal

"Fuck that, Boss. I am not waiting at some shit-assed base camp while you deal with Ludmilla the Crazy and whoever she brought along for the demented rollercoaster ride. I'm on the mountain with you, and that's it."

I swiped the SUV keys, left Cameron a note saying we'd return soon, and hit Alaska State Highway 3 North from Anchorage to the historic town of Talkeetna nestled in the boreal forest of pines, spruces, and larches. Here and there, a stand of birch trees offset the green and brown of the taiga. Our trip brought us near to the confluence of the Susitna, Chulitna, and Talkeetna rivers.

"Nick, Denali is the highest mountain in North America, and your …. well, perhaps we should talk more."

"Can't even hear you, Kayne. Uh uh. Hell, we fought the Big Bads in the Himalayas, man. I do plane rides now like fuckin' Howard Hughes. Nothing to worry about here."

"There's your exit. Interesting how you remember things, my love. I recall the Head Lama at the Tian Cho-lei Nyingpo Monastery helped you align your spiritual center to keep you from throwing yourself into the abyss. And, I might add, we have the most recent incident of the tunnel in Whittier. Claustrophobia and acrophobia can be paralyzing."

"Listen to me, my Studly. No drugs in this body. And you know what I'm talking about. I can do this -- just a matter of manning up. You're married to a *man*, Dude, a former cop, and quite a man he is."

Kayne mugged. "Oh, the masculinity. My hero!"

"Do not make me throw you a beatin'."

The clapboard sign on the roadside read, "Welcome to beautiful downtown Talkeetna." Main Street resembled a movie set in a frontier town of the mid-19th-century. We passed a post office, a repurposed sawmill, three trading posts (Nagley's Store- since 1921), the Talkeetna Roadhouse eatery, and a cigar and donkey store, in addition to many tourist cabins. The quaint environs screamed Gold Rush and mountaineer outfitters out the ass.

Standing at the north end of Main Street, the Fairview Inn ruled the roadside landscape. It is a two-story frame structure with a hip roof and a dazzling vertical sign at the end of the white wooden facade announcing, "Saloon." Its eponymous vistas were indeed magnificent – the rivers, the forests, and the snow-covered peaks of the Alaska Range.

"Nick, the sensible thing, in this case, would be for you to ...."

I interrupted -- something I rarely do, but I was not giving in.

"We're done with that, Boss. Hey, this place reminds me of Lake George, New York, with higher mountains – frontier primitive chic. No gay bars within five hundred miles. What do the boys do for fun?"

The Denali National Park's Walter Harper Talkeetna Ranger Station was a few blocks from the Talkeetna Historical Society. Local artists and musicians seemed to populate the shops and cafés throughout the town. Country and Blues could be heard in the crisp morning air.

I was getting pretty nervous-goofy, and it was evident to both of us why.

"Let's find us the hottest forest ranger in the borough and get Officer Brawny to send in the Mounties in their tight uniforms, and ... well, you get where I'm headed."

"Please roll the window down, my love. You are steaming up the windshield. I continue to protest the criticism of your libido – it never goes down -- by explaining that you are a hot-blooded Italian American – part of your personal charm."

He continued, "On another note, I believe we should avoid local law enforcement regarding this stage of the case. Considering the spiderweb of conspiracy surrounding this adventure, I am reluctant to trust anyone. And furthermore, our friend, Regina Netsilik, assured us we are unofficial collaborators with the CIA, an agency that flies well under the radar."

The Ivory Knife

"Then it's you and me, Boss, on the top of the world. The top of the fuckin' world, kickin' ass!"

Kayne pointed to the left.

"There, Nick. Parking seems to be back by the runway."

Talkeetna Air Taxi – The Glacier Landing Company.

"Holy shit, no!"

Thomas Paul Severino

Chapter Forty-Nine: The *Angakkuit*
Talkeetna, Alaska

Nick Sechi's Journal

"Tell me."

"Um, the planes. Very small."

"Yes. The largest is a twenty-passenger. I can fly it, but it is too big for our purposes. I think we are at a significant impasse in the case, my love."

We left the car at the air taxi parking lot and walked out into the crisp Alaskan sunshine in the rustic town. I shot a glance at the aircraft lined up to the left of the runway.

I gulped. It was put up or shut up time.

"I meant what I said before, Kayne. Let's do this."

Kayne looked at me with some honest skepticism. He pointed to the Tulugak Trading Post. The vintage building was hung with snowshoes, fishnets, iron-toothed bear traps, and a two-man, push-me-pull-you cross-cut saw. A somewhat faded totem pole was set just to the right of the front door. Its tower of native Arctic beasts watched all who passed by. We entered beneath a spring bell triggered by the front door. It bounced and rang with a clear metallic sound.

Touristy shit was everywhere. A few customers wandered the premises examining the souvenirs and curiosities. An older woman, whom I took to be the proprietress, eyed us with interest over the shoulder of two visitors. She was working on something artsy-crafty.

I tried to look interested in the many Alaskan history and cultural items but could not get passed our present predicament. We were indeed at a standstill.

"You have your professor of psycho-criminology face on, Boss. Are you about to give the teacher's pet a full-fledged lecture? Just like when we first met at Florida Global U, with your ice blue bedroom eyes and seductive ways."

"Crikey, Nick. Not that again. I recall that you took a rather sensual interest in your teacher, and therefore, how could any red-blooded Aussie bloke survive your carnal interests? You and your lightning bolt – swept away with explosive results like a muscled-up Nikola Tesla making sparks that incinerate the night. And my absolutely academic intentions all but incinerated."

"Yeah, right."

We were standing next to a stuffed grizzly. The beast had reared up on her hind legs, and a threatening growl was frozen on her bared teeth and snarling muzzle. The monstrous golden-brown beauty with her devastating manicure was to be a part of what came next.

Dr. Sorenson continued, "Seriously, let's review, Nick. Lieutenant Colonel Sidorovna is headed for Denali. There, she will rendezvous with her comrade, the one who possesses the Ivory Knife. They will not give it up easily."

"Two against two, Boss. Yeah, she is bad-assed with the martial arts, but that is a unique feature of Sorenson and Sechi Consulting Detectives. We box. So, bring it."

"The likelihood that the Russian agents who throughout this case have brought death in their wake will be on the mountain hunting our fugitives is certain. They are chasing her and us. How many and how armed, we can only speculate."

... and Kayne never guessed.

"Also, please consider the summit of Denali is a world of thin air, rocky tors, and glaciers. There are, in fact, two peaks, north and south. the summit elevation is 20,310 feet and usually holds fifteen feet of snow. Five large glaciers flow down the slopes of the Denali massif."

He faked interest in some Inuit soapstone carvings – a man with a seal, a polar bear, a mother and child.

"There are two ways in and out -- flight or mountaineering. Our choice will be flight as we are hardly 'men of the trail,' and time is of the essence.

The Ivory Knife

Similarly, aircraft will have put her on the mountain as she is in a hurry to meet her companion and complete the plan of destruction and sabotage from North America's highest and remotest place. This may have already happened. Your tracker device is somewhere in the Yukon. We cannot be sure if she has started her ascent or if she is even here."

"She is here, Dr. Sorenson. You may count on it."

***

"The woman you seek stood right where you are. Last evening, just before closing. Only she and I were here in the post. I know of her plans to meet her lover on the mountain. She flew up to Denali less than an hour ago."

Poldine Stickman sat at a wooden table at the back of the shop and carved. She explained that she was an elder of the Koyukon, an Alaska Native Athabascan people.

"My tribe has lived as they have for thousands of years. My family is among the first to create this township."

She hiked a thumb over her right shoulder at a vintage photo of a 19th-century motley crew of trappers, women, and children standing before the trading post and squinting into the camera.

Ms. Strickland was in her seventies with a small body and the gray-haired weather-worn face of a true outdoor pioneer. She had eyes the color of a humpback whale's skin set in deep wrinkles that suggested mystery and magic. When the elder looked up at us, they were filled with tiny lights in the blue-gray.

Poldine of the Athabasca was dressed in traditional garb but not a showy costume to attract tourists. Authenticity flowed from her very appearance. Her gnarled hands worked at her scrimshaw carving as she spoke.

In a voice like a teller of sacred tales, Poldine Strickland said, "The Russian woman goes high on the north mountain peak to retrieve the *ulu*. The Ice Knife holds death in its grasp, the suffering and extinguishing of many. Sidorovna has a very malicious *tuurngait*, and with this fetish spirit, she defies the gods."

Kayne whispered, "You are an *angakkuit*, my Mother. Your power is great."

Deep carving cuts were followed by a pause.

"It is as I suspected. It is you who possess the powerful spirit. The Raven protects and guides you. He hovers over you in the spirit realm. But, Man-with-Sea-Ice-in-his-Eyes ...."

Her words were accompanied by an upward look at Kayne – an intense stare. Her eye-lights seemed to flash.

"No, Dr. Sorenson. I am fading like a flame of a seal oil lamp in the north wind. My time is drawing to a close."

She waved a dismissing hand.

"Age, progress, and those horrible Christians and their single approach to divinity ... the flame is slowly extinguished. I and my kind will soon disappear into the mists. For I am the last of those who live in both worlds. But what I tell you of the Gatherer-of-the-Dead Woman is true. My helping spirit, my *tuurngait,* guides me to the truth only."

She rubbed the carved ivory with a cloth coated with lamp oil carbon. She lightly scraped the surface with fine steel wool.

"How did you get her to tell you her story, Ma'am? Why did you not go to the police?"

Poldine sniffed and grunted at what she considered the ridiculous nature of my questions. She was lost in her carving as she said, "I may do this, you may not. I am Inuit."

"I beg your pardon?"

Kayne said, "The state of Alaska only allows indigenous Alaskans to use ivory for tools, decorations, and art. Tusks, teeth, and bones of whales and walruses are highly controlled to protect native species."

Our little Ice Jedi froze me in her gaze.

"What is this? This? You are a haunted soul, Arctic-Fox-in-Summer, red with green eyes. There is fear all around you. Give me your hands."

The Scrimshander set aside her art piece and held me close.

The Ivory Knife

Twinkle twinkle – eyes that went into me like a scanner ray. She moved one withered hand up my arm.

"Ahh, you are a strong warrior but flawed. Your spirit resists the help of those who hold power over the world."

She closed her eyes and rocked. Her voice became almost a murmuring wind in tall trees as she said, " I call Silla to come and dwell inside you. No, do not keep him away. Breathe him in. One of the old gods, he is the breath of life, the spirit of the sky, the wind and the weather, the substance of your soul. Open to the Wind Indweller. Become Warrior Fox. Let go of your fear. "

The *angakkuit* continued to sing softly in her native language. She kept her eyes closed and her head slightly back. Now, Poldine rocked as she held onto me. The fringes on her clothes rustled like tiny snakes coming to life.

The front door slammed in the shop, but its sentry bell made no sound. As if someone turned on a large ceiling fan, hung fabrics lifted, and art hangings shifted, dangling pieces of bead, wood, and crystal fluttered, clacked, and tinkled. Someone was fucking with the lights.

I felt cold, like taking a naked ice plunge but then quickly warm and soothed. Something seemed to rush away from me, replaced by a sense of calm and strength.

Poldine Strickland stepped back to her table and picked up her ivory.

"The Mighty Hunter is inside you now, my Red Fox. Trust him to guide you. Do not doubt, and do not allow fear to possess your spirit. This one ...."

She nodded to Kayne.

"This Man-of-the-Seeing-Sky will be your strength as he has always been. As you are his. For you catch each other's fire and keep each other from the *killait* – the holes in the ice. Yes, heed him in all things and catch him when he falls."

Poldine Strickland, the Angakkuit of the Koyukon People, turned to Kayne, holding her scrimshaw in front of her like a talisman.

"Now go and stop her."

Thomas Paul Severino

The portrait in the ivory was Lieutenant Colonel Katsitsanóron Isapoinhkyaki, aka Katya Sidorovna, of the Russian Foreign Intelligence Service.

Chapter Fifty: *Kahiltna*
Denali, Alaska

Nick Sechi's Journal

"Freaked me the fuck out, Boss. What the hell was that?"

Kayne pocketed the ivory and said, "The *angakkuit* can bestow gifts and extraordinary abilities to people and items such as tools, my love. That's our plane."

As we boarded the DeHavilland DHC-3 Otter. I was without the usual fear, only excitement about the hunt. My innate cockiness seemed to be fired up.

What does the Fox Say? (busta rap move) Boom boom, cha boom boom.

Our Sky Otter was a single-engine design, fitted with a turboprop and a set of wheels that extended and retracted below skis. Pilot Sorenson and our ground guy checked it out, and I was about to climb into the front passenger's seat when two folks came hurrying across the runway.

Poldine Strickland and a younger woman came up to the plane carrying bundles.

"This is my granddaughter. Take off that shit and put this one. Ana, take their puffy jacket shits and burn that trash. Be dead in ten minutes up there."

In the plane's cabin, we exchanged our outerwear for knee-length parkas, pants, mittens, and boots made from caribou and seal skins. Layers of insulation -- one of each of our two parkas had fur next to our skins. Socks also had animal hair on the inside.

Looking like real caribou hunters, we prepared for takeoff. Poldine scrambled into the back seat. Kayne and I turned to our passenger.

Before we could say anything, Poldine pointed a finger and said, "You two have no idea where you are going. Denali is huge and filled with power. Do not question me. Fly the damn plane."

Down the runway and up we went into the misty blue Alaskan skies.

***

Above the three-river basin, the air was crystal clear as we sailed over stands of evergreens in the deep green taiga forests. We figured we had about three hours of good light. The colors of the magnificent landscape were dazzling.

Above the green-brown Alpine meadows, the Denali Massif wore a skirt of navy blue streaked with rocky diagonals of gray and black. The foothills seemed to play 'johnny ride the pony' as they piggybacked higher and higher into the air before being frosted with brilliant white snow, glistening in the morning sun. The north and south summits were trailing shrouds of creeping glaciers, scarred by crevasses and soaring ice columns. The two mythical peaks reigned like snow giants over the entire mountain group towering at 20,310 feet above sea level.

Kayne kept the aircraft on a steady course into the gigantic mountain mass. The cabin was exceptionally quiet, caused by engine design – prop rather than turbo. Poldine reached forward and touched my shoulder.

"Where?"

I responded, "She is on the South Peak, the higher one."

Turning to Kayne, I added, "It just seems like the right place to hunt, Boss. Can't say why."

Truthfully, it was like the mountain was magnetized and pulled us onto her soaring flanks. As she sat back, I heard Poldine say something like, "Silla." She was softly murmur/singing her native chant.

The flight took about 45 minutes. We began our descent into an ice-age world of flowing rivers of dense ice, snow-covered mountainous landscapes, and the awe-inspiring scenery of a geological wonder.

"Dr. Sorenson, the glacier we are over is the Kahiltna glacier. It is the longest in the Alaska range running 44 miles into the river basin. There.

The Ivory Knife

The East Fork Base Camp is to the left, just below the tallest pinnacle. She is there."

Somehow I felt her there before we heard the words of our *angakkuit*.

***

"You must hurry, Stefan. That plane is landing."

"I do not have a signal. The upload cannot be completed."

"Set it so it is automatically sent when the connection is made. The virus will be released in the manner of a zero-day event. Operation Exquisite Fire will hide in the system and await the release algorithms. Our man in Kyiv will see to its completion. The fire will burn and spread. Death will follow."

At the weather station computer link, the shivering priest punched keys on the mobile phone, matching his strokes to the script on the curling paper that Sidorovna held. The codes fluttered in the wind.

He disconnected wires.

"It is finished. Run."

Thomas Paul Severino

Chapter Fifty-One: *Truyi*
Denali, Alaska

Nick Sechi's Journal

"At more than 18,000 feet," Kayne said, "We are near the Japan Alpine Weather Station donated to the University of Fairbanks. It is the third-highest weather station in the world. I have it on the GPS. Wheels up, skis set. Seat belts. Stand by for descent."

Weather station? I looked for cinder block buildings set into the sheet of the glacier — slow-spinning satellite discs, weather socks. Perhaps a dome and a tower — nada.

Our stretch of Kahitna seemed to split the mountain as if someone slammed a white sloping ice platform between two walls of rocky cliffs. Above us, the glacier snaked down from the heights. Below, the ice river slanted slowly and curvaceously into the lower elevations. Near our proposed landing, on the glacier's south side, was a group of low, crescent-shaped nylon tents trembling in the wind. No other structure could survive the forces of the gales or the frigid temperatures of Denali's icy kingdom.

"A bit different from bringing Da's Cessna down on the station's airstrip. The Outback is a bit warmer than our present location, my love. We are here as is our quarry."

Below us, two figures moved at a sprint from the base camp structures into the gaps and ridges of the cliff overhang. Each carried a large backpack.

"Looks like we have them digging into defensive positions. Where is the weather station, Boss?"

"See that metal pole with the cross-bar. That's it, Nick. Those little boxes and whirligigs are the instruments for transmitting data in real-time for use by the climbing public and the science community. The entire array is custom-built for extreme weather and altitude conditions."

Kayne made an expert landing. The Otter slid to a stop, braked by the airframe, which rocked in the turbulent air. We saw another plane peaking behind a rocky wall extending along the glacier floor as he swung the Otter to face the camp. The hidden aircraft listed to one side. It appeared a bad landing had fatally injured the right-side undercarriage.

I pulled down my Pit Viper 2000's ski sunglasses with style points up the wazoo and reached for the door handle.

"The Fox must take care. The woman is armed."

Our *angakkuit* prepared to step out on the glacier at my side. Kayne de-planed and went wide, our usual strategy when apprehending a suspect.

The Russian stepped out from the rocky pinnacle and hit her stance, both arms straight in front of her. She yelled into the glacial valley directing her shouts at us. The echo was fierce and fought with the wind.

"You were supposed to help me. But you hunted me like a dog. There is no side of truth in this battle, Sorenson. We are swamped with a corruption that deserves death and extermination. The people cry out for vengeance as they burn in the fires of greed. Let it be so! I call the *Truyi*!"

She knew exactly what she was doing. The demons in the hanging snow piles tempted her with present danger since her younger days among the Inuit. Kataya Sidorovna knew how to pull them down in a deadly embrace.

My police training kicked in, and I grabbed Poldine and spun into a snowbank. Drop and roll when the shots ring out, and this crazy woman was not kidding.

She fired three shots directly at us.

The rumble was soft at first. Then the sound built like a stampede. Piles of snow and ice rushed at us from the mountain heights above the reckless Russian spy. She lowered her arms and bowed her head. Katya Sidorovna disappeared, as did the opening to the cave behind her. Off to the left, Kayne was lost in a haze of white clouds.

Truyi, the snow that covers you with death ....

It raced for us like a ravenous beast.

Poldine scrambled up and caught my arm. She yelled, "Run to the side." The snow in the center was moving faster, and the volume of the massive spill was greater there. The white quicksand swirled around our legs and glued us to the glacier.

"Swim!"

This was incredibly hard to do in our Inuit gear. We were sinking as we were carried down the slope of the Kahiltna Glacier. I copied the elder by kicking my feet and thrashing my arms in a swimming motion. Like Poldine, I swam on my back. This kept our faces turned to the surface -- a better chance of getting oxygen quickly should we get buried.

We did not, but the Otter was pushed on its side and was crushed as it careened across the ice. There is no sign of Kayne, just a swath of deep snow covering the base camp from the cliff to the center of the glacier's expanse.

No, wait. A hand! There, where the fog of snow had cleared from the surface. We raced.

"Fifteen minutes. Fifteen minutes, Nick. That is all the time we have. Dig."

The elder and I attacked the snowy tomb like maniacs. It was like hacking at concrete. Poldine pulled a carved walrus tusk from her belt and chopped the hard white cover. I used a rock that had skidded down from the overhang.

Kayne had managed to create a breathing bubble in front of his face by pushing the snow about seven inches from his nose and mouth. We freed him, pulling him up to the new snow surface.

"Nick. In the plane. Ice axes. Please hurry."

The Otter had been pushed along the glacier's surface for about one hundred yards like a curling stone. It came to rest teetering on the edge of a crevasse on the opposite side of the ice valley. One wing and part of the undercarriage on the aircraft's left side hung into the abyss. The empennage, the entire tail section, including both the horizontal and vertical stabilizers, the rudder, and the elevator, were gripped by the ice but at a twisted angle. The nose was slipping on its side. One of the airscrew blades seemed to be gripping the edge of the opening like a beast clawing at the ice scree moments before an impending fall.

I approached the balancing act carefully. As I reached for the cabin door, my weight on the land side of the plane caused it to rock backward and loosen its pinnings on the icy edge. I could see the tool kit and a survival backpack in the cabin. The larger satchel was against the pilot's door, whose window looked straight down into the brilliant blue ice of the gorge.

After waiting for the Otter to stop rocking, I lifted up and in like I was crawling onto a spiderweb. It was a game of weight-counterweight teeter-tottering on the wrecked carcass of a $2.5 million plane.

Easy, easy, Nick. You know, Gravity, you are such a bitch. Just this once ... just this once ... gimme a break... one time, man.

My legs were in the air, out the cabin door as I stretched for the parcels. One. I tossed it over my back and heard it fall up the slope, scratching into the ice behind me. The fuselage rocked as if the interior motion was a personal affront. Her twisted metal groaned softly. When she got over herself, the Otter went stock still, just a tad lower on the rim.

C'mere, you pain in the ass ... come to Daddy.

I had the second pack, but its opposite end was hooked on the far door handle. I jiggled carefully but to little avail. The strap seemed to move further up the handhold.

Fuck!

The wind gusted, and the plane tipped further. I felt my legs catch on some ropes or cables.

It was there. I heard it. Like a sighing voice in the wind ... calling.

Silla.

I moved forward, stretched out for what I figured was the last time. With a jolt, the pilot's door flew open in the wind. Cabin stuff fell into the pit, tumbling like Alice and her friends into the rabbit hole. The strap slipped off the handle, and the momentum of the flapping door created a shuddering roll. The Otter crashed into the blue ice ledges that seemed to go on and on and on into the underbelly of the Kahiltna Glacier.

My parcel and I popped out like someone had pulled the cork on a bottle of Pino Blanc. Hanging on the edge face down, I watched the

The Ivory Knife

DeHavilland DHC-3 Sky Otter descend into Dante's ninth circle of Hell — demons imprisoned in solid ice ... forever.

Kayne pulled on the rope, and I slid back up with my prize. Poldine was securing one end of my lifeline to pitons from the tool kit, hammered into the ice.

As he pulled me into his arms, Kayne said, "We must hurry, my love. The light is dying. I fear that we are too late."

We weren't.

The avalanche carried most of the snow away from the cliff. The cave in the overhang was blocked by a drift that was easy to open. The priest clambered up and scrambled out, handing his satchel to Kayne as he climbed.

In Russian, he said, "Where?"

Kayne shook his head and pointed to our feet.

"Approximately seven meters below us, Father."

He removed the icon of the saving Virgin and handed it to the priest.

The abbot knelt in the deepening shadows and made the sign of the cross

Thomas Paul Severino

Chapter Fifty-Two: Denali Denouement
Denali, Alaska

Nick Sechi's Journal

"Inside, or we will die."

We had raided the Russian's broken plane for combustibles and coverings. The *angakkuit* packed us into the cavern, and Kayne lit a fire at the back. I messed with rescued radio and attempted to find help. Who was I kidding? The wind and the darkness grew with each moment as despair intensified.

Kayne spoke in the flickering firelight.

"Perhaps, when it gets light, we can see what we can do with the plane. Crikey, have I lost all my cognition? Nick, your phone. Bundle up and follow me, my love. Madam, keep him alive and stay close to the fire."

She nodded and pulled the shivering priest closer as we stepped into the snowstorm. Denali clawed at us with a vengeance. I followed Kayne into the freezing darkness.

The avalanche had not quite buried the weather station. I do not know how we found it, but Kayne has an exceptional sense of direction. I gripped the metal array and showed the flashlight feature of my phone on the white box, now about ankle-high from the ground. Kayne lay on the ice, opened the instrument, and punched at the display.

I could barely hear him yell over the howling gale.

"It has an emergency feature. Nick. Like an Amber Alert. Here's hoping."

The box flashed six times and went dead. We huddled against each other and followed our tracks back to the cave's shelter, glowing softly against the mountainside.

Poldine piled the snow almost to the top of the cavern's opening. The four of us hugged up. Kayne pulled out a flask and handed it to our

Koyukon friend. She passed it to the priest, who held up his hand. In Russian, Poldine said, "Father, your vow of holy temperance is not needed here. This is a sacrament. It will keep you alive. Drink."

He did. Kayne and I shared a swig of the Hibiki. No Saint Bernard dog brandy for my man. Only the finest Japanese whiskey -- always first class, baby.

"Do not sleep. You will freeze."

She started to chant, but Kayne interrupted. He launched into "Where the Dog Sits on the Tucker Box" in his silky baritone." The lyrics spoke of an Outback life, big skies, love and acceptance, and good old dogs. The Aussie slang was rich and colorful.

Kayne went on for about ten verses, including repeats attempting to keep us awake. I thought of Chouko and Alice snuggling by the library fire back home in San Francisco. The eyelids of the priest began to droop, and I felt exhausted as well.

We had enough in the flask for two more pass-arounds. I sang in Italian and Poldine in Inuit. Just a campfire singsong at 18,000 feet, singing and getting "knackered." Then the fire began to die.

The cold was deadly and invasive even through our native gear. It was like being submerged in a sea of ice. I wanted to sleep, but Kayne shook me.

I mumbled, half asleep. "Yeah, Boss, the auroras. Yep, seen 'em. Very cool. Too sleepy."

He jumped up. Stoked the fire and pulled something long and burning out. He climbed out of our hole. There was another noise in the wind, choppy and roaring. Spiraling searchlights lit the glacier floor and created light curtains in the falling snow. I thought a bit nutso that it looked like a hot dance club ... oh, never mind.

The helicopter descended like an angel of divine compassion. Hooded figures ran to us and grabbed us in tight embraces. Behind us, the Inuit and the Russian stumbled into the circle of light.

The Ivory Knife

Cameron Yakecen Jakobs and his new squeeze, CPT Ciarán Farrell, hurried the four of us into the Coast Guard Helicopter, and we lifted off the mountain.

Poldine's eyes seemed to glow in the darkness of the aircraft. Abbot Stefan examined the icon and kissed it, crying and praying in Russian. He searched for the hiding place in the back of the triptych. Kayne slipped my hand into his parka, and there it was.

The Ivory Knife.

Thomas Paul Severino

Chapter Fifty-Three: The Elephant's Foot
BurshtynPower Headquarters, Umatilla, Ukraine

Nick Sechi's Journal

"We need to see the Director of the Power Station immediately. We are here at the direction of the United States Central Intelligence Agency."

The head of security frowned over the card we gave him. He spoke in English.

"But you have no clearance. Your CIA has no authority here. It appears that you two are some sort of private investigators. I am afraid that I will have to ask you to head back to the city. Umatilla is private property."

I objected, saying, "Ukraine and the CIA have cooperation agreements. We just want to see the person in charge."

Kayne began punching his phone.

"I can have our special agent on the line to verify our credentials. This is of utmost importance. Officer, ahhh..."

He read the name badge, "Boyo ... I assure you we are not ... Oh, bloody hell!"

Kayne pointed.

"Look, a *kat*!"

The big guard went for it like a sucker. As he turned, Kayne dropped him with a kick to the solar plexus. We ran into the facility.

So, not smart to be sure. The security checkpoint at the entrance to the nuclear facility was as big and as heavily armed as the fabled Checkpoint Charlie. We were pursued.

"Halt. Stay where you are."

Five guards in black with bodies like Olympic footballers, five Sig Sauer P320s at the ends of five pairs of outstretched arms pointed at our two heads ... the natural response is to stop and grab some sky – or ceiling in this case.

"Down on the ground. Keep your hands in plain sight."

Not going too well.

***

"I apologize for assaulting your guard, Director Belous. I assure you that our intentions were fueled by a pending disaster beyond your imagination."

Vasyl Belous was a man in his fifties and emitted an air of restrained control. He had been BurshtynPower's General Director for eleven years. He reported to the Ukrainian Deputy for National Energy.

Addressing us in English, the Director said, "Dr. Sorenson. I am familiar with your work." He looked at me as his source provider.

"I see. My husband's blog. Fascinating, but at this time a total non-sequitur, Minister.'

The man held up one hand.

"My country is at war. Sir, we get threats to the nation's nuclear power grid daily. Frankly, I find your cases to be a bit on the fabulous side. You and your ... ahh ...."

"Husband. You can say it, dude. I *am* his husband, after all. Got a paper back in San Francisco and a shit load of wedding pictures. But this all can wait."

"Right. I believe your detective organization cuts corners and flaunts quite a few rules. In the energy industry, regulations are essential. And abiding by security regulations is critical."

"The Elephant's Foot."

The General Director was visibly shaken.

"Shall we name the Elephant's Foot that will erupt near the core of every one of the running nuclear power plants in this country after you, Director Belous? It is sure to rival the one at Chornobyl. That hole into the

The Ivory Knife

earth's crust continues to grow, a cancer of radiation burning into the earth. Director, please, you must listen to what we have to say."

The guy was stammer city.

"This is highly irregular. You seem to ... what exactly are you ...?"

"Please listen to me. You have a systems programmer, one Danilo Soroka. He has worked for the company for three years but has affiliations with a foreign government hostile to yours. He has for many years been one of a group of Russian spies working in the Kyiv government's energy commission. He is not at his desk currently. Our CIA contacts confirm Soroka has compromised the highest security protocols from an off-site location near the Moldovan border and has introduced a worm into the operating systems of your nuclear reactors. The virus was smuggled out of eastern Russia by way of Alaska and sent to this man."

"Dr. Sorenson, the security of our system is quite unbreachable, even during this unfortunate war ... one second, please ...."

He pressed a button.

"Get Pavlo in here quickly."

"Director, it is code developed by hackers in Belarus working for their Russian masters. The string of timed commands is named 'Operation Exquisite Fire' and is a Trojan Horse program."

"Named for the military stratagem found in Homer's *Iliad*, a Trojan Horse makes the system think it is harmless, part of the program."

The dude who, at that moment, walked into the Director's office and took up the conversation did not introduce himself or shake hands. He just started speaking at one end of the Director's desk like an automaton.

He went on with, "Then, at a particular signal, it could be a date, a time, or another piece of code, the virus is unleashed and disrupts the program."

"This is my Director of Technical Operations, Pavlo Dydenko."

Heyward explained our accusations.

"Impossible. Soroka is security Delta. He could not possibly ...."

We were interrupted a second time.

"These will prove you need to take these men seriously. Orders from the Energy Ministry. Vasyl, get us to the main systems console. Pavlo, and stand by. Dr. Sorenson, I apologize for my tardiness. Folks, we are going hunting for nightcrawlers."

Special Agent Rysam Keal of the CIA proceeded into the office with a companion, Regina Netsilik. He quickly convinced the Director to move his ass. Behind the newly arrived Americans, a diminutive third person leaned out, smiled, and gave a little wave.

"The Sechi."

"Hey, Benjamin. What's going on?

***

The kid's fingers were flying over the keyboard. To his right, Pavlo Dydenko had commandeered another computer console. They worked together to assess and mitigate the attack.

Monitors all over the room flashed emergency messages in red, yellow, and black. Lights were spinning cylinders of red, and horns sounded throughout the facility

"The worm has escaped the wooden horse, Sechi. Zero-day! Zero-day!"

As we stared at a large overhead flatscreen, Regina explained, "The malware has been introduced by a hacker who found a vulnerability in the system's software that was previously unknown. This is called 'Zero-day.' The intrusion of the Trojan Horse, carrying the worm, came through an email program. The infection has no signature and is extremely hard to detect. What has happened is this Zero-day Exploit has taken control of the central systems of the reactor."

Both security experts were typing and mousing like fiends. Pavlo pointed to his monitor. "There it is. Ben, you got it? There, that string."

"Yes. Yes. Stuxnet. Stuxnet. This is indeed a bad one. We need Horton and Maizie. I will get them inside."

I asked excitedly. "Are we fucked, Ben?"

The Ivory Knife

"Please step back a bit. Thank you."

Director Belous was freaking out as Kayne kept him away from the boy.

"He can do this, mate. The lad is a genius."

The folks around the console were in heightened states of controlled panic. Around us, people were exiting the facility in a rush. Outside, busses and vans were racing employees to the property exits and beyond.

"One fish, two fish, red fish, blue fish ...."

Benjamin entered commands as he chanted.

Belous asked, "What the hell is he doing? He is breaching our firewalls."

Kayne said, "Mr. Benjamin Waska is attempting to hook a worm."

The boy slowed his typing and said, "Come here, the Sechi. Look."

I moved closer.

Dydenko pointed to the monitor.

"*Bozhe layno!* The water level in the reactor chamber has remained safe. Small amounts were lost only."

"The Sechi ... Maizie, that lazy bird, has laid her egg, and Horton, the Elephant, will sit on it. All is well in Whoville. No fire. No fire." He began to rearrange the stuff on the computer desk.

Regina translated.

"My colleague here identified the Exploit and created a patch he calls 'Horton, the Elephant.' The vulnerability in the operating system has been plugged. Maizie's offspring, 'the egg,' is Ben's creation to isolate the invader and prevent another attack."

Pavlo said, "I don't fucking believe this. No one can do what he did."

Belous was speechless. He began giving orders to bring back personnel and alert the authorities that all was well at Umatilla.

"You fuckin' did it, dude. Holy shit!"

Thomas Paul Severino

I made to hug the little hero-geek. It was Regina who put her hand on me and shook her head. I remembered. Ben does not allow touching.

"How about we head back to Seattle, Benjamin? Levitch needs you on your perch bright and early."

She turned. "Gentlemen, I will call you from the plane."

Benjamin Waska stood up, replaced his chair, and then adjusted it slightly. He nodded to Pavlo Dydenko and Vasyl Belous without actually looking at them. Falling in behind his boss, he looked back and gave a little wave.

"Bye."

Chapter Fifty-Four: A Grocery Bill
Mariupol, Ukraine
Notes to the file by Rebecca Quinto

"Produce. Five thousand kilos. From the Black Sea farm cooperatives -- ready to eat, cook or feed to the pigs. Cabbages, potatoes, carrots, turnips – big red beets the size of your noggin'. It's all going to spoil real fast unless you take possession, Major. Otherwise, we turn east, and I'll sell it to the Ukrainians. No reason everyone should go hungry. Doesn't matter to me. Money is money."

"Who are you?"

"What does the flag say, Comrade? The ship's registry? You are a *umnyy paren'* -- a smart guy."

"Wait a minute. Georgia? Why are you speaking English?"

"Never learned Russian, pal. Too many consonants. Sounds like you're gargling. You want to go in Georgian? *Daelap'arak'e, amkhanago?*"

The soldier waved and shook his head.

The Agribusiness Provender came up to the Russian soldier and me. Kris said. "*Ehay's otna oinggay orfay itay, isay ehay?*"

Pig Latin. Seriously? Fuck, we're all gonna die. Kris did look good in his fake blonde mustache, business suit, and officious attitude. The kid is a born actor.

I pointed to the Russian.

"No Georgian. Go to English,"

Kris and I had practiced Georgian accents on the voyage from Varna. I hoped we were convincing.

"What's the problem, Captain Ignorovka?"

"They don't want the stuff. I think our comrade soldiers are out of money, Mr. Berdzenishvili. They only have what they could steal. Look at how they totally destroyed this city and its people."

From the deck of the disguised Bulgarian tanker, we could see the smoking ruins of the Mariupol steel factory and just about every building in the ruined city. Part of a church seemed to melt into the nearby bombed-out cityscape. The rest of the once-beautiful city was building skeletons, bomb craters, and rubble out to the foothills. The invaders obliterated the place, and the dead lay in the streets.

The Port of Mariupol was like a scene from the Last Days of Pompeii, with soldiers, ships, and people clamoring through the smoke everywhere. Everyone was seeking to get out. Every so often, an explosion could be heard. Panic was like a thick fog as far as the eye could see.

"Be careful Georgian woman. I can simply take this food. The dead need not be paid."

A soldier, returning from the ship's hold, was chewing a carrot. He spoke to the Major, who did not move his eyes from us as he listened. He tapped his clipboard, and the Major signed something. He gave the order, and his troop began to 'liberate" the food from the depths of the tanker. Cranes, nets, and hand trucks were commandeered by his army, and our stevedores lifted our cargo down to dockside trucks being emptied of the people of Mariupol.

Kris stepped with me to the railing. He pointed down to the mob held at gunpoint, watching the food pass over their heads and away.

"Wait, Major. Fair is fair. Russia is not a thief."

"What are you saying, Georgian pig?"

"I want them ... in exchange for the food. Give them to me, all of them. Those. The people of Mariupol. They are a hindrance to you now. The dead and the half-dead – they slow you down. You will be taken captive if you have to bring them with you. This entire city is coming down fast. Soon the water itself will be burning."

The Russian thought for a moment. Most likely, the commanding officer realized he was getting out from under an insurmountable

The Ivory Knife

problem. His takeaway was tons of badly needed food for his soldiers. I held my breath for the decision.

"What will you do with these Ukrainian pigs?"

"Why sell them, of course, Comrade. Have you no sense of enterprise?"

The Major barked to his staff, and they exited down the gangplank.

The refugees were guided to the ramp up and then down into the stern hold of the tanker. It was where we had secured the untainted food. Some of the sailors who were actually "The Flea," a few of his Ambassador buddies, NATO adjunct staff, jock footballers, his cousins, and relations – all dirtied up and looking like the cast of Les Misérables, updated. A few of our shabby mariners, both the men and women, lifted the elders and the children into their new place of refuge. Below decks, volunteer medical staff attended to our guests.

Where the hell is he? He just has to be in this mob. Via the Star Link, Eris had let him know we were coming. Don't let this be a fuck up.

One of the last groups to board was a trio of men in very rough shape, bent over in the rags of war and destruction. Matt Crowley, disguised as an ensign or something, intercepted the three stragglers and showed them the way into the ship's safety.

Before going below decks, one of these rag bags -- Mark, in dirty tatters galore, came up to me, and I thought I was gonna blow our cover right there. Kris came forward as the Major moved off and whispered, "Just get below decks. No sweet stuff, or the shit flies. Who's this dude?"

Mark played it cool but touched my hand with one finger as the boat rocked slightly. The Russian Major turned from the unloading of the supplies and the entrance of the refugees. He seemed to suspect some kind of ruse. As the port officer in charge, he moved up to us to check out the three stragglers. I could tell he was suspicious of possibly escaping enemy soldiers.

One of Mark's companions began to cough like a tuberculosis patient. Matt came between us. He said in accented English, "Port Major, I will make sure these refugees are quarantined. I suspect plague."

Matt repeated the last word in Russian.

"*Chuma.*"

The filthy fugitive coughed again, clutched his chest, and gasped for breath. The major and his attendants turned quickly and "got the fuck out of Dodge." The unloading continued, but the Russian occupation of our ship was thinning out as the operation went quickly.

Mark said softly, "This is Captain Ivan Illyich Korolenko, 11th Spetsnaz Brigade, and Corporal Jan Gonchary. They have had enough of war. Their families slipped out of St. Petersburg to Helsinki one month ago. I offered a ride."

I followed as Matt led the way to the forward hold. Our "health dude" said, "This way, gentlemen. Man, could you guys be any dirtier? Lovin' it, *tovarich.*"

Kris remained on deck to hurry the Russians off the deck and down to their troops.

"That all you got, Major-comrade? You could sweeten this deal up a bit with a few more."

The Russian exited the gangplank, and shortly after, about sixty more escapees hurried up and into the ship. Civilians, disguised soldiers – no one seemed to be checking as our mission was ending and the shelling of the port increased.

I ordered our departure in fractured Georgian as our "crew" untied our moorings. Engines rumbled.

As quickly as possible, we sailed for the Bulgarian port of Varna, hoping that our "Georgian" tanker would not come under fire. It did not.

I went below and joined Mark, Kris, and the rest of the rescue team to assist Matt, who coordinated the care for the sick, injured, and hungry in the tanker's hold. Stepping between people and equipment, I took Mark's hand and breathed a sigh of relief as we left the war-ravaged southern coast of Ukraine and headed to the western shores of the Black Sea.

"Another escape, beautiful. We lead charmed lives."

"Charmed and blessed, and your tux better be pressed. My opening is in four days, darling."

The Ivory Knife

I neglected to mention the tanker's name, registered to Gotha Maritime, Inc., out of Burgas. *Rezolyutsiyata* —The Resolution.

***

Addendum: As remembered by Kris...

"Saved the world. It's what we do. Should morph that into our family motto. Sorenson – 'Saving the World And Looking Damn Good Doin' It." Am I right or what? ... you guys, too, huh? See, there ya go, Uncle Nick ... bet you'll be glad to get back to where you can be bare-assed in your swimming pool.

"Yes, Dad. School, blah, blah, blah. I'm on it, Pop. Can I ask if being the main man on Operation Resolution pays out The Kris' big debt? Be thinking it does, Commander. It sure the fuck comes close, huh?

"Cousin Pesho – oh, my god, fuckin' NATO, guys, NATO! I want a medal. Yep. That's it. Gotta be.

"Anyway, Pesho is sending us back to San Francisco in style. Rebecca and Mark will most likely stay at 221 Baker, but I haven't had the chance to ask them ... yeah, and how about the two defectors? Mark needs to fill me in on that, and Rebecca has an opening in Ft. Lauderdale soon ... but they haven't yet come up for air. You know how these heteros are, always making with the sex – honestly, what's a gay boy like me to do? So scandalized!

"Anyway, I'm loving this group FaceTime, but I think I need to get into some good mischief before getting into Varna. Pesho has this staffer, Mikhal, who is cute as a bug – just all about sexy in his worn sailor kit.

"Oh, O.K., so yeah, so, see you all soon.

"Good-bye"

Thomas Paul Severino

Epilogue: Starlight
Lubin, Poland to Prague, Czech Republic

Nick Sechi's Journal

"Kinda cool, Boss, right?"

"To what are you referring, my love? The fact that we are now not glowing in the dark?"

"You are such a little nointer. No, I'm talking about how things turned out and this incredible train ride."

"Nointer, eh? Look at you, getting all Aussie slang on ya, man. Bonzer, lad."

I held his hand close as we sat together in the executive's compartment of the Polska Starlight, bound for Prague. From Kyiv, Agent Keal had us placed on a truck transport to the Polish border. In Poland, we were met by an EU attache and provided train tickets to the West. The accommodations were Orient Express lush, and the bed – warm and ready for action. Comfort was the byword as we made our way through mountain passes, rivers, and forested valleys. However, we made one adjustment in the accommodations.

Kayne spoke to the attache.

"*Mój przyjaciel*, this cabin is too big for the two of us. The refugees in third class ... bring those most in need in here. There are sick who could use that bed and the lav. We do not care if they are seen by the other passengers. This part of the world is at war, and humanity cries out."

I chimed in, "Also, please, some food in here."

Kayne stopped the exiting man. Slipping him some Euros, he said, "The gentleman in first class in the blue serge suit is a doctor. Please give him my card and ask him to look in on the passengers on the Starlight from Ukraine, in third class. Thank you."

We found a corner and sat together on the floor. Three families were allowed to be our guests. I entwined one arm in his.

Kayne sensed my need for closure. He spoke softly.

"First, boyo, I must settle my mind regarding the near-disaster at BurshtynPower. It was, as you Americans say. 'one close shave,' I have to admit."

"Sorenson and Sechi -- saving the world yet again."

Kayne hugged me against him. His ice-blue eyes and the closeness of his muscular form were warm and breathtaking. I had a tendency to get lost in this guy, big time.

He did a sweep of his pesky bang off his handsome brow and said, "No, Nick. It was Benjamin."

"You are right about that, Bossman. To think we were so close to reactor meltdown despite all the safety protocols in the aftermath of Fukushima."

"By the time he sat down at the console, the water had begun draining from the core. That is pretty close to thermonuclear disaster, my love."

I watched a few of the children sharing a bit of our room service. My thoughts went to how close we came to the creation of a nuclear wasteland smack dab between Russia and the EU.

"So, I understand that Benjamin has been invited to the White House. Care for a visit to DC, Nick?"

"Oh, hell yes. All those hot Secret Service Agents getting all ...."

Kayne looked at me with a comic expression.

"Just who exactly are you?"

"Gonna show you soon as we check into the Czech Republic, Kayne, my man, but finish what you were going to say."

He continued, "As difficult as it may be to ignore your uniform fantasies ... please allow me to add that a group of anonymous donors in Eastern Europe have created the Waska Autism Endowment. It will be the highlight of the President's honors."

The Ivory Knife

"Sorenson and Sechi, Inc. should make a gift, Boss."

He pulled me closer. "Umm hum. Absolutely."

"One more thing, Kayne. The Russian Spy network that was after Sidorovna and the Knife, they never did show. What's the deal?"

"Your hunky Irish-American, my love, Ciarán Farrell, during the time we thought he was ah, 'entertaining' our randy Cameron, the captain put the dogs on the spook who trolled us to Orso. Those Big Bads were rounded up and convinced to return to Moscow or face charges."

"That's good."

"Nick, Kristof said something about paying off a debt. I am unaware of this, I fear."

I said, "No drama, mate. And remember, Boss, money isn't everything."

He shrugged and let it go.

"Something wrong, boyo?"

'Nah. Just thinking the list of those looking to fry our asses gets longer and longer."

"Ahh, it would seem, then, that we should make every attempt to keep each other from falling through the ice, my love."

The hotel in Prague beckoned as the Polska Starlight raced to the West.

The End

Thomas Paul Severino

Research

Alaska

https://en.wikipedia.org/wiki/List_of_research_stations_in_the_Arctic

https://en.wikipedia.org/wiki/Trans-Alaska_Pipeline_System#Forming_Alyeska

https://en.wikipedia.org/wiki/Nuiqsut,_Alaska

https://en.wikipedia.org/wiki/Ulu

https://en.wikipedia.org/wiki/Snow_knife

https://www.nytimes.com/2017/03/30/world/europe/alaska-russia-sale-150.html

https://en.wikipedia.org/wiki/Inside_Passage

https://www.powerandmotoryacht.com/voyaging/cruising-the-inside-passage-to-alaska-on-a-marlow-explorer-61e

https://en.wikipedia.org/wiki/Ketchikan,_Alaska

https://en.wikipedia.org/wiki/Denali

https://en.wikipedia.org/wiki/Portage_Glacier_Highway

https://en.wikipedia.org/wiki/Prudhoe_Bay,_Alaska

https://en.wikipedia.org/wiki/Ruth_Glacier

https://en.wikipedia.org/wiki/Fairbanks,_Alaska

https://en.wikipedia.org/wiki/Talkeetna,_Alaska

https://en.wikipedia.org/wiki/Mount_Juneau

https://en.wikipedia.org/wiki/St._Nicholas_Russian_Orthodox_Church_(Juneau,_Alaska)

https://en.wikipedia.org/wiki/Glacier_Bay_National_Park_and_Preserve

https://en.wikipedia.org/wiki/Wrangell%E2%80%93St._Elias_National_Park_and_Preserve

https://en.wikipedia.org/wiki/Disenchantment_Bay

https://en.wikipedia.org/wiki/Aurora#Images

https://en.wikipedia.org/wiki/Raven_Tales#Northern_Athabaskan

https://en.wikipedia.org/wiki/Whittier,_Alaska#Geography

https://en.wikipedia.org/wiki/Anchorage,_Alaska

https://en.wikipedia.org/wiki/Joint_Base_Elmendorf%E2%80%93Richardson

https://www.talkeetnaair.com/

The Arctic

https://en.wikipedia.org/wiki/Arctic_Institute_of_North_America

https://www.russiamatters.org/blog/chinas-arctic-ambitions-could-make-or-break-us-russian-relations-region

https://www.cnas.org/publications/reports/navigating-relations-with-russia-in-the-arctic

https://foreignpolicy.com/2022/04/04/arctic-council-members-russia-boycott-ukraine-war/

https://rusi.org/explore-our-research/publications/commentary/ukraine-war-and-future-arctic

https://www.wilsoncenter.org/event/ukraine-and-arctic-perspectives-impacts-and-implications

https://time.com/6156189/russia-ukraine-conflict-risks-arctic-climate/

https://www.worldpoliticsreview.com/amp/articles/30434/for-nato-russia-ukraine-war-forecasts-tensions-in-the-arctic

https://arctic-council.org/about/states/the-united-states/

Australian Slang

https://en.wiktionary.org/wiki/Appendix:Australian_English_sexual_terms

https://www.krakenlyrics.com/slimdusty/wherethedogsitsonthetuckerbox-93d130c4

Autism

https://www.easterseals.com/explore-resources/living-with-autism/autism-signs-and-symptoms

https://www.easterseals.com/shared-components/document-library/2018-autism-fact-sheet.pdf

https://www.medicalnewstoday.com/articles/326841#summary

https://www.verywellhealth.com/what-is-an-autistic-savant-260033

Bulgaria

https://www.dw.com/en/nato-or-moscow-bulgaria-torn-between-russia-and-the-west/a-61036527

https://www.britannica.com/place/Bulgaria/Government-and-society

https://en.wikipedia.org/wiki/Bulgarian_royal_family#Tsardom_of_Bulgaria

https://www.euractiv.com/section/politics/short_news/bulgaria-offers-to-help-moldova-with-ukrainian-refugees/

https://ec.europa.eu/migrant-integration/news/bulgaria-takes-first-steps-welcome-those-fleeing-ukraine_en

https://www.dw.com/en/nato-or-moscow-bulgaria-torn-between-russia-and-the-west/a-61036527

Indigenous Peoples

https://en.wikipedia.org/wiki/I%C3%B1upiat

https://en.wikipedia.org/wiki/Inuit

https://en.wikipedia.org/wiki/Indigenous_peoples_of_Siberia

https://www.sheldonmuseum.org/vignette/tlingit-fishing/

https://en.wikipedia.org/wiki/Tlingit

https://alaskatrekker.com/alaska/alaska-natives/

https://en.wikipedia.org/wiki/Totem_pole#Meaning_and_purpose

https://en.wikipedia.org/wiki/Inuit_clothing#Fabric_and_artificial_materials

https://en.wikipedia.org/wiki/Angakkuq

https://en.wikipedia.org/wiki/Koyukon#Notable_Koyukon

https://en.wikipedia.org/wiki/Inuit_religion#Anirniit

https://en.wikipedia.org/wiki/Silap_Inua

Miscellaneous

https://pencils.com/pages/the-history-of-the-pencil

https://en.wikipedia.org/wiki/Great_Seattle_Fire

https://en.m.wikipedia.org/wiki/Zero-day_(computing)

https://en.wikipedia.org/wiki/War_crime

https://www.npr.org/2022/04/28/1095277848/ukraine-russia-war-crimes

https://en.wikipedia.org/wiki/Moose

The Ivory Knife

https://en.wikipedia.org/wiki/Detection_of_fire_accelerants

Russia

https://foreignpolicy.com/2022/02/25/arctic-ukraine-russia-china-eu-invasion-nato/

https://en.wikipedia.org/wiki/Russian_espionage_in_the_United_States#Transition_from_Soviet_to_Russian_intelligence

https://en.wikipedia.org/wiki/Arkhangelsk

https://en.wikipedia.org/wiki/Siberian_regionalism

https://en.wikipedia.org/wiki/Gulag#Conditions

https://en.wikipedia.org/wiki/Intelligence_agencies_of_Russia

https://en.wikipedia.org/wiki/Russian_honorifics

https://rusmania.com/top-monasteries#Siberian%20Federal%20district

https://en.wikipedia.org/wiki/Russian_Canadians#British_Columbia

https://en.wikipedia.org/wiki/Russia_men%27s_national_ice_hockey

https://en.wikipedia.org/wiki/Our_Lady_of_the_Sign

Seattle

https://en.wikipedia.org/wiki/Seattle

https://en.wikipedia.org/wiki/Seattle_Underground

https://www.baconmanor.com/

https://en.wikipedia.org/wiki/Great_Seattle_Fire

https://en.wikipedia.org/wiki/Pike_Place_Market

https://en.wikipedia.org/wiki/Space_Needle

https://en.wikipedia.org/wiki/King_Street_Station

Ukraine

https://www.mcgill.ca/oss/article/did-you-know/there-radioactive-elephants-foot-slowly-burning-hole-ground

https://en.wikipedia.org/wiki/Eastern_Slavic_naming_customs#Affectionate_diminutive

https://en.wikipedia.org/wiki/Mariupol

https://www.defense.gov/News/News-Stories/Article/Article/2994894/slovakia-to-supply-s-300-air-defense-system-to-ukraine/

https://world-nuclear.org/information-library/country-profiles/countries-t-z/ukraine.aspx

Vancouver

https://en.wikipedia.org/wiki/Vancouver

The two sets of song lyrics in Chapter Twenty-Eight:

"The March of the Ukrainian Nationalists" was written by Oles Babiy to music by Omelian Nyzhankivskyi in 1929.

"On the Hills of Manchuria" is a waltz composed in 1906 by Ilya Alekseevich Shatrov.

Afterword:

Thank you for reading The Ivory Knife: A Kayne Sorenson Mystery. I hope you enjoyed the story.

Nick and Kayne return soon in The Death of the Hungarian Tutor: Cases from the Private Files. An excerpt follows.

More adventures may be found at tomseverino.com or on Amazon.

Until next time…

Thomas Paul Severino

The Death Of The Hungarian Tutor
Cases from the Private Files

The Kayne Sorenson Mysteries

Thomas Paul Severino

Thomas Paul Severino

Introduction: The Private Files of Sorenson and Sechi, Inc.

221 Baker Street, San Francisco, California

From the Case Files of Nicola M. Sechi

Why private?

The answer is somewhat complicated.

Confidentiality has been a hallmark of Sorenson and Sechi, Consulting Detectives, Inc. since my husband and I founded the firm. Whereas all of our cases are handled with confidentiality, certain of our adventures are classified as secret. Should these private files come to light at an inopportune time, certain of our investigations could result in the unnecessary suffering of innocent parties or have other disastrous consequences.

I call one such investigation "The Case of the Secretary General's Lover." This affair will never see the light of day. Revealing details of that adventure could affect world diplomacy's course with unnecessary and disastrous consequences. Suffice it to say, we chose to leave that *affaire de coeur* alone – solved, sealed, and done.

"The Death of the Hungarian Tutor" involves international intrigue and criminal machinations that could greatly tip the political scales in Eastern Europe for evil purposes. The account contained herein has been edited for security purposes.

"Murder in the Highlands" resulted in court cases that have recently been settled. The firm feels that due diligence has been paid regarding the course of justice and has released that account with the court's approval.

Likewise, others of our mysteries involve high and even low-profile scandals that have been brought to just and honorable conclusions. Public knowledge of these mysteries would only calumniate the reputations of some beloved members of our communities. Regarding "The Case of the Portuguese Infanta," we have received information that justice was served, so the story may be told. Where love and passion are involved, our strategy is to tread carefully.

Some cases came about before we formed our partnership. The victims of terror and crime have found their evil ways into our lives from our early years, and we chose to intercede for good. "Saints of Wilton Manors" is one such episode. Kayne's records and my journals reflect a world that seems to cry out for heroes when the wicked are on the prowl.

A few of these endeavors we have undertaken together or individually may excite the reader. Action and adventure are our business, and so these cases are offered for the education and edification of our readers.

I met my husband, Kayne J. Sorenson, Ph.D., in Ft. Lauderdale. He was my professor of psycho-criminology, and I was a police officer eager to become better at crime-fighting through higher education. Our beginnings may be found in *Seed Blood: A Kayne Sorenson Mystery*. Several hair-raising and action-packed adventures followed, and as our reputation for serving justice and defending the defenseless grows, our firm's docket is often filled with the most strange and treacherous maladies that plague humanity.

As you review these exploits and quests, you will meet some unforgettable members of our family and associates who provide support, frustration, and even rescue. Along with these allies, our dangers are filled with some of the most infamous villains ever to threaten all that holds us inches away from the brink of insanity. Sorenson and Sechi stand vigilant.

As each adventure presents itself, be guided by the oft-spoken words of Kayne Sorenson ...

"Nothing is what it seems, my love."

Made in the USA
Columbia, SC
28 December 2022